ABOUT THE AUTHOR

Rebecca Murphy is a writer from Cork, living in Wicklow with her wife and two dogs. *Blood and Water* is her debut novel. She was the winner of the RTÉ *Today Show* novel competition and the recipient of a Faber Academy Scholarship. Her influences range from Anne Enright to Stephen King, by way of Maeve Binchy. She has a degree in Drama and English from UCC.

AF147827

Praise for Blood and Water

'*Blood and Water* is a profoundly moving exploration of identity, the shame that echoes through families and the silent grief of losing a long-held dream. The prose is vivid and beautiful. On the human condition, Murphy writes with wit and a startling clarity. Here is an astonishing new voice in literary fiction.'

SOPHIE WHITE

'A complex, compelling and deeply moving story of loss, love and family.'

ANNA CAREY

'*Blood and Water* pulled me in from the first page and held me there. Rebecca Murphy writes with such warmth, wit and emotional honesty that the characters feel utterly real and heartbreakingly human. It's the kind of book you fall into completely, emerging hours later feeling like you've been somewhere else for a while. Tender, atmospheric and quietly powerful, this is a beautiful debut that will stay with readers long after they turn the final page.'

STEFANIE PREISSNER

BLOOD AND WATER

REBECCA MURPHY

MERCIER PRESS

————∞◇∞————

FOR RACHEL

————∞◇∞————

MERCIER PRESS
Cork
www.mercierpress.ie

© Rebecca Murphy, 2026

ISBN 9781917453851
eISBN 9781917453868

Printed and bound in the EU.

FOREWORD

A quick note before you dive in ...

Thank you for being here. This story is very close to my heart, and it walks through some heavy territory: infertility, loss, grief and mentions of suicide.

I'm sharing this so you may decide if you are in the space to take on these themes right now.

Take care of yourself.

REBECCA

PART ONE: ARRIVAL

CHAPTER ONE

Susan flinched as a splash of cold salt water whipped across her face. Mick, the captain, laughed. Susan returned the look with an embarrassed smile.

'There'll be plenty of that where we're going!' he roared, his head stuck out the window of his wheel-house, his eyes barely watching the sea ahead. He laughed again and retreated inside, leaving Susan to turn toward the horizon, gripping the wooden sides of the small vessel. Seasick and sea-shy, she was grateful to be the only passenger. She tried her best to make a good impression on the red-faced sailor with his big hands and kind smile. In the distance, a small island started to take shape in the mist of the horizon, arching up like an uneven triangle, emerging slowly as they put-put-putted towards it. The sun began to loom over the island's eastern cliffs. Bursts of purple heather tumbled down the gentle slopes to greet her as small herds of donkeys, like wandering grey puddles, flicked their tails and brayed to each other. She spotted birds in the distance, small dots circling by the cliffs at the mouth of the port – gulls perhaps – terns maybe? She searched her memory for the names of other birds along the coast, but they remained out of reach. Jen would know. She shoved the name out of her head and returned to the skyline. The birds screamed at no one in particular and dived into the sea, clambering for the next meal to bring back to their nests, hidden, safe in the side of the precipices, untouched and unreachable.

The mainland vanished from view as the little boat chugged through the blue. On either side, the spit of the sea foam danced in the swell of the boat – it floated away across the Atlantic. She followed it with her gaze, imagining sitting in one of its bubbles, carried away, disappearing into the depths. Her stomach disliked the thoughts of bubbles and she swallowed, taking a big gulp of sea air. Mick gave another laugh.

'Mick, is there a shop on the island?'

He took his hands off the wheel and leant out his window again.

'Sure, what do you need?'

'Well, I didn't bring anything with me.' Her cheeks reddened. Food and supplies had not been a concern as she careened down the motorway, her only mission to abandon the car at the ferry port and disappear.

'Ah, I'd say we'll manage something all right. None of us have starved to death lately.'

Mick roared again and returned to his steering wheel, correcting the slightly off-course boat.

Her ancient Toyota sat ten kilometres across the sea at Kilbrean Port – hopefully locked and the windows up. The seagulls would be shitting all over it. Souvenirs from the coastal skies for when, or if, she returned. She rubbed her eyelids, took another deep breath and shook her head away from the land behind her.

The *Lord and Lady* pulled into Dune Island a few minutes after noon. The sun advanced on the harbour and the surrounding green hills, lush with heather, offered no shelter as Susan gingerly stepped onto the concrete pier. Her backpack pressed sweaty against her spine and her shoulders felt clammy under its straps. This end of the island was home to a tourist shop offering mostly ice cream and maps. Susan caught a vinegary whiff of chips from its direction and her belly rumbled. The long concrete pier jutted out from a small gathering of buildings, including a shop and some public toilets. Their paint was sun-bleached and peeling. On one side of the pier, boats – both visiting and resident – bobbed in the lapping, gentle ocean. On the other side, a small stony cove entertained crowds of Sunday day-tripping mainlanders. Children screamed as they splashed in the waist-high water, their shoulders reddening in the Irish summer sun. Susan watched as the small, fat toddlers, pink with excitement, stumbled towards the water, arms outstretched, their tired parents chasing behind. Her eyes began to close as the travelling caught up with her.

A honk sounded behind her. She turned to see Mick waving as the boat pulled away from the shore again, a lazy plume of diesel smoke wafting out of its chimney. The acrid smell floated towards her nostrils and stung; the taste of the fuel was uncomfortable in her mouth, bitter and pungent. She lifted her hand to wave as it moved out of view, back towards her old life. She turned back to the buzz of the pier and picked up her bag. The handles pressed into her flesh as she strolled in the direction of the hill Mick had pointed her to. The stiff grass of the island poked out of the stone walls hugging the harbour, the boundary marking the battleground between the sea and the land for real estate.

A granny in a floppy hat and her best sundress wandered past her, a cartoonishly large ninety-nine dripping down her leather hands. She licked her wrist in a daring rescue as a child whinged behind her.

'Nan, that's mine!'

The lady caught Susan's eyes and rolled her own. Susan smiled at her and at the child, who scrunched up his brown eyes, scowled at her and brushed past, arms crossed and furious. The woman shrugged.

'Children these days, eh?'

Susan pursed her lips and nodded like she thought she should, feeling a small twinge low in her belly. A group of older teenagers sat at the edge of the pier, their scruffy trainers dangling inches above the sea. The cloud of smoke from their rollies reminded Susan of misspent college years, drinking tea and smoking spliffs on a broken sofa, watching stoner TV and planning her magnificent future. She considered asking for a drag but decided against it; she already felt the youths eyeing the weird lady, blonde hair blown askew, face windburned and tired, hanging around in her own sweat. She distracted herself by seeking the pub. She'd been told the sole pub on the island sat near the mouth of the harbour, away from the tourists, so the locals could hide from them, but also close enough that a savvy visitor might stumble in for a pint to escape their sand-caked children for an hour or two.

The sun squatted directly above the island, baking its inhabitants as she left the small port and screaming children behind her. As advised, the pub wasn't hard to find – it seemed nothing on the island was. All roads appeared to lead to the port and the main road from there found its way to Peggy Quinlan's Pub. *Peggy's Place* was painted an immaculate red, with window baskets of pink and purple surfinias cascading down its walls to the floor. A sign pointed to a small beer garden at its rear, nestled between the pub and the hill that overshadowed it. Some small tables and benches sat in the sun. Connected via a small, narrow slip of a wall lay a separate dwelling, whitewashed with a well-maintained tiled roof. Despite the heat, a lazy plume of smoke drifted out of the chimney, and a gentle smell of turf filled the air.

The door to the pub was mahogany with glass panels coloured blue and yellow, with deep swirls that distorted what lay within. Susan stepped inside, nervous in the empty quietness she found as she crossed the threshold onto the black-and-white-tiled floor. The bright sunshine outside gave the interior a cool darkness, a welcome escape from the sweat and salt of the cove. She had been here before. It had felt bigger back then to her table-height self, bewildered at the new faces. Today, it was more proportionate to her adult size. There were no other customers inside, but she heard a hubbub of voices coming through a small door that appeared to lead to a beer garden. She suspected the locals skulked there, enjoying the quiet gossiping. The interior smelled like stout and fried chicken, and Susan's stomach complained again. As she glanced around, a stern face popped up from behind the long bar counter to her right. Susan jumped.

'Jesus Christ!'

The stern face broke into a laugh, and greying blonde

hair fell from a loose bun, tied with an old blue scrunchie. The bartender dragged herself up from her stooping position and gave a weary groan.

'Jesus is right, I'm getting too old for all this bending. Now, what can I do for you?'

'Peggy?'

Susan left her suitcase by the door, stepped towards the woman and extended her hand. She received a firm rattling in return.

'I'm Susan Shaw. Em … Frank's niece.'

Peggy leant back and surveyed her.

'You are and all. I was expecting some young one, but sure, it's been a fair while since we saw you around here.'

Susan had no memory of this woman, the keeper of the island's social centre. She responded as best she could.

'Sadly, I guess I haven't been a young one for a while. I've been told you have all the, eh … bits and pieces?'

'Straight to business so is it? You have the letters and all that, do you?'

Susan slid the by now damp backpack off her back and gasped with relief at the loss of the weight. She rummaged through its contents and produced a plastic folder, signed documents highlighted and colour-tagged. She handed Peggy the signed solicitor's letter. Peggy checked it over, glancing now and then at Susan as she stood, shiny-faced from the heat.

'You're not a scammer so. Look, sit yourself down there, we'll get you a plate of chips and a few goujons and get you all sorted.'

'No, no, I'm grand, honestly,' Susan told the obligatory Irish lie. Peggy silenced her with a narrowing of her eyes.

'Sit. Down. Do you want to go outside? There's a bit more craic out there?'

Susan resigned herself to a delicious, greasy fate but was in no rush to leave the cool silence and return to the sunshine. She pointed an awkward thumb towards a table at the back of the lounge.

'I'll just make myself comfy over there. Thank you.'

'Not at all. Sit down and relax. My youngfella Daniel will be out to you in a bit.'

Peggy left Susan to her own devices as she slipped away, singing to herself. Susan wandered past tables with reserved signs and sat in the corner, surveying the interior of the pub. The red foam-cushioned seats, with their equally cushioned backs against the wall, offered bliss after a long day of car journeys and seasickness. Susan sat in silence; only the ticking of a cuckoo clock, carved from driftwood with gnarled edges and a swinging pinecone, filled her mind. She inhaled and glanced down at the paperwork still in her hands. The words 'estate', 'Frank Shaw', and 'bequeathed' jumped out. She glanced at her phone reflexively, but there was nothing new to see. She had deleted her apps, but old habits died hard. The mainland and all its connections, noises and notifications were behind her. It would be easy to send a two-word message, 'I'm safe,' but that would open too many doors. Susan kept them clamped shut.

A handsome teenage boy with Peggy's firm look emerged from the door where she had exited, carrying a notepad and pen. He walked towards her with purpose.

'Can I get you anything?'

'I heard something about goujons and chips?'

'We've scampi as well if you'd prefer. Freshly caught this morning.'

She considered this, a sudden memory of lemony breaded fish spilling out of the past.

'Sounds great.'

Daniel made a note.

'Any drink?'

Susan bit her cheek, thinking. It was the middle of the day, but this was life now; she had nowhere to be, nothing to do, and no responsibilities. She thought about her last drop of alcohol, back before months of careful dieting, restriction and caution. There was no reason for that now.

'Go on, I'll have a glass of Murphy's so.'

She wanted to sound as though someone had been trying to convince her. Daniel didn't seem to notice as he scribbled the order down. He left Susan to the silence of the empty pub. The roar of laughter from outside the back door made her shift in her seat. Her body had started to cool; the sweat under her arms had dried, and there was a slight stale smell from her clothes. She hoped the cottage had a working shower and decided to run into the ocean if need be.

Time lagged in this place. Her pulse and breath slowed, responding to the slow tick of the clock. She sat in the calm and waited, the smell of stale beer mixing with the wafting of fried food from the kitchen. Daniel emerged again and headed for her table, one hand holding an overfilled basket of chips and scampi, the creamy stout in the other. He placed them with precision, and Susan thirsted for the creamy coolness of the glass dripping condensation onto the pub table.

As she tucked in, Peggy emerged from the door again with something wriggling under her arm.

'Now,' Peggy said as Susan half-choked on a prawn, 'I need to give you him as well.' She held a small, unimpressed terrier in her arms. Susan swallowed the prawn in perplexed silence.

'Walter, Susan; Susan, Walter.'

The dog sighed. Walter was a gruff, stubby-legged mutt with some Jack Russell and God knows what else. Peggy handed him over like a stuffed ham.

'He was Frank's. Congrats on your new dog.'

Susan and Walter sized each other up – neither was overly impressed with what they beheld.

'Em ... I didn't know there was a dog.' Peggy raised an eyebrow.

'I don't want a dog ... No offence.'

Susan's father had a dog once; his death had given her the only memory she had of her father crying. He never let another pet into the house. She had followed his lead, despite many debates with Jen. She shook the name away again and made an apologetic gesture towards the hound. He rolled pleading eyes to Peggy, who plastered on a grin and gave him a scratch behind his ears.

'Look, sure he's a lovely little fella. No bother at all.'

She leant towards Susan, staring her right in the eye, a slight scowl across her brows. Her tone was firm and final.

'I do not have the time for a dog. OK?'

Susan nodded and realised they were stuck with each other for now.

'Right. OK. Got it.'

Peggy called for Daniel, and he wandered over, gripping a large bag with *Red Mills* blazoned across it.

'That'll do him for the next few months, but he'd eat his own shite if you let him.'

Susan made a face at Walter; he seemed to shrug, unapologetic. Peggy offered Walter another gentle ear scratch. He leant into her hand and gave a satisfied grunt.

'Take good care of him. He's a good boy.'

Peggy placed a set of keys next to Susan's plate and turned to wander out the door behind the bar, disappearing into the darkness of her house. The dog hopped down off the seat and gave himself a quick shake. He cocked his head towards the exit. Susan shook her head, perplexed.

'I'm still eating.'

He exhaled, hopped onto the chair and curled into a croissant, his soft, wet nose tucked into his tummy. His tail was too long for his body and swept over his snout like a sleep mask. Soon Susan heard gentle snoring and returned to her food. A few minutes later, the pub came to life; two young people stumbled in at first, then the rest of the students from the pier poured in. They were older than the teenagers she usually taught – more facial hair, more confidence – but not by much.

Susan was tired but curious, content to watch the busy life going on around her from her cosy corner.. Peggy and Daniel flitted in and out of the mysterious door behind the bar, their trays overflowing with baskets of chips, chicken wings, goujons and deep-fried prawns; round ramekins of mayonnaise and sweet chilli sauce nestled amongst them. They waltzed around the tables, dispensing their goods like confetti. The invaders fell upon the food like locusts. Peggy seemed to know everyone by name and handed out kind words and stern admonishments to whoever needed either. She paused, chatting to the redheaded leader of the group, a young woman in her mid-twenties, if Susan had to guess. They pretended not to be talking about her, but she caught the glances they cast her way. She studied the map and letters she had brought with her to the island, running the set of keys through her fingers. She finished the bowl of fried food and knew the next step awaited. She yearned for the journey to be over, to arrive at a destination and rest. Walter took his time stretching himself awake. His claws tippy-tapped across the tiled floor while he ignored the affection lavished upon him by the pubgoers. Susan tried to pay, but Peggy waved her cash away with a flick – then clasped her hand, and the goosepimples rose on Susan's skin. 'I'm sorry about your uncle, pet. He was a good egg.'

CHAPTER TWO

Walter led the way home. He stopped to wee at regular intervals, accompanied by a glance back to ensure Susan was following. She cooed gratefully at him; he responded with withering looks. The orange of the *Montbretia* spread wild in the ditches and filled her eyeline as far as it could follow the road. She smelled its freshness and heard the bees working in the summer heat. Not dressed for this weather, her sunglasses slipped down her nose and, even with her polo neck wrapped around her waist, her T-shirt clung to her. Her jeans felt painted to her skin. The hiking boots, which had seemed like a sensible choice when packing in a panic, weighed her down as she stomped along the stony road. The straps of her bag cut into her shoulders, the pinching claws of its clasps squeezing snatches of skin between them.

The hill leading to the heart of the island stretched out before them. She followed Walter's chubby bum up the gravel path until a long stone wall appeared beside her, peeping out of the hedgerow. Walter stopped a few feet ahead of her at a small, rusted red gate hanging on one hinge. Here, the gravel gave way to carefully laid cobblestones, weeds and grass poking up between them. Algae from the winter still tarried like an oil slick, leading from the gate down the path towards the cottage and its whitewashed walls. A single-storey dwelling, its gutters were home to wildflowers and birds' nests – a family of starlings popped in and out of the drains, their heads to one side as they bickered with each other. In the garden to the front of the house, bathed in sunshine, bird feeders and baths lay empty and crusted with dirt and neglect. Blue tits and blackbirds combed the lawn searching for insects, still hopeful for the return of sunflower hearts and peanuts. The cottage, its garden and its inhabitants ignored Susan and Walter until the sun-burned warmth of Susan's forearms spurred her into action. She lifted the broken gate and opened it with care; the starlings retreated to the peak of the roof while the smaller birds shot into the overgrown blackthorn bush lining the stone wall and sheltering the cottage from the wild Atlantic winds. Walter glanced up at her, waiting.

'Go on then,' Susan urged. Walter shook himself, then walked toward the front door of the house, a solid wood rectangle of red that matched the lopsided gate. Six small panels of glass sat in the upper half of the door, thick with grime and unusable as windows to anything other than muck. Fumbling with her bags and the dog food, Susan turned the solid Chubb key, leaning her body into the door. It gave more easily than she expected, the years of care not undone by the recent neglect. She half-stumbled into the cool of the entryway.

The hall in the cottage where her father's family had lived was dark even in the afternoon. Only occasional sunbeams from the open front door alighted on dust. It smelled of months-old loneliness. Susan stood still, memory weighing on her shoulders. Framed photographs of her grandparents, distant relatives and parents filled the wall like a giant jigsaw puzzle. Here and there, a light square of virgin wallpaper, blank squares where photos used to be. She wondered if the photos were buried with him. Who would have decided that? Who curated the end of Frank's life? The faces on the wall were long gone, and her uncle had entrusted her with every possession he had on this earth. She glanced at the gaps where the missing photos would have been – almost every possession.

She heard the click-clack of claws on the tiled hallway and glanced down at Walter following behind. He looked around the cottage and gave a yawn, trotting down the dark corridor to the living room. Susan followed her four-legged guide past the doors to the bedroom and the bathroom. The door to the sitting-room was teak with glass beer-bottle panes. Nudging it further open, Susan glanced around the darkened living space. A couch, a small kitchen sideboard and a table. A unit of doors and drawers with brass handles. Most of Frank's life was in this room – a life she knew nothing about. She tried to imagine the people who could have come and gone here, who might have sat with him at the table, sipping tea of a winter's evening while the turf fire smouldered.

Walter hopped up on the settee and made himself comfortable, pulling a small blanket over his fat, round body. Small snores emerged from his snout, and Susan realised the guided section of the house tour was over. She returned to the hallway, leaving him and his bag of food to rest. The bedroom door opened with a soft squeak and the space surprised her with its light. It faced the front of the house, a wide window catching the daylight and filling it with sunshine. The double bed was unmade. Clean, pressed linen sat at the foot of the bed; placed there by Peggy, she assumed, and ready for her to prepare. She dropped her suitcase and backpack with a thud and almost cried with relief; tears of pain stung as the feeling returned to her arms, along with fiery pins and needles. She sat on the edge of the bed, considering her next move. She was drained. The locked box in her gut, where she stored her emptiness and fear, was beginning to leak. Its familiar darkness seeped into her. She swallowed hard, forcing it back inside. *Shove it down.* She lay down on the naked mattress, closed her eyes and curled up.

When she awoke, the sun had moved to the other side of the island, sinking beneath the horizon. The house was quiet, Walter still napping. She moved to the sitting room and sat next to him, her hand in his fur as he snored.

The silence of the house suffocated her. She remembered why she'd come here, remembered what she'd come from. The clock in the corner ticked.

The sun had started to swap places with the moon by the time Susan found the energy to move again. Even Walter had awoken and grown impatient with her. He pawed at the bag of food, nuzzling at its stringy clasps, and giving an irritated whinge in her direction. She shook herself back to life and apologised to the terrier. He grunted, sitting down, waiting. His old bowls still sat by the back door of the kitchen, waiting for him. She lifted them, and a wave of nausea swept through her. So much in this house held the trace of a man she knew almost nothing about. As she moved through the cottage, the otherworld pulled at her like a current beneath still water. The veil between life and death felt thin in this dark, empty house – the faces on the wall, the often dark feelings she'd brought with her.

Walter tucked into his bowl of dog nuts, ignorant of Susan's morbid thoughts. She searched for the kettle and ran the tap for a minute to clear out the dust. She pawed around the kitchen, looking for matches or a lighter, then lit the stove of the old-fashioned Aga. She'd always wanted one of these, but her middle-class notions of a farmhouse kitchen bore little resemblance to what faced her: a stubborn heap of metal with doors and handles and clasps. She stuck to the nearest ring and lit it. Thankfully, it sparked to life, the flames licking and kissing the bottom of the heavy kettle. Opening cupboards and presses, she remembered she had nothing to fill them with. No tea, no coffee. No milk or bread. She cursed herself and her rushing. The doorbell rang before she could berate herself any further.

Daniel stood on the front step. The outside house light, still working and bright, cast a harsh beam on his face, and he had soft, fuzzy hair on his top lip. He rolled out his words.

'Eh, my mam asked me to drop these to you.'

He handed a plastic bag over, bursting with basics. The bread, milk, tea and eggs she had been cursing the absence of. Oh, Peggy, Susan thought, I could kiss you.

'She said to come down for your dinner too this evening,' Daniel said. 'She does a great lasagne in fairness.'

Lasagne sounded great, but the tiredness and sweat of the day were still rolling down Susan's back and thighs.

'I'm a bit knackered. But thanks.'

'No bother.'

Daniel tipped the peak of his baseball cap and turned away. He had a gentle but gruff manner that was familiar.

'Daniel?'

He turned back, his face open and curious.

'Is Mick your dad?'

He flashed the mischievous grin of his sea captain father.

'He is, yeah.'

He was a good lad. She turned back toward the dark of the cottage and fumbled for a light switch. The bulb in the hall flickered on, then cut out.

'Oh, for fuck's sake,' she muttered. She heard a screaming whistle from the kitchen and rushed in to rescue the kettle as Walter watched her, unimpressed.

'I'm doing my best here, bud.'

He wagged his tail.

'Scrambled eggs?'

He wagged his tail harder.

'I should get you to make all my decisions for me, shouldn't I?'

He started to lick his arse and Susan laughed.

'Maybe not.'

She went to bed when the heat of the Aga faded and she could no longer sit in her own quiet torment. She lay awake in the new sheets until dawn started breaking and studied the inches of the ceiling, marking the cobwebs out of ten. Occasionally, she reached for her phone, spotted Jen's name on the notification screen, and thought better of it. She tried to count sheep, but it only made her frustrated. Sleep came within her grasp but slipped away again at the last second, disappearing back into her subconscious as the nighttime thoughts, drenched with guilt and sorrow, wrestled back control.

Dawn broke early on the island, and what a dawn. Lightning streaks of red and yellow danced across the sky and sea as the sun peeked up on the horizon. The birds started their chorus, calls and songs and chirps flying in the bedroom window. The sound was raucous yet harmonious, and soon she found herself drifting off on a bed of song.

CHAPTER THREE

———◦◦◊◦◦———

Susan found herself in Peggy's for lunch again, facing down her famed Irish lasagne. It drowned in a creamy sauce alongside greasy chips and coleslaw and Susan wondered how long her waistline would survive the island. She thought of the swelling, bruising and bloating from treatment that had all but disappeared from her abdomen, and swallowed the thoughts back down. She pondered her glass of Murphy's Stout, the sound of the ticking clock turning her thoughts over in her mind. Walter snoozed next to her on the lounge seats. From time to time, he lifted his head, and Susan offered a chip. She had made her peace with being well trained by a small dog.

She jumped as the front door of the pub flew open with a bang.

'Oh shit, sorry!'

It was the red-headed woman, back with the students. The gaggle of youths stomped in behind her, smelling of seagrass and fresh air, with a whiff of delicious weed snatching towards Susan.

'Sorry we're disturbing your lunch again!' the student-wrangler apologised.

'Not at all, I'm just enjoying my Peggy special.'

She gestured towards the plate piled high with food. The woman's face flashed between a quick grimace and a broad smile. She cast Susan a curious glance under her fiery fringe.

'I'll leave you to it then.'

The youths filled the empty seats and tables, the quiet oasis of the pub was chock-full of noise and laughter. Susan lifted her handbag onto the chair next to her, crossing her legs and folding in on herself. The woman was chatting at the bar, legs swinging from the stool as she laughed through her conversation, giggles bubbling.

Susan unfolded a detailed map of the island, acquired from a little stand in the cool porch. She pored over the shapes and lines and 'landmarks' – churches and bird-watching spots mostly – of her new home, trying to decide how to spend the rest of her day. She found a tag labelled 'Dune Island Distillery' and gave it a quick circle with her marker. It lay a fifteen-minute walk away on the other side of the island – an excuse, flimsy though it was, to avoid it for another day. There were two main beaches and swimming areas here, the cove she had already walked past on her way from the boat, and another golden spit of sand just over the hills from the cottage. A swim could consume two hours of the day if she planned it correctly. The chips sat heavy in her belly and she thought of herself sinking like a stone. She made another mark on her map across the yellow shore. A shadow fell over her shoulder.

'We're having a party there tonight if you want to pop by.'

It was the girl with the red hair, her blue eyes sparkling. She blew cold air on some chips in her hand as she waited for a reply. Susan thought the party sounded like a nightmare. She searched for a polite reply, but the girl raised her eyebrows in realisation.

'Sorry, you're probably thinking a party with a bunch

of random students sounds horrendous. Fair enough. Oh, also, I'm Amelia.'

She stuck out her hand, then pulled it back.

'Sorry, chip grease. You'll just have to pretend.'

Susan tried to remember how conversations usually worked.

'I'm Susan. Thanks, nice to meet you. I'll see about the party.'

'Do! There'll be music and beer – you know, I suppose, standard party stuff. And look, you'll know me now!'

'Is it for someone's birthday or something?'

Amelia gave a smiling shrug.

'This crowd doesn't need much of an excuse. Basically, the weather is nice, so we're going to go drinking on a beach.'

'That does actually sound like fun. I'll see how I'm getting on. Thank you, though.'

Susan hadn't expected a shock of warm kindness this early in the day, in the coolness of the pub, from a random stranger who owed her nothing.

'Oh god, don't mention it. Anyway, I might see you later, yeah?'

Susan blushed and felt annoyed with herself. She pursed her lips and tried to look mysterious. Amelia shuffled back to the crowd, seeming to forget all about Susan and her blushes. Walter followed her to the snug, spotting an opportunity for adoration. Susan took a breath and returned to her map. She spotted a tag labelled 'The Wailing Crag'. She circled it with the Sharpie.

The students had finished their food and the dart board, badly placed by the back door, was gaining their attention. Periodically, an oblivious punter came in from the beer garden and narrowly avoided a misthrown dart with a yelp; each time Peggy gave a snarl for them to be more careful, and when her husband walked in, she turned on him with frustration.

'Mick, you need to move that bloody dartboard before someone takes their eye out.'

Mick groaned. He looked tired, his face red from the wind and sun at sea. He grabbed his pint and left the bar, beaming as he saw Susan.

'Sure, there she is now!' He roared, and Susan's cheeks flushed with embarrassment.

'How are ya getting on?'

'Ah grand, Mick, thanks.'

Mick raised an eyebrow towards the empty lounge seat beside her and plonked down with a relieved groan. Daniel appeared and placed another glass of Murphy's in front of her with a wink. She winked back and brought the cool, creamy drink to her lips. Bliss. Mick laughed, full of admiration.

'Jaysis you're some woman for a stout are you?'

'Ah, sure when it's this good!'

Susan caught sight of Walter, belly in the air, Amelia and the others fawning over him. Amelia looked up, noticing Susan watching. The tip of her pixie nose turned pink. She beamed sweetly at Susan, her face lighting up with fun. Susan smiled back before she could stop herself. Mick rolled his neck, making a deep cracking noise that sent Susan back to the table.

'You've met Amelia, then? She's here every year with the college lads.'

'They're all students, yeah?'

'They come every summer, eat us out of house and home, drink the taps dry, then feck off again for another year. But sure, it's a bit of life around the place.'

He sipped again.

'How's the house?'

'Oh. Grand. A bit abandoned but seems in good shape.'

Mick was serious for a change.

'Frank kept it well in fairness.'

Susan was unsure what to say.

'Imagine,' Mick continued, 'your dad, Frank, grand-parents, all in that tiny little place. Mad, isn't it?'

She had history in the house; her own loneliness didn't belong there.

'You couldn't make it to the funeral?'

She glanced at Mick, ashamed. He gave a kind shrug.

'Look, it was a bad weekend to be getting out here, I wasn't even running the boat myself, the winds were that bad.'

Susan didn't want the excuse Mick offered. She had her own reasons lined up like coats by a front door.

'A lot was going on back home –'

'Dublin, is it?'

'Yes. Back in Dublin. I couldn't travel at the time.'

Susan's heart had started to quicken, memories she'd rather leave locked up threatening to emerge. She shoved them back down. Mick had a milky moustache on his top lip.

'It was a quiet one anyway,' he sat back and slapped his legs for some reason, 'I don't think Frank would give a shite about his funeral anyway.' He laughed again.

'There's not many of your family left, is there?'

'No. Only me now.'

'The last queen of the Shaws.'

She smiled, accepting Mick's mocking in good grace.

'Well, I did arrive on the *Lord and Lady*, Mick.'

'Oh fierce notions, Susan, fierce notions!'

He paused and leant back, his hand pointing towards the far end of the bar.

'You've seen the pictures on the wall, haven't you?'

Susan followed his finger and shook her head.

'Take a look there in a bit. You might see a few faces you know –'

Peggy appeared and interrupted her husband.

'Susan, love! Was the grub all right?'

'Oh, it was delicious, thank you. And thanks again for the supplies last night.'

Peggy dismissed her with a swat and returned to the bar, tea towel tucked into her apron. Mick tapped his fingers on the pint glass and seemed to consider his next words.

'C'mere, have you been down to see JP yet?'

'In the distillery?'

Mick nodded, solemn.

'No. That's tomorrow morning's plan. Hopefully.'

Mick said nothing.

'I've been avoiding it to be honest.'

Mick's face was understanding.

'Will he be in here this evening do you think?' Susan asked. Mick gave a firm head shake.

'He keeps to himself especially since … well. Himself and Frank were good buddies. He took it pretty hard.'

Susan found an odd solace, knowing someone mourned Frank. The pressure to be his last relative was suffocating

– it cloyed at her insides. Someone else mourned him, someone else missed him. She thought of the week ahead, of exploring further into what was Frank's and was now her world. A cold dripping of dread moved through her body, a fear of both things known and unknown.

'What's JP like?'

Susan noticed Mick was planning his words and the dread grew larger.

'He's a nice lad. Very obliging. But em … he's developed a bit of a taste for the oul merchandise shall we say …'

Mick gave a quick look towards the bottles of Dune Island Gin displayed at the bar.

'I wouldn't ride in there all guns blazing, if I were you. Just give him a bit of time to adjust.'

'Thanks, Reverend Mick.'

Mick was back to himself again with his booming laugh.

'Last time I give you any advice ya smart arse.'

Mick's kind eyes were warm and welcoming. He pointed at the back wall again.

'Go on and take a look there, I'll get another drink in.'

Susan swallowed, sliding out of her seat and weaving her way through the busy pub towards the back wall. She had sat near here yesterday on her first arrival – too tired and sweaty and overwhelmed to see beyond the map and the legal documents. The wall of Peggy's pub lined with photos of young men and women in sports teams, celebs in the pub, and even one of a white-haired US president sipping a pint at the bar. In this photo, Peggy, her own hair young and wild, leant over the bar – her face a picture of delight.

There was only one photo that Mick could have been referring to – it popped now that she was looking for it. Two young men beside each other, holding a giant fish out in front of them. The faces were framed by their seventies long hair and decorated with giant moustaches that kicked up dust in Susan's memories.

Her father and Frank stood together in this picture, taken before her father left the island, and barely glanced back. They must be only teenagers, but they had the look of adults, like everyone in the past seems to. Derek's muscular frame contrasted with Frank's weedy shoulders. The sun glinted off her father's milk-bottle glasses; in the background, the open sea spread out behind them. She reached out her hand and pressed a finger to her father's face. He seemed proud; Frank's pose seemed forced.

Behind her, a fresh pint was settling in front of Mick. He gave her a thumbs-up and pointed over her shoulder again. She searched the faces on the wall, spotting another photo of Frank – newer, and with a different man this time. This man was as tall and lean as her father had been short and blocky, his hair a sandy colour, his face handsome and gruff. Frank had lost the skinny arms and gained the muscular, stiff posture she remembered from the few times she had met him. The two of them held a plaque between them, with Peggy's bar in the background and a row of Dune Island Gin bottles lined up and posed.

'Irish Gin Awards: Best Small Craft Gin Maker 2015:
Dune Island Distillery'

This man with her uncle was JP, and his sad, angry face was waiting for her on the other side of the island.

CHAPTER FOUR

—◦◦◦◦◦◦—

Frank
Dune Island, 1978

Until the day he died, Frank said there was no one like Fiona.

'She was wild as a hawk.' He'd said to JP, on more than one occasion, when the gin they were distilling had loosened his memories and unmoored his words.

Fiona had never seen a hawk. There weren't any on the island, and Fiona, apart from the day she was born and one trip to the city to buy a communion dress, had never left it. Her escape to 'the big place' would have been secondary school across the slim channel on the mainland. But she never made it that far.

The day before Frank went to big school, they sat on the spiky grass, looking out to sea and the Wailing Crag peeking out over the Atlantic. They were twelve and eleven, counting the ladybirds that swarmed along. Frank squashed one with his thumb just to hear Fiona scream.

'Frankie, you're a monster!'

He waved the squashed insect in her face. She punched him. He rubbed the bits of broken ladybird on her dress. The dress was navy with yellow trim – the dark colour hid the guts and legs smeared across it. Fiona was not impressed.

'Well, Mammy's going to kill you now anyway.'

They both laughed, the crash of the waves stealing it away.

The last day of summer was here. Frank's Mam had lovingly ironed and laid out his uniform on the bed. He would join Derek on the first ferry and travel across the sea. There, he would sit amongst the mainlanders, squeeze himself into what they expected of him, and learn the things that a small primary school with two teachers and twenty-four students couldn't teach him. Fiona had one more year before she made the jump. She seemed to find the restrictions of time and ageing dreadfully unfair, as if Frank himself were responsible for the order of their birth.

'But WHY do you get to go but I can't?'

''Cos you're only eleven, Fiona.'

'You're only twelve!'

'I'm thirteen in three weeks.'

Fiona rolled her eyes. Frank pressed on.

'I'm too old to be learning five times tables with a bunch of kids in Mrs O'Grady's class.'

'But what if ... what if ...'

She was searching for words to put on her fears. Her loneliness.

'What if what?'

Frank had enough of his own fears without having to help Fiona with hers.

'What if they're not nice to you?'

'Who, the teachers?'

'No ... the big people.'

Despite the growing number of visitors to Dune Island, Fiona's perception of anyone not from there seemed to be of a race of mysterious giants. Frank shrugged.

'I'll be grand.'

Fiona was quiet, picking at the insect entrails on her dress. When she spoke, her voice was sad, thoughtful – a voice pulled from a future she didn't have.

'What if something happens and I can't mind you?'

His throat tightened. He swallowed it down.

'You're not supposed to be minding me. I'm your big brother.'

Fiona threw him a side-eyed look. She had already hit a growth spurt that Frank hadn't, threatening to outgrow him even with their eighteen-month age gap. Frank shrugged again.

'I'll have Derek.'

Her look intensified. Derek was no use. Not if there were girls around to impress or boys around to look tough with. She spotted Frank's teary eyes.

'No crying! You can't be crying over there, Frank.'

She squeezed his hand.

'Suppose you can cry here with me and then you won't want to cry over there …?'

'Yeah, maybe.'

There was no maybe about it. Not if he wanted any chance of surviving the big people.

They sat looking out to sea, in the place they came to almost every day of every year, in all weathers, since Fiona entered the world face red and fists waving. They had sat there with their mother, watching for their father's boat to return from the mainland. But mostly they sat alone, the stones leaving imprints on their legs, watching the world go by and making each other laugh.

That ended today.

They would have the weekends, but there would be homework – essays and maths – and Frank would need to do it alone. He knew Fiona knew this. She knew it deeper than he did. In twelve years, they had never spent a day apart. Now real life was coming for them – timetables and uniforms and a ferry that would carry him away every Monday and bring back a slightly different version of him every Friday evening. The Irish twins pulled apart.

'Sure you'll be coming over yourself next year.'

His voice was weak and unconvincing.

Fiona looked smug. She turned her face out to sea, like she was casting her mind into the future. Her face darkened, and she returned to the stone wall with the spiky grass by the pier.

'Ah yeah,' she said. Non-committal.

The wind was picking up, the sun going in. Frank gathered himself to go home. Fiona pouted.

'Do you want to go climbing?'

Frank shook his head.

'They're too slippy.'

Almost forty years later, JP sat nursing a whiskey, he listened as Frank retold the story, booze loosening the box of memories once again.

'She wouldn't leave,' Frank said, his eyes misting.

'I thought she'd follow me if I just left her. She must have gone over the rocks after … after I left.'

They both stared into the hearth, the flames flashing amber in their pupils. JP leant forward, topping up Frank's glass.

'It wasn't your fault, Frank.'

'I could never imagine her in that uniform, JP … why was that? Why couldn't I ever do it?'

Frank's memory was a series of violent flashes.d

Walking from the stony shore to the path.

A scream. Bloodcurdlingly familiar.

Yellow-trimmed dress bobbing in the ocean. Blonde hair, dark and wet. Small hands thrashing.

He ran. The waves threw him back. Against the rocks. Again. Sea water flooding his lungs. Again. The sea spitting him out on the steps, half-conscious.

Fiona's head slipping below the surface.

A man passing by ran for help.

His mother.

Her screams. Her sobs and wails. They settled within him, made a nest in his nerves, and re-emerged like Shelob throughout his life. Any moment of doubt, of fear, of worry, of challenge – he heard her screams. He was twelve again. His sister was dead.

Derek's face, grey. Fiona's limp body carried from the sea. He grabbed Frank. Lifted him to his feet. Shovel hands shaking him.

'Where were you? WHERE WERE YOU?'

Where were you, Frank thought. Where were you?

CHAPTER FIVE

—◦◦◇◦◦—

Susan couldn't remember the last time she had nothing to do and no one to do it with. She walked back to the cottage, passing shiny tourists and islanders alike. Everyone was good-humoured despite the humidity. Susan surprised herself with the genuine pleasure that had started to creep into her body. The island was starting to work, she thought. Real life was sliding away from her, the past shuffling into the distance.

In the cool of the bedroom, she tipped her suitcase out fully. Her swimming costume sat right at the bottom amongst the extra underwear, socks and make-up she had grabbed in a hurry. She sorted her small pile of clothes into even smaller mounds. The drawers were dusty – a quick wipe with a cloth and they were ready for her to set up camp. She stuffed the empty suitcase into the wardrobe, built flat into the wall, its glossy painted doorknob rattling as she turned it. The door didn't quite close, pressing against its hinges with a dull scrape. It would do. It would all just have to do.

Her swimming costume was neglected and showing signs of it – the panel covering her breasts almost thread-bare, her nipples pressing close to the surface of the fabric. She thought of the school tour with her students in Paris, how her fellow teacher Tracey had lost her bikini top on a slide at the water park. The absolute consternation. She laughed to herself at the memory and the laugh faded into something else – she should text Tracey. Let her know where she was. Let someone know. She closed the door on that thought before the guilt could spill through, slid her togs straps over her shoulders and flattened them.

She was surprised that Frank had a full-length mirror in his bedroom. She stood in front of it and wished she hadn't. Pasty – both in hue and texture. She had lost a lot of muscle tone over the previous twelve months, and though she didn't think she was overweight, her body was untoned. Her blonde hair was still thick and glossy, her brown eyes still shone out of a face that looked much younger than it was. Much younger than she felt. She patted her belly full of lasagne, turning to the side with her hands over it out of habit – the old pose, the old check. Her eyes stung. She turned away before her reflection could say anything else. Her breath caught. Something wet pressed against her leg – Walter's nose on her skin. She bent down and scratched behind his ear.

'Are you OK, boy? Why are you so needy, my little man?'

She gave herself a break from observing her flaws and pulled on a pair of shorts and a cotton T-shirt. The fresh clothes felt so refreshing against her skin, still clammy from being outside. She slid her feet and neglected toe-nails into her Birks.

In the kitchen, Susan found a carrier bag and packed a small bottle of water and a bowl for Walter – leaving him behind in the house seemed more cruel than taking him out into the hot summer day. He was just a tiny dog, still adjusting to new people and a new life. Besides, she sensed he would and could take himself home if he wanted to.

The sandy shore was quieter today than she had expected, the day-trippers gone until the following weekend. She felt like a true islander, taking in the Atlantic Ocean on a random Monday afternoon. It was a wonder how soft and golden the sand was. The tumbling dunes, filled with sea thrift and grass, proceeded from the roadside and dwindled to the sand, which piled and flowed and troughed along towards the sea. The beach gave way to a few feet of colder, harder sand mixed with tiny, round, gleaming pebbles, before the water washed in and claimed the land.

She had flashes of being here as a small child, marching in front of her parents towards the water. A bright pink bucket and shovel – not her choice of colour – swinging wildly in her tiny fists. The sea hit her like a wall of cold, salt on her lips, a scream of joy breaking out of her. A sting from a jellyfish that set her crying for hours; her mother stressed and her father annoyed. They hadn't stayed long here and hadn't been back.

There would be jellyfish today, Susan realised. The tide was in, the sun was high. Unless there were seals in the water, hunting them. Susan wasn't sure which was worse.

'Now Walter,' she said, 'no pissing on me if I get stung, OK?'

Walter hopped down the dunes. He plopped onto the sand, kicking up a fistful into his face. He shook his head and sneezed a few times. He stood waiting for her as she picked her way through the sharp grass.

Even in the late afternoon, the sun reflected off the sea so brightly it blinded her. She slipped off her sandals and let the water kiss her toes as it ran in and out – it was cold, but alive in a way that the sea in Dublin never was. The sparkling water held a dangerous draw. This side of the island faced east – the sun was at her back, casting her long shadow into the ocean. The dark patch rippled along with the waves, disappearing as the bright foam splashed and consumed it.

Her swim was just what she needed; the cleansing immersion of the ocean washed the sweat of the summer heat and yesterday's car journey from her. The cold, salty brine entered her ears, nose and mouth, the drops cauterising her, the sea wind pushing her back and forth within the currents. For an immeasurable time, she lay on her back, floating, allowing the currents to drift her back and forth. Her brain went quiet for those few moments; and the only sound in her ears was the sound of her own breath as she submerged herself beneath the waterline. She returned her feet to the bottom when she heard a sharp yip from Walter. She was chest-deep, and he knew the dangers of this more than she did, apparently. She dunked her head under the water one last time, ignoring the visions in the darkness that formed behind her eyelids when she did.

She returned to shore, stripping self-consciously under her too-small towel, forsaking underwear and pulling the T-shirt and shorts back over her sticky, sandy legs. She sat with her wet braid soaking her neck in the warmth, feeling the wind lift the beads of salt water off the hairs in her arm. She was already starting to freckle, just one day into summer. Her arms had tiny brown spots popping up across her pale skin, and she knew without looking that her face was the same, with a red tip on her sharp nose to match.

A woman with two little boys, twins, hassled past her, laden down with bags. She offered Susan a weary look, the children running to Walter – on his back, awaiting his worship.

'Sorry,' the woman started, 'is it OK if …'

She gestured at Walter and to the kids.

'Oh yeah, he loves it.'

The kids ooohed and aahed and stroked his upturned chest, fluffing his hair as they did. He lolled his head back, tongue hanging out, his tail giving happy swishes.

'They're well used to dogs then?'

'Obsessed. They have me tortured to get one. As if they're not enough work as it is.'

Susan responded with a flat smile and a bite of her tongue. She couldn't find it in her heart to care about the problems of parents.

'Anyway, thanks. Come on, lads.'

The two boys protested.

'NOW.' She barked, and they gave a final pat to Walter and wandered sadly away, waving to Susan and the little dog. Dinosaur swimming shorts and matching sun hats. Baby skin shiny from suncream, bits of sand stuck here and there. Hair bright baby-blond, grasping hands still learning to navigate their world. Walter returned to her side, his soft body pressed against her legs.

'I think you like me, Walter.'

Walter gave a non-committal lick of Susan's salty knee. She patted his head again. They sat together, enjoying the sound of the waves tossing in and out in the dying hours of the afternoon. Susan's stomach rumbled – the sun had started to lose some of its heat, anyway, and the hairs on her arm were perking up. The few humans had started to leave the beach, and the oystercatchers and curlews were emerging, running like lords of the dance with the sea covering their toes. They took no notice of the woman and her dog, watching the afternoon slide away across the sea.

She couldn't do a second meal in Peggy's in one day – that was a line she wasn't willing to cross just yet. Once again, she turned to scrambled eggs and toast for her dinner. She knew at some point she would have to fill her cupboards with something more substantial – but for now she needed sustenance, not anything fancy. When she finished eating, she glanced at the clock – it was 8 p.m., and now the whole night stretched in front of her like a rickety bridge. Tiredness wasn't there to save her this evening – her long lie-in and day of not much had made sure of that. She ran through her options with Walter.

'We could go to the pub'

His ears remained unmoved.

'So that's a no.'

Further proof I've lost my mind, she thought to herself, I'm consulting with a dog. She decided there were worse ways to make decisions, so she pressed on.

'We could stay here and play solitaire.'

While looking for a box of matches to light the stove, she had found an old dusty deck of cards hidden in a drawer in the old dusty sitting room. All fifty-two were present and accounted for. Walter still seemed unimpressed.

'All right … how about a walk?'

His ears lifted and she gave them a scratch.

'You're never going to say no to that, are you?'

As she stepped out the red door of the cottage, the sun was sinking into the peachy sea, the sky ablaze in a fiery sunset red.

Nature's night shift on the island was no less chaotic than the day. As the dusk approached, midges and grass-hoppers began to croak, swarming and chirping their way around the bushes and long grasses that bowed to Susan as she walked along the quiet gravel path. A hungry bat would flit above her head at times, making her start. Soon she grew used to the different sounds and sights of the island twilight, the gentle scrape of Walter's paws and his panting adding to the soundscape of her stroll. In the distance, she heard the curlews whistling, their haunting cries eerie in the fading light.

Susan's walk looped her back towards the cottage, conveniently and not entirely accidentally taking her past the golden bar of sand where the students from the lunch-time invasion were setting up their camp. Already, a giant bonfire was springing into life – small sparks spitting into the sky from the driftwood, licking the setting sun. She spotted coolers full of ice with bottles sticking out like the roots of a tree – a few young people sat around on picnic blankets, others had their own circle of guitars and a djembe drum, busy in their world of tipsy music.

Blaring music from a nearby speaker fought with the musicians for attention. She listened, didn't recognise the song, and suddenly felt very old. Then the music turned and ABBA came pouring out. She watched the young people, the dancing, the fire and the beach – surreal, something from a movie or a dream of youth. She had been standing there watching far longer than was normal when Amelia came skipping towards her, a hip flask in her hand.

'Hello!'

Amelia called to her, her voice full of friendship and mirth. She was a bit glassy – whatever was in the hip flask was doing its work.

'Hello yourself. Having a good night?'

'Oh … yes. Long hike today, so need to drink to dull the aches and pains.'

'Any excuse, I suspect.'

'The cheek!'

Amelia laughed again and offered the hip flask to Susan. She declined, Amelia waggled it, offering again. Susan shrugged and took a slug. Liquid fire slid down her insides.

'Jesus.' She handed it back, coughing and laughing. Amelia took a slug, then slipped the flask inside her pocket. Susan noticed a small tattoo of a bird on her inner wrist as she did. She looked away. Amelia gave a cough herself and rubbed her throat.

'That'll put hairs on your chest.'

'Great. Exactly what I'm after.'

Susan leant back against the rock she had been resting on. Walter had left them both, wandering towards the students, sniffing out snacks and belly rubs. Amelia watched him.

'He's getting very fat.'

'Are you body-shaming my dog?'

'It's not his fault, in fairness, we've been spoiling him

the last few weeks, he's been there every lunchtime eating our scampi.'

Susan felt queasy at the thought of it.

'You eat that stuff every day?'

'I know, and you know what the worst thing is?' Amelia said, 'I'm supposed to be a fucking vegan.'

'Ha!'

Amelia looked pleased. Susan spoke,

'I think he's just been lying around Peggy's, eating chips since ...'

'Your uncle died?'

'You've been doing your research then.'

It was Amelia's turn to give what Susan suspected was a rare blush.

'Sorry. Peggy mentioned it yesterday.'

'It's not a secret, you don't need to be sorry.'

Susan wasn't hugely surprised at how quickly news spread on an island of fifty people. Amelia sipped her liquor again. She opened her mouth and bit her lip.

'How long are you around for?'

Susan shrugged.

'For the summer, I guess. Maybe longer. It's all a bit complicated. Yourself?'

Susan knew the answer, but she liked hearing Amelia speak in her champagne voice. Susan caught her scent; she smelled of the sea and soft detergent.

'We're here for the summer. We go up into the cliffs and count the birds.'

Susan's eyebrows lifted before she could stop them.

'You count birds. What, like, the seagulls and stuff?'

'Oh god no, they're boring bastards. The more unusual ones – puffins and that. I can show you them sometime if you'd like.'

Amelia gave a flirty wink as she said this, giving Susan a jolt. Susan was out of practice, but this seemed more than friendly. She replied as her mind panicked.

'That would be nice. Maybe, you know, uh, once I've settled in a bit.'

'Sounds like a plan.'

They both stood awkwardly for a moment before Amelia stuck her hands in her pockets.

'I'm going to head back to the lads. Do you want me to send the dog back over?'

'Jesus no, keep him. He's a pain in the arse.'

Amelia turned away, then wheeled back around.

'Oh, and by the way … do you still have your map?'

Susan dug it out of the pocket of her shorts. Amelia took it, pressing a small line under a house-shaped icon with her fingernail.

'That's where we're staying.'

Susan peeked at the key – 'Dune Island Hostel?'

'Yeah, not very imaginative, is it? I'd have gone with Sandy Shores Inn or maybe Rolling Hills Lodge, something a bit more, I dunno, romantic?'

Amelia looked off in the distance, eyes a bit glazed. Susan smirked.

'A romantic youth hostel?'

'Yeah, it's pretty grim either way, isn't it? Anyway, you know where to find us. You know, if you need anything.'

Susan and Amelia looked at each other, an odd current buzzing in the still air between them. Susan broke the silence.

'That's good to know,' she ventured. 'Just in case.'

'Exactly!' Amelia's stillness was broken, her bounce returned as she retreated, giving Susan a wink. 'It was really nice to see you, Susan.'

Susan blushed again and looked for Walter. He waddled towards her, tongue lolling in the heat. She spun away from the beach, the party, and the students and headed for home.

CHAPTER SIX

At night, Susan slept and her pain awakened. It crawled out of her heart, around her lungs, up her spine and surrounded her sleeping throat. It spidered across her brain, dragging memories to the surface that she spent the daytime pushing down. She awoke in a panic in the pitch dark, reaching with her fingers between her legs, expecting to find hot, wet copper. She remembered where and when she was, and lay back on the cool sheets until her breath and her heart slowed.

She rested late the following day, lying in the warm bath of the morning sun, dozing in and out of stressful dreams. She leant over the bed and grabbed her map and the folder of documents from the nightstand. She flicked through accounts, statements, land deeds and legal documents – fighting to understand this new world she had inherited. Her degree in English had not prepared her for this. Walter pushed his way into the bedroom, the door's dodgy catch giving way beneath his gentle nudge. He hopped up on the bed beside her, his coat brushing her arm as he rolled himself into a bagel. They lay together, his fur a sleeping bag around her fingers, as the sun drifted across the island sky. When she could no longer lie in the quiet comfort, when the knowledge of what lay ahead refused to settle, she moved – ready, although not quite willing, to start the day.

Susan walked the gravel road into the glare of white summer light. She passed some tourists and tipped her head, 'hello' – like a local. She wiped the sweat from her forehead, Walter panting beside her.

'All right, pal?'

His tongue lolled as he looked up at her. A blackbird scrabbled in the ditch nearby, pausing to trill hello to his wife nesting in the heather. His partner sang back to him. Susan considered joining their conversation, whistling to them of her own woes. She imagined how they'd listen to the tangle of her life, confused as she was, before flying off to their own.

Every inch of the island buzzed – birds singing, loud shocks of blooming colour dazzling, and the crash of the Atlantic was never out of earshot. In the brief milliseconds when birds were silent and the sea took a breath, a goat or donkey sauntering through its day would disturb the brief peace. The whole island, serene and gentle though it seemed, heaved with life. Chaos hummed beneath its calm.

Beyond the hills in the distance, the ocean shimmered. A lighthouse – borne of sweat and genius in the early twentieth century – sat stubborn and immovable off the craggy cliffs. Susan wondered whether her great-great-grandfather had stood in this exact spot once, watching builders and engineers swarm like ants on the rock, adding piece by piece until the great beacon stood ready to light. Generations of sailors had followed its beam home, and now Susan kept it in sight as she descended into the valley to survey her new empire.

A different sound reached her – the put-put-put of distillery mechanics and the rumbling of furnaces, grinders and mixers. The distillery sat in the snug valley, separated from the ocean by a series of lush hills. A collection of grey squat sheds and polytunnels poked out of the shell of an old farmhouse, contrasting with the green of its surroundings. She'd expected it to be bigger – her impressions of distilleries summoning visions of belching chimneys, building-high still pots and fires stretching into the sky. This place was peaceful. It sat amongst its surroundings, not quite belonging, but comfortable nonetheless. Well-maintained wooden posts fenced in the sheds and polytunnels. Susan spotted a gate, secured with a heavy metal clasp – she remembered to close it behind her as she stepped in, even if all that could escape were whiffs of botanicals and the sound of boiling pots. She picked up her pace as she approached what looked like the hive mind of the set-up – a low-roofed white shed with potted plants by the door and a pair of mucky boots on a mat outside. Walter gave himself an excited shake and trotted on ahead of her.

'Get back here!'

'Hello?'

A deep voice from within the office gave her a start. The tall, sandy-haired man from the pub photo popped his head out, surprise on his weathered face. Thick grey socks, big toes poking out.

'You must be JP?' Susan forced warmth into her voice, aware she had arrived uninvited and unannounced.

'I am.' He replied, studying her. Susan drove on.

'I'm Susan.' She paused, hoping for a flicker of recognition. Something. He stared, unmoved. 'Frank's niece?' she continued.

He folded his arms. He was semi-present, like someone awoken from a dream.

'Were you asleep?' It was out before she could stop it – rude, she knew, but the silence had pushed it from her.

'No?'

She didn't believe him but chose to move on.

'I thought I'd pop by and say hello. Since you know …'

'Since you're my new boss, is it?'

JP spat it out. Susan's jaw tightened. She hadn't come here for a fight – she hadn't even figured out what she had come here for.

'That's one way of looking at it, I suppose.'

'Is there another way?'

Susan tried to find a reply, but JP drove on.

'It's all right though, I'm sure you have years of experience running a distillery, or in sales, or merchandising or marketing?'

JP's immediate sarcasm was surprising. She blinked then and stared JP straight in the eye.

'You know I don't have the experience, JP. So let's figure it out, yeah?'

It was JP's turn to be surprised. He folded his arms again. Susan calmed herself and tried a new tactic.

'I thought maybe I could get a tour of the place?'

Walter's tail knocked over a plant pot,, and JP's face softened. He bent down to the happy dog, who leapt and kissed his face.

'Ah, there he is now.'

JP's big hands scratched behind his ears. Walter's tail was almost wagging off his body – it was the most animated Susan had seen the dog since they had met.

'You're a good little fella, aren't you?'

'Peggy said he'd eat his own shite if I let him.'

JP laughed.

'Ah yeah, he's an awful dope all right. We had to bring him to the vet over in Skibb once because he got into one of the whey stores and ate his way through it.'

'You and Frank?'

JP stood up quickly, ignoring her question.

'I heard you arrived a few days ago.'

'Yeah, I was just … you know, settling in, getting the house sorted and that.'

He seemed to search around for something else to say. Susan continued.

'It's looking well actually, the cottage. I expected it to be in more of a state.'

'Why would you expect that?'

JP's tone was sharp.

'Just as it's been empty for so long.'

'It's not been that long.'

'I suppose …'

Susan couldn't figure out where the hostility was coming from – the only safe subject seemed to be the dog. She opted for silence – she had waited out many a teenager throwing a strop, she could manage it with a man in his fifties too. They both stood, stone-faced. JP rubbed the back of his neck, then sighed.

'All right, a tour then.'

He turned and walked back into the office, seemingly unfazed about whether or not Susan was following.

The distillery spread across a series of stifling-hot

greenhouses – a botanical garden with machinery tucked away in the back. The scent of herbs and spices calmed her, loosened something in her chest. She wanted to learn their names, all of them. JP trudged her through the area, describing the different botanicals in a hassled monotone, throwing the names out left and right at a speed she couldn't grasp. She made a mental note to bring a notebook next time and to find a herbology guide somewhere and somehow.

JP paused to pinch a small amount of whatever plant they were passing. It almost looked like a bush of bright daisies. He passed it under Susan's nose, surprising her with the delicacy of the gesture. She inhaled deeply. The scent was soothing and fresh, and for a moment the knot inside her eased.

'Wow, what's that?'

'That's chamomile.'

'Like the tea?'

JP chuckled, then seemed annoyed with himself.

'Yes, like the tea.'

'I didn't realise how pretty the plant is.'

'That was … that was Frank's favourite one to infuse. He loved the flavour and the smell of it.'

Susan tried to imagine her gruff uncle enjoying a botanical gin infused with chamomile. The thought danced across her brain like oil across water. JP saw her face.

'He was a man of fine taste.'

They swapped sad looks. Susan spoke.

'You two were close?'

JP's eyes turned to stone.

'Not particularly.'

He turned again and walked on, leaving Susan standing in the cloud of his mood. They reached the end of the last greenhouse, the door opening out into the afternoon sun. For once, the outside temperature was welcome and Susan took a deep breath of the salty air coming in from the sea.

On the other side of the fence from where they stood, a small herd of cows were lazily grazing and flicking flies away with their tails.

'They're yours too,' JP stated.

'Cows?'

Susan pointed at the herd in disbelief.

'Yep.'

JP seemed amused, warming up a bit. Maybe he was just grumpy when he woke up at three o'clock in the afternoon, Susan thought. He continued,

'The cows actually came first, before the distillery. The O'Learys over in Kilcrea make craft cheeses and that – so they send the waste whey back to us to make the gin.'

Susan made a face.

'I know it sounds odd, but it's fairly common. Now the cows don't really produce enough whey anymore for the amount of gin we make, so we buy in some as well. But these ladies still get their bit in. Frank liked having them.'

The cows had started wandering over to them, their big eyes filled with curiosity. JP leant on the wooden fence, stretching his hand out to give the lead cow a rub down her long, wide nose.

'Is it just the gin you guys, em, we make?'

'Yeah, we're not in the whiskey business sadly.'

'Do you think we should be?'

'Arra, I have a few ideas, all right.'

Susan saw a way in.

'Sure, we can have a chat about them once I know what the fuck I'm doing.'

JP was surprised, but Susan could see he was pleased – a pink tinge was in his cheeks. He gave a cheeky half-grin.

'That'll be a while so.'

He reached out and placed Susan's hand on the cow's head.

'This is Minnie. She's the best milker. She bosses the rest of them around the place, but she's as gentle as you can get with us.'

Susan rubbed the smooth nose, feeling the soft breath of the animal as Minnie moved towards her chin. The cow rubbed her block of a head against Susan's palm, using it to scratch her short fur. Something about the warmth of the animal, the simplicity of the exchange, made Susan's throat tighten. Minnie stopped, shook herself off and wandered away, hooves kicking up the dry muck behind her. The rest of the cows followed her lead, marching to the opposite end of the field where the grass was lush and less spoiled by their trampling.

Susan leant on the fence, her shoulders almost touching JP's arm. The skylarks were kicking off in the field next to them, the long marshy grass giving them room to grow and nest and trill in peace. Swallows flew to and fro from the eaves of the greenhouse behind them; swooping and soaring above their heads. Susan wondered if she could feel this content forever on the island. Whether the knot could stay loosened. Whether the dreams would stop. JP seemed to read her mind.

'Will you stay long?'

The words fell out of JP's mouth and Susan had sensed they had been stored in the back of his mouth since they had met. She loosened her own tight jaw and allowed some truth to slip out.

'Honestly, JP, I have no idea.'

He seemed to appreciate the honesty, and the distress that lurked underneath it.

'It's starting to get dark.' He muttered, looking far out to sea where the dangling sun was starting to lose some of its brightness.

It was barely evening, but Susan knew she overstayed her welcome.

'I'd better head ... I've kept you long enough. Thank you.'

Susan saw that when the anger and hostility dropped away – what remained was pain. The half-smile he gave her as he waved goodbye, even the full grin he gave Walter as he fished a treat from a dusty jar in the office, the beam as he rubbed the dog's ears – the eyes never matched. A sorrow she couldn't quite name lurked in him. Her own grief recognised it.

'I'll see you for a pint down in Peggy's at some stage, yeah?'

'You might yeah.'

She took that as a win and started back home.

CHAPTER SEVEN

Frank

Since Fiona's death, Frank's mother had struggled to care about anything, so every weekend he washed, dried, and ironed his trousers, his shirts, his jumpers. He even pressed his tie, each wrinkle pushed out by the steamy heat of the iron. He arrived at school on the ferry each Monday tidy and exact, ready for another week of morning porridge, rainy PE and teachers handy with their rulers across your hand.

First year had been all right. He started two weeks late, already defined by what others saw in him: the boy with the dead sister, the boy whose brother won GAA trophies, the boy with weak arms and a face that blushed without warning. The dead sister covered a multitude – even the most vicious of the boys wouldn't touch him.

By third year, that protection had run out of road. The girls found him endearing. The boys found him strange. He was thin and gruff. He liked PE until the other boys, already growing their chests and shoulders, started slamming him into the walls. The teachers blew their whistles impatiently.

'Francis Shaw, would you get up please?'

He would pick himself up, his head ringing, his neck

aching, and another series of bruises purpling somewhere on his arm.

One day, he sat in the changing room after another slam, holding his head in his hands. He heard a rustling and stood up immediately. Michael, another third-year, walked in almost on tiptoes. He had a mischievous face and darting eyes.

'You all right, Frank?'

Frank shrugged, turning his back and studying the lockers intensely. He blinked the tears away. When he turned back, Michael had moved closer.

'It's shit that they do that to you.'

Frank blushed and his eyes stung again. Michael seemed to notice them but ignored them, even as Frank pushed his voice out through a thick gullet.

'Ah, sure they do it to everyone.'

'No, they don't. Only to some people. Like you. And me.'

Michael bit his lip and gave a grin.

'Anyway, I just wanted to say I was sorry.'

The rest of the class came bursting in. Michael sprang away and returned to his locker. Suspicious looks fell on them both. Frank dressed as quickly as he could and escaped the changing room for another day.

A week later, another PE class, another slam. This time, his ribs burned. Later he changed slowly, his back to the room, buttoning his shirt with minute movements to avoid the bruises. A punch landed sideways across his ear, more like a slap, but it sent him tumbling over the bench anyway. Frank picked himself up and faced Jack, a large townie with a bad temper.

'Looking at my brother were ya? I'll fucking kill you, ya dirty bender.'

Frank's head rang. He looked around for confirmation that others were seeing this, hearing it. A changing room full of boys and young men, their faces a mix of embarrassment, adrenaline and fear. Michael – Jack's brother, someone Frank thought was a friend – hid in the corner, his face burning with mortification. Frank held his hands out in front of him, palms towards the angry young man.

'Jack ...'

Jack stepped towards him, jerking his head forward in a threat. Frank flinched and heard small sniggers of laughter around him.

'Don't fucking look at him again or I'll break your fucking legs, ya little queer.'

He turned and walked out. Frank picked up his clothes, bundled them into his thin chest and headed towards the bathroom stalls.

Derek was behind the school hall with a blonde from the girls' school, having a smoke. Frank sought him out, a cherry bruise spreading across his ear and his cheek. His older brother swung an arm around the blonde and pulled her close. He took a quick look at Frank's ear and grimaced.

'I told you to stop messing.'

'I wasn't messing, Derek. I was just getting changed.'

Derek offered the cigarette. Frank shook his head.

'Derek ...'

His brother tilted his head, as if he knew what was coming.

'Wha?'

'Is Jack Deasy in your class?'

'Is that who hit you? What did you say to him?'

'I didn't say anything? Can you talk to him? Can you tell him … can you tell him I'm not a bender?'

Derek and the blonde laughed.

'I mean … I could …'

A shrug and silence.

'Will you though?'

'No.'

'He'll stop at me if you tell him. Just tell him I wasn't looking at his brother. I don't look at anyone.'

A look of disgust passed over Derek's lips in a moment. Frank caught it and the fire of humiliation burned even brighter. Was his brother disgusted at his desperation? At the possibility of him looking at other boys? At the lying?

'Who's his brother?'

'Michael Deasy.'

Derek chewed his lip.

'And when I'm gone next year? What about then?'

Frank took the cigarette and inhaled. He coughed, his eyes watering. The girl gave another laugh.

'You need to toughen up, Frankie. You're old enough now to sort your own problems out.'

Frank's mouth tasted of bile. He hated his brother. He hated Jack. He hated that squealing weasel Michael.

He hated himself.

CHAPTER EIGHT

———∞◇◇∞———

Despite the cool breeze that swept through the cottage windows, hot, crawling alarm slid down Susan's spine again. Still wearing her pyjamas, she dug through the wardrobe for her abandoned hiking boots. The summer heat still threatened her feet with blisters – but Amelia had been clear that she would need proper boots, to guard against the rocks, and ticks.

She had cornered her in the pub the night before. Susan sipped on the distillery's produce – for research, she told herself – and saw the students, tourists and island residents mix and laugh and get tipsy together. Amelia sidled up alongside her, face flushed from the heat of bodies and alcohol.

'I'll bring you for that walk tomorrow. To see the puffins.'

Susan looked around and pointed to herself in mock confusion, feeling the warmth of the gin loosening her tongue.

'Me?'

'Yep – see you at nine.'

Susan made a face.

'Ten a.m.'

'Fine. It's going to be great!'

'You haven't heard how much I complain when I'm hiking.'

'I don't think you'll be complaining.'

Amelia had thrown her a smug smirk, and Susan's mouth went dry. She'd coughed and taken a sip of her gin, searching for more excuses.

'What about your students?'

'They're travelling around other islands for the next few days.'

'You don't know where I live.'

'Don't I?'

Susan had run out of invented obstacles and resigned herself to her fate.

'Oh, and wear your boots!'

After Amelia retreated, Susan caught Mick raising her eyebrows at her.

'What?'

'I'm not saying a bit!'

It was half past nine and too early for gin. Walter lay on the bed; his hair had formed a fine layer of dander across the duvet.

'It's just a walk, Walter, it's just a walk.'

He paused, licking his paw to throw her an unconvinced look, then returned to grooming himself. Something tight and painful thudded in her chest. Her stomach gurgled with cold nausea. A knock on the door – bile rose in her throat. She pulled on a jumper and ran to the door in her socks, throwing it open.

Amelia's blue joyful eyes shone at her from the doorstep.

'You're early!' Susan cried. Amelia laughed.

'Chill out, I finished breakfast earlier than planned. I can wait out here? Or …'

She looked past Susan into the sitting room. Susan

pushed her tongue against her lips and swallowed her indigestion.

'Yeah, OK, fine, come in. I'll be a few minutes.'

Susan rushed back into the bedroom, leaving Amelia to wander in. She heard her squeaking open the sitting-room door, then her happy greeting as Walter wandered in to say hello.

'Oh, who's a good boy, who's a very good boy?'

The thumping of Walter's tail against the wooden floors mirrored her frenzied heart. She sat on the bed and took a deep breath, rubbing her fingers together. She pulled one of her boots on, groaning at the weight of its leather, and the thick socks needed to stop them from from shredding the skin on her heels. She called to the sitting room.

'Do I really need the boots?'

'Yes!'

Susan pulled on the second one with a grunt. She was ready and she could no longer avoid the arrangements her brave, tipsy self had made. Amelia was on her knees in the sitting room, rubbing Walter's upturned belly.

They turned left out of the gate of the house, a sloping walk that eventually forked into two. One road led towards the beach where Susan had spent a sandy afternoon earlier that week; the other led further inland towards the heart of the island. Amelia swung a left at the fork, beginning the climb away from the sea. Susan followed, blowing out her lips in anticipation of the sweaty trudge ahead. Walter skipped alongside her, his fitness already improving from his faithful following of her island walks.

'Where exactly are we going?'

'Does it matter?'

The island was a criss-cross of gravel paths, cow tracks and hill-walking ways across springy beds of heathery hills. The graveyard was the highest point of the island, Susan remembered noting it with her marker on the map.

'How do you know your way around here so well?'

'I told you, I come here every year with the college.'

'Every year?'

'Yes.'

'So you're one of those eternal students then?'

'I'm not a student, Susan.'

Amelia turned to her, a single eyebrow raised in mock shock and continued.

'I'm a lecturer.'

'Oh ...'

'Jesus. How old do you think I am?'

'I dunno, like twenty-four, twenty-five?'

Amelia looked pleased and turned back towards the road, not offering any more.

'Come on now, keep up.'

Susan puffed out her chest and forced her legs, short but muscular, to power her on. Until Amelia stood bright-eyed and bushy-tailed on her doorstep, she hadn't realised that the redhead was taller than her. Not that she didn't appreciate a taller woman. Or that she should be appreciating any woman. She shook her head, frustrated with herself. They walked on, the incline increased. The sweat of the island pooled where her hair met her neck. She spotted that Amelia had an undercut in the same spot, a clean-shaved line that kissed the tip of her spine.

Susan followed the vertebrae down her back where the muscles rippled through her tight tank top. She glanced away as Amelia chatted on, her tone becoming oddly officious.

'What do you know about Irish sea birds?'

'Not much, it's mostly seagulls in Dublin.'

'Plenty of them here too.'

'I'm good with flowers and gardening stuff, if that makes up for it?'

Amelia gave her a side-eyed look.

'It helps.'

Susan remembered her father squatting in their garden, his gloved hands clutching mounds of dead and dying weeds and vegetation. His aggression with weeds was only matched by his gentleness with everything else. Soft pink flowers held between his fingers as he breathed in their scent. He would point them towards her, invite her into his world of flora. She would lean in, press herself against him and be enthralled.

Amelia's teacher's voice continued, giving a lecture she had clearly delivered many times.

'So puffins are actually relatively common around the Irish coast. You'll find them in the Skelligs, as we all saw in *Star Wars*, but you'll also find them around the east coast, and of course, here on Dune Island and other islands around the south coast. There are loads of chicks around at the moment, actually.'

'Cool.'

'It is very cool.'

'I can't believe you're such a nerd. You seemed so slick when I first met you.'

'Three days ago?'

'It's been a long week.'

As they walked on, Susan settled into Amelia's bubbling presence. She fought off the clawing sensation of rising tension and ignored the growing awareness that she was walking a very dangerous tightrope. She told herself it didn't matter that every so often Amelia would send a glance her way, her lip slightly bitten. It didn't matter that each time this happened, Susan felt a small jolt deep inside her in a place she had forgotten about. They were out for a nice walk, Susan decided. She was learning about puffins, terns, little egrets, great egrets, and the many types of gulls that filled the island around them and the skies above. She pushed away thoughts of the phone, lying abandoned on her nightstand, its notifications still lighting up. Amelia didn't seem to notice Susan's internal fires, or care how much petrol she poured on them.

'How did the distillery go yesterday?'

'Oh, fine ...'

'I heard JP can be a bit testy?'

Susan gave a derisive snort, and Amelia smirked.

'I'll take that as a yes.'

'I don't think he likes me very much.'

'Why wouldn't he like you?'

Susan shrugged.

'Did your uncle ever talk about him?'

Susan liked Amelia, but she wasn't about to go into the intricacies of her family's ups and downs and lack of communication.

'So Amelia, where are you from?'

'Galway.'

'So you're a vegan lesbian from Galway? Ground-breaking.'

The quip came out before she could stop herself.

'I'm not a lesbian,' Amelia said.

An unwelcome note of disappointment pinged within Susan. Amelia's face was indignant.

'I'm queer, actually.'

'Of course you are.'

Amelia threw her head back and laughed, the most genuine laugh Susan had heard in a long time.

'You're such a grump.'

They had reached the graveyard, which Susan knew spelt the end of the hill. The roadside brambles gave way to a stone wall that ran the length of what had been the islanders' resting place since people first settled here two hundred years ago. Susan leaned against the wall when Amelia paused by it and watched her point through the graves.

'We'll walk through here, it's the best view you'll get of the island, then we'll go down to the cliffs and the Wailing Crag if we have time.'

'What exactly is the Wailing Crag?'

'You'll see! It's a stunner!'

The gate was old, cast iron, and well-maintained by the community. It slid smoothly along its hinges, closing with a gentle clink when Susan pushed it back into place. Instant peace. Her ancestors were around her – she could almost hear them whispering, holding her in their curiosity and wonder. *She's here. The last of us is here.* Susan paused, breathing in the honeysuckle carried on the wind.

The graveyard covered the top of the hill, and a stone-stepped pathway brought them up into its centre. They stood and admired the panorama of the island, the Atlantic stretched out on all sides. On a clear day like this, the mainland – and all the shadows it held for Susan – was in perfect view to the north, the small bobbing boats of Skibbereen skittering around in the foam. To the west stood the lighthouse, its torch dark. When evening came, it would fire up, waving its light around the ocean and away from rocks and dangers. To the south, nothing but water; the next land was about two thousand kilometres down in Portugal. To the east, the cliffs they were about to visit, and beyond that again, the sea. The never-ending, all-consuming Atlantic, lifegiving and alive itself. A hungry mouth with its lips around the island, ready to swallow it down. One step and she could disappear. The thought held her for a moment, then the breeze swept through her hair and brought her back. At this altitude, the wind blew from all directions. Susan closed her mouth to stop it from stealing her breath. Walter's ears helicoptered, eyelids squinting against the breeze.

'Do you want to … em … stop by anyone?'

Amelia, awkward – a first, in Susan's experience.

'I … I actually don't know where Frank is. Or anyone else, really.'

'You weren't here for his funeral?'

Susan bit her lip in self-disgust and shook her head. Amelia moved past it.

'Your parents aren't here?'

'God no.'

'They weren't … massive fans of the island. Or Frank. They didn't talk.'

'We can look for his grave if you want?'

Amelia's voice, usually full of mischief, was gentle and kind. Susan pressed her nails into her palm.

'No ... that's all right.'

She wasn't ready yet – and wasn't sure she wanted to do it in someone's company. She started descending towards the east. Amelia caught up with her in a few strides, and they fell back into an easy stroll past the graves. Some were new, their marble still glinting in the sun, fresh flowers placed on the grassy knolls before them. Others were barely legible, yellow lichen crawling over the lettering, their stone edges crumbling. The grass was well cared for between each plot, and the ground was uneven but easily followed. Amelia opened the gate, gesturing for Susan to walk through with a flourish.

'Madam.'

'Thankee kindly.'

Susan let out a strong exhale when she stepped through – the air seemed lighter out here, the forced solemnity of the graveyard had begun to feel oppressive. Despite the heat of the summer so far, the next section of the walk was boggy – a winding inlet from the sea kept it sodden all year round. They squelched through the mud, their heavy boots splashing through the brown liquid. Susan resorted to lifting Walter over a large puddle, his stubby legs dangling uselessly in her arms. Amelia placed a hand on Susan to steady her, then observed her keenly.

'I know you didn't want to wear them, but you do look very good in those boots.'

Susan shook her head, annoyed at how pleased she was.

'Do you always say every thought that comes into your head?'

Amelia looked a bit surprised but amused.

'Doesn't everyone?'

'No ... but I like it.'

'Well, I'm glad you like it. But even if you didn't – tough shit.'

They both laughed and continued walking. Susan stopped, something bothering her.

'How did you know my parents were dead?'

Amelia gazed at her.

'I know a lot about you, Susan Shaw.'

The hill descended, then sloped back up closer to the cliffs. Poor Walter was struggling again, and Amelia took matters into her own hands, plonking him into her backpack and slogging along with his head sticking out, tongue lolling to one side. Susan laughed her head off at the sight of it, this thrilled lazy terrier on his royal litter.

'No wonder you've got so fat,' she scolded.

'Oh, he's fine ... But maybe we'll leave him in Peggy's next time.'

'Next time?'

Amelia winked, and Susan blushed again. For fuck's sake, she swore to herself. Get a fucking grip.

'Here we are!' Amelia announced. The cliff they were on was at the bend of a U-shaped inlet on the coast. From where they stood – about six feet back from the edge and four hundred feet above sea level – Susan could see the buzzing of activity to and from the cliff faces on her left and right. Amelia lifted Walter out of her backpack with a small kiss on his head. He shook himself down and went off for a sniff. Susan was concerned.

'Don't fall off, you dope!'

'He'll be fine, he's not that much of a dope.'

Amelia grabbed a pair of binoculars from the pack and handed them to Susan. They were warm from Walter's furry body. She pressed them to her eyes and followed Amelia's finger. Amelia was leaning against her, the warmth of her breath on her neck as she spoke.

'See that big clump of sea thrift by that branch. That fluffy pink flower, just to the right of it – you see that big cavity in the cliff?'

Susan gasped as a fluffy baby puffin popped into view in her lens. It darted in and out of the burrow as its black-winged parents went to and fro, their vivid orange bills bobbing as they dropped fresh, tiny fish into their child's mouth. The chick lowered its head and squawked from its tiny beak, roaring at its hassled parents. Amelia gave a gentle elbow into Susan's ribs. Susan pulled the binoculars away, smiling, her heart feeling a familiar joy. Amelia's face filled with delight.

'See? I told you it was cool.'

They sat watching the puffins for about an hour, on the useless rain jacket Susan had packed in her tiny bag just in case. Their arms touched as they took turns using the binoculars, Amelia nattering away, boggling Susan's mind with her bird and nature knowledge. Susan was fascinated by it and by her.

'Do they always only have one chick?'

'They're actually called pufflings.'

'That's ridiculous.'

'I know. And yes, only one per year.'

'Just one?'

'One is all you need.' The phrase echoed. She watched

the birds go to and fro, doting on their child. Her heart was sore. She shook it away.

'Wow. Is this about as close as you guys get to the birds?'

'Yeah, it's best just to mind our business.'

'That must be hard for you.'

'Fuck off!'

Susan liked making Amelia laugh – the abandon of it, head thrown back, the sound bubbling up then roaring out before the wind stole it. She missed this. Making someone laugh. Walking with someone. Talking. Amelia ran her fingers through her red hair and something stirred in Susan that she hadn't felt in a long time. Amelia caught her gaze. Held it. Her hand found Susan's – just resting there, gentle but deliberate, warm. Jen's face flashed across her mind. Long chestnut hair. Green sad eyes. Susan pulled her hand away and looked back at the cliffs where the black-and-white birds soared. Amelia stood, breaking the moment.

'All right then, time for the Wailing Crag.'

'Is this another sweaty uphill trek?'

'Not even a bit, you've been to the top of the island already. All downhill from here.'

They gathered their stuff and turned in the direction of home, and apparently the Wailing Crag.

'So what is the Wailing Crag?'

'It's a rock formation, it's down near the dunes and the stony cove.'

'Erosion?'

'Very good!'

Susan thought to herself that teachers of all types were always the same.

They walked side by side closely, hands and elbows gently brushing as they walked through the long grass, descending towards the shore.

'Anyway, the legend is that some pirates kidnapped a local chieftain's wife and her baby from the mainland and brought them here. They held them both hostage, and rather than submit to them, the woman threw her baby into the waves, then turned to stone in her grief.'

Susan's blood ran cold and she turned away, nausea rising in her throat. Amelia, feeling the mood shift, tried to lighten the moment.

'Yeah, another cheerful Irish legend. So the crag is in the shape of a weeping woman, leaning over the sea, crying into the waves.'

She knew this wasn't something she wanted to see.

'Amelia, I think I should go home now.'

She stopped walking. Walter stopped also, pressing himself against her leg, ready for home too.

'But we haven't seen it.'

'No, I think I need to go now. Thank you. Maybe another time.'

Amelia's face was concerned, with a bit of hurt mixed in there, too, Susan thought. She pushed down the guilt. There was so much in that locked box already; some more wouldn't do any harm. *Shove it down.*

'Can we go please? I don't feel well.'

'Yeah, of course, we can go home.'

The walk back was silent; they no longer moved side by side comfortably. Susan kept a distance between her and Amelia, forcing herself to look down at the grass, weeds and heather under her feet. She counted the small pebbles that lined the road beyond the marshy hills. Small breaths, she told herself, small breaths to get through it all.

They passed by the beach and Susan knew it wasn't far. They reached the fork that indicated her house was around the corner and Amelia took her hand, pressing it between both of hers. Walter walked on ahead, oblivious.

'I had a nice time today. Sorry, you're not feeling great right now.'

Susan couldn't speak, she just nodded, not sure what she was agreeing with. Her hand burned between Amelia's flesh.

'We're having a party tomorrow in the hostel if you want to come. But no pressure.'

Susan croaked out her words.

'Thank you.'

She found herself pulled into a hug. They stood, breathing in each other's scent, until Amelia stepped away. Her red hair smelled like lavender, with sea salt from the morning's walk. She left Susan at her gate and continued towards the port, her footsteps fading on the gravel. Susan pushed open her front door, stumbled into her kitchen, and hot, heaving sobs poured out of her.

CHAPTER NINE

—◦◦◦◦◦—

Susan was awake but her thoughts moved slow, dragging through her head like honey off a spoon. The Xanax she had desperately dug out of her bag the night before, mid-sobs, had done its work. A day lying in bed while the weather continued to be glorious seemed sinful, but she was in no hurry to climb out of the warm duvet. The rays of the dawn sun fired in the window like darts, falling across the bedroom and landing amongst the folds of the bedsheets. Walter had broken in and was tucked up by Susan's hip within reach of her hand. His tail swept across his body and over his nose, his ribcage rising and falling in soft little pulses.

Susan reached for her phone, a morning routine she hadn't quite forgotten yet. Before she realised what she was doing, she had unlocked it, noting the missed calls and text messages from various, increasingly worried contacts. Jen's name jumped out from the din. She ignored them all, opening only the email app. A reply from her solicitor was neatly sitting amongst the spam emails and the newsletters she never read. She glanced through it, turned the phone off and put it away again, deciding to let the battery die this time rather than charge it again. Jen knew where she was; Susan's note made it clear what she wanted. Didn't it?

She pulled herself out of bed, giving Walter a pat on the bum. He popped his head up and dragged himself to his feet, stretching out before hopping off and following her into the rest of the cottage. Her breakfast cereal bowl from the day before was turning crusty in the sink. She opened the back door to let Walter out and some air in; a stiff breeze from the west came through and cooled the dark kitchen.

The island was less safe with Amelia on it – the tension that had flitted between them, the abyss of bad decisions waiting outside the door – too dangerous to return to. Waiting for the kettle to boil, Susan looked around the small room, at the drawers she had not yet opened, and presses not yet explored. She decided today was the day to do some digging.

The garden and shed felt like a safe place to begin the clearout – a necessary job and one less likely to carry family baggage amongst the dusty garden tools and old buckets of bird seed. The grass had grown so long that only Walter's ears and the periscope of his tail poked above it as he pottered about. The electric lawnmower kicked into life. She razed through the wilderness, the visiting birds perturbed by the sudden disturbance. The local robin waited on the garden wall for any unearthed insects – his black beads watching her as she worked. It was early in the day still, but there was no let-up in the sunshine. Once the grass was cut, she grabbed a glass of water and sat on her back step, surveying the work. It was a start. The bushes and trees would have to wait until the songbirds had moved on from their nests. She had learnt that much from Amelia on their walk. Amelia. The scent of her lavender hair came back to Susan, and with it the warmth of the hug, the hand on hers, the moment she had pulled away. Her stomach turned. She had let someone in, even for a second, and the guilt settled in her now.

She stood up, winding the lawnmower's cord around itself as she walked back towards the shed. She spotted something shiny lying in the now-shorn grass. A speckled green egg, cracked and empty, lay abandoned on the lawn. She picked it up and it sat in her palm like an offering. She didn't know the type of bird it was. Amelia would. Jen might too. She dropped the shell and saw it crack.

The birdseed in the shed was in good condition, sealed up for the winter against invaders and damp. She grabbed the feeders hanging in the garden and refilled them, setting them against the fences and tree branches dotted around the small space – a space that nonetheless felt bigger with its new haircut. Walter seemed to appreciate the change, rolling on his back and scratching himself off the tight blades of grass. She could almost imagine having people over on a sunny evening, a barbecue smouldering, cool bottles of beer clinking as friends laughed and chatted. Late-thirties easy-listening tunes playing from a small speaker, getting more aggressive, louder and retro as the booze flowed and they reverted to past selves. Someone would put on a playlist from their college days. That wouldn't happen, though; her Dublin friends would never travel all this way, even assuming anyone was still talking to her. For now, she had herself and a friendly dog. She could get her own beers and perhaps invite some islanders over once she got to know them. *Maybe I could invite Amelia.* It was an unexpected thought, but not entirely unpleasant. She remembered Amelia's party that night; she could almost taste the rollies and the cheap booze. Something in her warmed to the idea.

The starlings watched her, waiting for a chance to slip in for a root around when the garden was unattended, so she left them to it. She hopped in a cold shower to cool down and followed it with a cup of tea to warm up – anything to delay what came next. But the tea ran out and the excuses ran out with it. She began to open the presses and the drawers and wade through the leftover mementoes of not just her uncle, but the entire Shaw family. A family disappeared except for her.

There were hoards of family photo albums, documenting over sixty years of life on the island. Her grandfather standing next to a prize heifer, looking like he won the lotto. Two boys and a little girl sitting on the wall of the pier with their ice creams, the washed-out sepia giving them all the same aura. She guessed they were pre-teens. She was sure the two little boys were Frank and her dad. But who was the little girl? Another islander, a distant cousin, maybe? She traced a finger over the children in the photo, their 99s melting down their hands. Frank was mid-laugh, her father more reserved, as always. The little girl wasn't even looking at the camera, her head turned to the side, looking out to sea.

A blonde little girl, a profile much like Susan's.

She found a photo of Nanny Shaw and three children – she was about the same age Susan was now. Nan held the children close to her, a hand over Frank's face as he laughed through her fingers. The little girl was barely out of toddlerhood and clung to her legs. Susan's father looked uncharacteristically cheerful. This girl wasn't a cousin or a friend. They looked like a perfect, complete family unit. She could picture her grandad behind the camera, beaming. She turned it over. Just a year – '1970'. Who was this child? How had Susan never heard of her? She stared at the photograph, at these people who made her, whose blood ran through her veins, and not one of them had told her a thing. The kitchen walls pressed in a little closer. She put the photo down, picked it up again. She knew nothing. She came from nothing she could name. There wasn't enough tea in the world for this job.

She moved to the small pile of notebooks that she had found in one of the drawers, labelled with Frank's name and the dates in her uncle's careful handwriting. She paused, wondering whether to dive into reading what was essentially someone's diary. Her pragmatic nature took over. Frank was dead, what did it matter? It was unlikely to bother him beyond the grave that his niece was glancing through his journals. They all seemed incredibly boring to her anyway, ledgers mostly – records of cows and yields. She found nothing about the little girl. His ideas about gin started to seep in as the journals went on. They were interesting, she admitted to herself. She enjoyed his drawing of the plans for the distillery and his sketches of the flowers and herbs he wanted to cultivate. Aside from these occasional nuggets of her uncle's personality, each journal contained more of the same mundane details of farming life.

Her stomach growled the time at her, and she put the ledgers back in the drawer. She'd only made it a few years in – at least twenty more to go. The morning was unproductive, but she had managed to not think about home or Amelia for almost two hours, and that was a win.

She washed the cups and plates from the previous day, placing them with a clink on the draining board. Outside, small blue tits and sparrows found their way back to the bird feeder with delighted chirps and trills. The sorrow of her family's memories lifted as she watched them twitter to and fro, baby birds waiting for their parents to feed them, mouths open expectantly.

With a clang, a magpie swooped, clambering his way onto the delicate bars of the bird feeder. The small songbirds scattered with a disgruntled squeak. He barely noticed his own disruption – balanced awkwardly, considering his move. Susan breathed and he turned his head towards her, accusing. They stared at each other for a moment. He pecked at a sunflower seed, spread his wings and flew away with a jack-jack sound cast back in her direction.

The little girl staring out to sea. Susan couldn't shake her. She was a piece in the puzzle – why her father never wanted to return to the island where he grew up, why the brothers cut all connection to each other. It was too late to ask either of them. But she had an idea of where to go for answers.

Peggy rested on a bench outside the pub, the sun on her face.She dug a knuckle into her calf, grunting as it pounded through one of the knots. She looked up and spotted Susan approaching.

'Good afternoon, Miss Shaw, how are you getting on?'

Susan sat next to her, determined to get straight to business before she lost her nerve.

'Peggy, can I ask you something?'

Peggy's face lit up in surprise.

'Of course, darling. What can I do for you?'

Susan dug into her handbag, producing the photo of Granny Shaw and the three children. Peggy's face seemed to crack for a second, and Susan saw the look of sadness and recognition pass over it.

'Who's the little girl?'

Peggy sighed. 'That's your aunty Fiona, my love.'

She seemed to wait for Susan to respond, but continued in the blank space between them.

'You know, the little one who died?'

Tears ambushed her, sudden and inexplicable.

'What?'

'Oh dear ... I'm sorry, love, I thought you would have known. I'd have thought Derek would have at least...'

Derek, her father, never mentioned anything of the sort. Peggy's face showed a quick look of annoyance. It disappeared as quickly as it had shimmered across it.

'No... I never heard anything about her.'

'Oh... oh, it was awful sad. I was only small myself when it happened. I know Frank was with her, and my own dad was the one who pulled her out of the water, but ... you look very pale, are you all right?'

The ground shifted underneath her. How had her father never mentioned this? Was this why he hated the island so much? Was this the wedge that drove the brothers apart? Peggy placed a hand on Susan's shoulder

'Susan, I need to go back inside and do a bit of work. Come on in and let's get you something to eat and a cup of tea.'

Susan followed Peggy like a zombie.

She picked at an egg and cress sandwich in the soothing summer light, the revelations about her dead aunt reverberating around her head. Peggy was back at work but seemed to keep a close eye on her, popping by with hot sweet tea and a few comforting words, until Susan was speaking in full sentences again. Fiona's life and death was a bomb from the blue, but now that the smoke was clearing in Susan's mind, more about her life and family finally made sense.

Young voices echoed in from the beer garden, stragglers from the student gang she assumed. She remembered the party that evening. The family drama of the morning made it seem like a much-needed, harmless adventure – another way to pass the evening, and a great excuse to avoid any further trauma in the family albums and journals that lurked in sitting-room drawers. She decided, against all her better judgement, she was going to go.

CHAPTER TEN

—◦◦◇◦◦—

The hour of the party arrived, and the decision she had avoided making now seemed silly. She could stay home; but sitting alone in the quiet heaviness of the house – now even more full of questions and sadness – for another night was even more unbearable. She made a mental note to buy a TV next time she crossed to the mainland. She wondered when that might be. No time soon, she thought. No time soon.

She sat by the dressing table, squinting into a small portable mirror she found in a dusty cupboard under the bathroom sink. The bedroom lights were too dark for her task, but the best option in the house. Once the sun went down, the broken lightbulbs and half-working lamps left her in a kind of half-life – not quite darkness, not quite light. She was getting used to that.

She emptied her makeup bag onto the table before her. Grabbed at the last minute before she left the mainland, it had been a 'just in case' piece of luggage. Just in case of what exactly she wasn't sure. A bunch of college students inviting her to a party, perhaps? She felt ridiculous then immediately wistful – who had she become that the thought of a party seemed ridiculous? Her younger self, almost always hungover or on a comedown, would be appalled.

Susan grimaced as she inspected the equipment before her – drying-up foundation, worn-down concealer, mascara past its prime and an eyeshadow palette crying for a face to show off. The sponge was a bit crusty but usable, a shake of the mascara bottle revealed a liquid inside with at least one more night left in it.

She scrutinised herself in the mirror, examining her thinning lips. She saw her aunt in her face again and wondered once again at the magnitude of that loss. Crow's feet had quietly appeared at some stage, and a worried furrow started to groove itself into her forehead. Her tools and equipment would have to do. She was still pretty, and young too, even if she didn't feel it. Her spark, crushed, pushed down under the drain of the last few years. Somewhere underneath her brow, she knew that the embers of that younger self still smouldered. She bit her lip and set to work.

Susan's hair, swept into a neat braid, behaved itself in the wild Atlantic wind blowing her towards the hostel. Guided by the sounds of music she didn't know, she strolled through dirt tracks. A warm shiver of anxiety spread across her chest every few steps, her mouth dry. She resisted cracking open the bottle of Island gin nestled under her arm. She'd found it in the press that day – a perk of the job, she figured. She'd left Walter snoozing on the couch and regretted it – his clicking claws and his cynical humour were a comfort already. She considered turning back to join him for a cuddle. A small voice inside her told her to cop on, so she kept walking in the dying light, the red sun seeping throughout the sky as it whispered goodnight. The bluetits rattled in the hedges to each other as they settled in for the evening. Swallows danced over the heather, swooping and chirping to each other, snatching flies out of the dusky sky. The air was cool in her lungs, and the smell of the honeysuckle sweetened her breath. It reminded her of childhoods at Inchydoney beach, her fingertips brushing the sweet flowers as she stomped towards the sand, her parents trailing after her.

She approached the front door of the hostel and recognised a small group of people, young and nervous, smoking outside. They started when they saw her, hiding the spliff behind their backs. She walked right past them. She wasn't going to let a bunch of students know they scared the shit out of her. The hostel was an old farmhouse, hollowed out and refitted with bunk beds, kitchenettes, and a large common area painted easy-clean grey. It was filled with bean bags and old, scavenged couches with seats that dipped in the middle, forcing anyone sitting on them to roll towards each other in a triangular conversation. A large table in the middle of the room held a bucket of yellow liquid, wafting scents of sugary lemon and cheap vodka. At intervals, someone would grab a ladle from the table and help themselves to a glass of the concoction. They'd sip it, make a face, down it and go again. Susan made a note to avoid the punch – for now.

She spotted Daniel sipping a can of Dutch Gold in the corner. Their eyes met, he gave a nod, then looked away. She looked back towards the front door, considering a quick exit. Amelia stood in the doorway, smiling at her. Susan's heart skipped against all her better judgement and Amelia bounced over.

'You came!'

'Yeah, I had to put off a lot of reading and sitting around until tomorrow, so I hope you're grateful.' Susan cast her eyes down and laughed. Amelia's body language was relaxed and confident.

'We've lots of couches and old field journals around here if you feel a yearning. Come on, gimme your jacket, have a drink.'

Susan's breath caught in her chest. She'd been clinging to the bottle of gin in her hands like a life buoy. She placed it down on a table, slipping off her leather jacket and draping it over Amelia's hands. Amelia shooed her towards the party, then turned and walked off to the coat room.

OK, get it together, Susan. She muttered to herself and let her eyes wander around the room. She spotted the punch bucket again, its volume dwindling as the minutes passed. She marched towards it, ignoring the looks of the students around her. Grabbing a glass and a ladle, she poured a generous helping and knocked it back. She flinched as the bitter astringent burned its way down her throat and a voice within whispered, *'Desperate times, Susan, desperate times.'*

The homemade yakka did its work. A warm, tingly fuzziness spread throughout her body; the music seemed more familiar, more in tune with her desires and needs. The lights were too bright, she thought – a real party needed lights to be dim, dingy and confusing. After two further portions of the rocket fuel, she switched to a more sensible gin and tonic and started chatting to the nearest group. She acted charming and relaxed and found that they weren't completely horrified at this old lady attending their party.

'Have you been to the island before?' They were

curious, figuring her out. She enjoyed the attention, the booze motoring her words.

'I was here years ago, as a kid, with my family. Not since, though.'

Susan opened her mouth to explain more when she felt a soft hand at her elbow. Amelia stood at her shoulder, two drinks in her hand. Susan threw her a drunken smile before she could stop herself. Amelia returned it while handing Susan one of the drinks. The cool glass, ice clinking was soothing against Susan's anxious palms.

'You haven't resorted to the field journals then?'

Susan shook her head. The shyness came flooding back – and underneath it, the room tilting slightly, the realisation that she was drunker than she had been in a very long time

'Come on, let's sit down.' Amelia cocked her head towards one of the less dilapidated sofas. Amelia took her hand to lead her. Susan froze. They paused a moment, both embarrassed. Susan broke the silence, feeling her Dutch courage push her on.

'Lead the way so.'

They slid onto a red corduroy couch in a quieter area of the common room. Their hands came apart as they did, and Susan sighed to herself, with relief. An old standing lamp from the nineties threw some pathetic warm light across their corner as they tried to find a comfy spot between the poking springs.

'This island life is just all glamour, isn't it?' Amelia mocked Susan's discomfort.

'Some of us have bad backs, you know. We can't all be twenty-four.'

'I'm twenty-seven, not twenty-four. And you're hardly ninety.'

Susan gazed into her drink, embarrassed, the ice clinking against the glass as the tonic fizzed. The warmth of Amelia's hand still lingered in hers. She relaxed into the back of the couch, the soft cushions sucking her in, and chose her words carefully, the gin and lemon punch loosening her tongue.

'You can take that as a compliment, I suppose.'

She raised her eyes. Amelia held them for a second before Susan dropped back to her drink. The distance between them had shrunk – when had that happened? It no longer seemed to matter. Amelia shuffled towards the back of the couch, her head just inches from Susan's, elbow resting on the cushion behind her, hand cupping her own face.

'I never asked what you do for a living.'

'Well, I recently came into possession of a herd of cows.'

Susan noticed Amelia glancing towards her lips and she liked it. Amelia caught her gaze again.

'What did you do before that?'

'I'm a teacher.'

'Primary?'

'God no. Secondary. English.'

'Sounds riveting.'

'I actually love it. Mostly. I've been on a break for a little while.'

Susan crossed her legs and rested her drink on her knee.

'What about you? How long are you lecturing?'

'I've been doing my doctorate for the last … two years, I guess.'

'So you are a student?'

'I'm a PhD! Not an undergrad. I don't eat Koka noodles and vodka for dinner anymore.'

'You're missing out.'

Amelia snorted, her laugh made Susan's face feel warm, and it was her turn to inch closer. The pull of the younger woman was hypnotic, her confidence, her comfort with herself in the space. Her red hair rested just above her shoulders, her fuzzy undercut peaking out on one side. She was stunningly beautiful, her skin glowing with joy and laughter. Susan felt the gaze of the undergrads on her again, envious as their suspicions were confirmed. She enjoyed their attention as much as she enjoyed Amelia's. Amelia's hand brushed against hers, and the hairs on the back of Susan's neck stood to attention at this forgotten sensation.

She looked at Amelia seriously, allowing the alcohol to open up her voice.

'You know I'm much older than you, right?'

Her age was only the start of their problems, Susan knew. But it was the easiest one to mention at this stage.

The tip of Amelia's tongue licked her lips, almost too quickly to be seen. Susan saw it. Susan liked it. Amelia leant in, her breath smelling like gin and elderflower, sweet magic casting a spell. Susan followed the curve of Amelia's chin, down her long neck, the soft milkiness of her breasts peeking out under the open top button of her shirt. They looked at each other, their breaths starting to rise and fall in sync.

'I don't care how old you are. I want to kiss you. Can I?'

Susan replied by kissing her fiercely. Her hand slid up Amelia's neck and into her hair. Her fingertips, out of practice but re-learning quickly, pulled her face toward her as their soft lips met. Their tongues brushed against each other as the warmth spread throughout Susan's body. The kiss deepened, and another sensation crawled its way up her insides. A tightening, a clenching, an unpleasant shiver of horror. Her subconscious flung open the box of guilt and pushed it up through the booze. She pulled away, leaving Amelia confused and breathless. Susan yanked herself off the couch like a marionette, a wave of punch-drunkness washing over her as she did.

'Sorry ... I just ... I just need some air.'

'Do you want me to come with you?'

'No! No, you stay there ... talk to your friends ... I'll probably be back.'

'Probably?'

Susan turned and tripped her way through the room towards the door, the students watching her as she did. She didn't want to think about Amelia, still sitting on that couch. She thought of Amelia's tongue, tracing shapes along the inside of her lips. A pleasant current lodged between her legs despite the anxiety. She stopped herself, leaning against the front door frame, most of the kids pretending not to take notice. They shuffled off the mossy front steps as Daniel regarded her in the semi-darkness.

'Are you all right?'

He was smoking a giant spliff, the red of its burning end casting an odd, eerie glow.

'Gimme that.'

She grabbed it, her fingers clasping expertly around the end of the smouldering cylinder. It tasted earthy and potent – it was good stuff. The kids these days had no time for the hash of her youth. The weed was strong and pure, and another type of warmth and softness moved through her. Her body decompressed and she felt her vertebrae breathe between each other, her shoulders loosening, her neck moving freely. The tension released, she was aware again of the heat and tingling between her legs. She swallowed the dread down and allowed her mind to be fuzzy again. She glanced at Daniel as she handed the joint back over, happy to let him be her conscience.

'Should I go back in?'

He laughed his father's big, hearty laugh. It seemed ridiculous coming out of someone with bum fluff on his top lip.

'Absolutely!'

'You're a bad influence.'

'Sure you're on your holidays.'

He offered her the joint again, but she shook her head. Through the window, Amelia was still on the couch, sipping her drink and laughing with another woman. Susan noticed, and was immediately annoyed with herself. She clenched her teeth and gave them a rattle, hesitating.

'Would you go back in for fuck's sake? What else are you going to do for the night?'

Susan thought about going home, bringing her pulsing body with her to a silent, empty house seemed wrong somehow. She thought of lying in the white bedroom, thinking about Amelia, moving her hand inside herself.

'Jesus!' She shook her head again. This was bad. Daniel leant back against the pebbledash wall. Others slipped back inside as Susan dilly-dallied. Daniel called after them.

'Here, Matt, give us the bag there for a second.'

Matt had the face of someone who'd never been asked for anything without a 'please'. However, he handed Daniel a small plastic bag without delay, loping back into the party. Susan smirked.

'Aren't you a bit young to be hanging out with these lads?'

'Aren't you a bit old?'

Susan cackled.

'Touché. You're very cosy with them.'

He was too busy fishing something out of the bag to look at her. His tone was jovial and droll.

'Ah, sure, they only want me for the cheap pints.'

Neither of them believed that.

'Now,' Daniel asserted, 'this'll get you going.'

He handed her a small pink pill, an M branded right in the centre. It took Susan a moment to realise what was happening.

'Are you actually fucking serious?'

'Sure, what else are you going to do tonight?'

'Stop saying that!'

She examined the pill in the light seeping through the front windows. She thought of what it offered, a brief explosion of happy hormones, and escape from everything she carried. All going well, of course.

'It's good?'

'They all seem happy out, don't they?'

Daniel popped his own one, followed by a slurp of Dutch Gold. Susan accepted the situation.

'All right. I can't let you do it on your own, can I?'

She threw it back and grabbed his can to wash it down. Cheap beer and ecstasy hadn't been on her list for this evening, but fuck her lists, fuck her plans. Fuck everything. She and Daniel looked at each other and burst out laughing. He looked worried.

'Don't tell my mam.'

Susan had forgotten how delicious the air could be. It had been so long since she had tasted it quite like this. She sat on the arm of the couch, eyes closed, breathing the oxygen in, then out, then in, then out. Her hands rubbed over and back across the fabric in time with her breath. Occasionally, someone passed by her, and she grabbed them.

'You have to try this!'

They joined her in the act of breathing, some on her wavelength, others not, all polite. Even those on her vibe eventually grew bored, but not her. She sat and breathed in, enjoying the chill through her nostrils, down through her trachea and into her lungs. The oxygen moved into her blood and ran through her body; life tingling all the way to her fingertips. The hairs on her arms seemed to fall and rise, fall and rise, with every breath. The blood in her veins burned; it pushed the darkness and regret out of her brain. Only the good nerve endings and synapses were allowed to fire right now, and she revelled in it.

'You came back in then?'

Susan looked up, the beams of light fracturing into her blown pupils as the rays haloed the redhead.

'Oh wow ... Amelia ... you're so ...'

'... what?'

Amelia was concealing a smirk.

'Just ... so ...' Susan's words failed her. She finished in a burst, 'Gorgeous!'

Amelia laughed.

'You're having a good time?'

'Yes. Aren't you?'

'Yeah, it's been an interesting night.'

Susan felt the air lose some flavour.

'You're not ... you didn't ...?'

'No, I don't think my professor would be very happy if he found out.'

Susan's hand brushed against the fine hairs on Amelia's arm, that warm tingle again, this time down in her centre. She sensed Amelia watching her reactions, searching her face for something to worry about.

'I'm sorry. I should have asked you if it was all right.'

'What? No, why would you? You don't need to worry about that.'

She sat on the couch, which made Susan lose her balance on the arm and slide next to her. So we're back here again, Susan thought. Her mouth was dry. She reached for her glass of water, but Amelia had already placed it to her lips. They stared at each other as she sipped. Amelia's breath was still sweet and hot, and she blushed as they gazed at each other.

'I think ... I think you're gorgeous too, by the way.'

Susan realised that, regardless of the method, both of them were intoxicated. Their judgement was off, and they shouldn't make any more mistakes tonight. They shouldn't be this close, touching, stroking. They shouldn't be leaning towards each other, breaths stuttering. Amelia's lips on hers again, less precise this time, more wanting and hungry. Amelia kissing her all over, as though her entire body covered hers, consuming her in a shimmering light. The heat building and throbbing, she was ready to explode. Deep moans escaped her as she heard a whisper in her ear.

'I miss you.'

She pulled back, bewildered.

'What?'

Amelia was similarly bewildered.

'What? I didn't say anything.'

The voice in her ear, its soft accent, its deep tones. It wasn't Amelia. Oh god. Here it was again. The fear fought its way through her chemical euphoria, riding on a wave of nausea. She pushed Amelia off her.

'I'm so sorry.'

She ran out into the night, guts churning as the cold air entered her lungs. She held her mouth shut until she was out of sight of the hostel, then vomited booze, bile and tears into a spiky bush. Her clothes tangled in its thorns as she tried to extract herself. A giant rock embedded in the side of the road invited her to sit, and she rested, staring out over the island, down to the sea, the moon lighting the quiet loneliness before her. She thought back to the voice.

'I miss you too.' She replied in a whisper, tears leaking across her face.

She sat until she heard footsteps approaching. Amelia held Susan's jacket, outstretched, in her hand. Susan lowered her head, humbled as she slipped it around her shoulders.

'You shouldn't be nice to me.'

'And yet ...' Amelia murmured. She pushed Susan's hair back out of her face.

'Come on, let me walk you home.'

She slipped her hand into Susan's, leading her down the darkened road.

'Are you all right?'

Susan tried to speak, but realised the words weren't making sense anymore. They walked on in silence until they reached her front door. Susan heard her keys jangle in her coat pocket as Amelia searched for them. Amelia opened the door, guiding Susan over the front step and into the bedroom. Susan pushed her off as gently as possible, while Amelia tried to help her undress for sleep.

'No ... no.'

Amelia took a step back. She disappeared into the sitting room and returned with a glass of water, placing it on the nightstand as Susan fell back into bed, still dressed, grateful for the darkness seeping in and whisking her away from reality.

CHAPTER ELEVEN

Frank

Frank hated the sunshine. It clawed at his pale skin, leaving red spots and dark freckles in unattractive patterns across his face.

The sun had been easy to avoid until his twenty-first year – summertime in Ireland lasted a manageable fortnight, the rest of the time the big orange burning globe in the sky ducked in and out of sullen clouds, taunting its pasty avoiders below.

It was different here. The desert sun scorched down, unrelenting. His sweat ran from the cropped hair on the back of his neck, down through his combat fatigues, gathering in his leather boots by the end of the day.

A dry, unforgiving heat.

He sat on his bunk wishing, for once, that the cool breeze of the Atlantic might wash over him. He closed his eyes and smelled the scent of honeysuckle on the ocean wind. Later he dreamt of dragging waves on a rocky coast, screams, hands reaching. His father roaring. His mother sobbing.

He awoke with a shout, fellow soldiers jumping to their feet, ready for the rockets to fall on their heads.

'Jesus Christ, what?'

'What? Frank!'

'You're at it again, for fuck's sake!'

A boot hit his head. He issued his apologies and rolled over. Sleep never returned on nights like this. He lay, his eyes empty, watching the shadows move across the wall.

During the day, he was back in the sun. The blue beret perched at an angle did nothing but insulate his clammy forehead. His muscles strained against his swelling skin.

Rúairí, a dark-haired Donegal lad, wandered up to him. They gazed out across the border, the peace they were keeping, thoughtful in each other's company.

'There's not even a wee argument going on out there, let alone any kind of fighting,' Rúairí said.

Frank's lips were dry; they cracked as he replied.

'Please God, it'll stay that way.'

'Ah, it'd be nice to have a bit of action, no?'

Frank didn't agree, though he was ready for anything – his daily routine made him so. Five miles before breakfast, even here, round the camp in circles, as the sun scorched through his skin and his white T-shirt hung off him with sweat. The older soldiers laughed, complacent paunches beginning to protrude under their fatigues. The soldiers his age watched, seeming to search him for the weaknesses he was desperate to outrun. Rúairí watched him most of all, Frank noticed. Rúairí had a cow's lick under his beret, and a fiancée called Mags back in Letterkenny, that he mentioned twice in six months. Frank adjusted his gun; the strap worn. It twisted as he moved.

He knew what Rúairí meant. The days here passed so slowly during the lulls. No rockets to observe, no crossings of the blue line, no militias gathering at borders that needed to be calmed. They entertained themselves between patrols with cards, playing football with local children with Irish accents or telling stories of women back home. Frank didn't have stories, so he made them up. Beautiful blondes buying him pints of Harp in the village pub. Martin from Wexford had eyed him up a couple of times.

'Aye, I've seen that ad on telly too.'

Frank laughed to hide his embarrassment and went back to planning the next story. The next one would be the one that made them see he was just like them.

'Any word from home?'

Rúairí's gentle lilt awakened him back to their patrol. Frank shook his head. The last dispatch had informed him of his father's poor health. It seemed likely the next one would bring death. And then what? Home? Decisions? Responsibility?

His mother was already dead. She had disappeared slowly after Fiona died, her screams turning inward, poisoning her until, one by one, when he was eighteen, gone from school and no longer reliant on her, her organs just stopped working.

Derek would never move back to the island.

It would be up to him.

Rúairí's shoulder brushed off him. The hairs on the back of Frank's neck stood on end, and he swallowed, then stepped away, shaking his head.

'How's Mags?'

Rúairí's dark eyebrows lifted in surprise.

'Grand, I suppose.'

Frank grunted and walked away, returning his view to

the horizon and the blue line they were protecting. He tried to ignore the squeezing anxiety in his chest, the cold sweat on his neck.

That evening, Rúairí found him again. The dorm was empty but for the two of them, sitting on Frank's bunk, closer than any lad should sit to another lad. His hands, as he moved closer to Frank's, were strong and tanned. Like Frank, he was raised by the sea. Even in the stink of the desert, even in the sweat of the sun, Rúairí, like Frank, brought the Atlantic with him wherever he went. Could Rúairí tell, in the moments between being awake and being asleep, before sleep brought the screams, when the thoughts Frank pushed away could crawl into his mind, he'd imagined sinking his nose into the space where Rúairí's neck met his shoulder? He'd imagined inhaling his scent, the smell of soft sweat and sea-salt, a smell of home – if home was warm, and welcoming and not filled with death and loss.

But flesh and blood Rúairí sitting on his bunk was too much – too real, too close. He was so close he could almost smell that sea salt. He jumped up and walked out, kept going until the warm air hit him, and ran until his legs collapsed under him, and all that was left in his brain was thoughts of rest and water.

Chapter Twelve

When Susan awoke with a pain, it was still dark outside, the sun was starting to appear on the distant horizon. She flung the covers off herself, sprinted to the hall, pushed through the bathroom door and landed on her knees, head straight into the bowl. She vomited everything left in her, the acid burning her gums as her body expelled its contents. She sat back after the first retch, took a breath, then sat up again for another turn. She was finally empty and lay down, her head against the cool tiles. All she could do was breathe deep into her abdomen and mutter to herself.

'Oh god, oh god, oh god.'

She heard the sitting-room door creak and a horror passed across her.

'OH GOD.'

Amelia peeked around the bathroom door.

'Heya ...'

'Oh fuck. I'm sorry.'

Amelia laughed, and Susan died a little bit more.

'Why are you still here?'

It sounded angrier than she'd intended.

'I wanted to make sure you didn't choke on your own vomit.'

Susan pulled herself to her feet, the room spinning. She pushed past Amelia.

'You can go now. Sorry for keeping you.'

Amelia made a face.

'Yeah, you're welcome.'

Susan stopped, leaning her head against the bedroom doorframe.

'I'm sorry. I just can't believe the state I got into.'

'Let's blame Daniel.'

Daniel. The little shit. She couldn't blame him, though, could she? Had he forced her to take the pill, or drink the yakka, or the gin? Or smoke that delicious spliff? Or drink whatever one of the kids had handed her in a mug – a brown shot that tasted like cough medicine? Had he forced her to slide next to Amelia on the couch, or to bring her lips to hers, put her tongue in her mouth, run her hands all over her neck? Had he ignited this inferno of guilt, summoning Jen's voice at the worst possible moment? Her legs buckled. She continued into the bedroom, flopping onto the duvet. Amelia followed, almost shy. She went to the window and opened it, letting fresh air into the stuffy bedroom, stinking of booze and sour vomit. Susan groaned and clutched her head.

'Did you ... did you sleep on the couch?'

'Attempted to anyway. I thought the hostel couches were bad.'

Susan glanced out the window. Dawn was breaking, but sleep was pulling her under. She held up the duvet, gesturing for Amelia to join her. The younger woman gave a wry smirk, peeled off her jacket and trousers, and climbed in.

'Sleep now,' Susan mumbled.

She took Amelia's hand and rolled over, wrapping the soft arm around her. Amelia nuzzled into Susan's hair, breathing her gentle breath on to her neck as they both drifted off to sleep.

Amelia's quiet snores woke Susan as midday approached. Her tummy had settled, but her head still clanged. Her brain was sticky, mouth dry. She peeled Amelia's arm from her waist and slid out of bed, backing out of the bedroom, watching the sleeping form lying on her tummy. A strange shakiness in her limbs – only food could save her.

Tea and toast. Beige food only. She nibbled at the edge of the bread, swallowing small pieces to prevent any catastrophes in her belly. The two paracetamol from the bottom of her handbag seemed to be helping; her brain was no longer attempting to crawl out through her eye. A yawn from the next room. She popped the button on the kettle and pushed the toaster down with a spring. Amelia stepped into the sitting room in her T-shirt.

'Good afternoon.'

'I'm making some tea and toast for you.'

'We can do better than that, surely.'

Susan opened the fridge. Butter, milk, eggs. Some fresh strawberries she had grabbed from a stall on the side of the road the day before.

'French toast?'

'Ooh la la.'

It took Susan less time than she thought it would to mix everything up. The steps of the recipe she held in her head were soothing. Step one: crack the eggs; step two: whip them up. Her booze-soaked, drug-addled brain needed instructions. The eggy mixture soaked into the bread. She coated both sides, then flung it on the pan with an industrial-size pat of butter. Amelia sliced the strawberries.

'Is that vegan butter?'

'Sure. Maureen got it in especially for you. Vegan eggs too from tofu chickens.'

Amelia laughed again, rubbing her unkempt hair out of her face. Susan set the toast down in front of them both, piled high. Amelia admired the stack.

'I didn't know you could cook.'

'I used to love it.'

'What happened?'

'Life, I guess.'

Susan had no energy for lying or deflecting. Walter appeared from his bed and interrupted.

'Oh, you're interested now there's food, is it?'

Susan threw a crust, and he gobbled it. They both dug into the plate, eating in silence as the food deflected the awkwardness. Finally, when the last piece was gone, they sat staring at each other. Susan decided to take charge of the situation.

'Look, I'm really sorry about last night.'

'Which part?'

'All of it. I shouldn't have drunk so much, or taken pills, or ...'

'Kissed me?'

Amelia folded her arms as Susan continued.

'No. I shouldn't have.'

'You didn't want to?'

'I did but ...'

'What about kissing me the second time? Are you sorry for that too?'

Amelia was poking her with her words, annoyed and frustrated. Susan looked at her without blinking.

'Yes.'

Amelia's face fell. She flicked her eyes up to heaven and shook her head. She stared at Susan, determined.

'Well, I'm not sorry.'

The nausea rose again. She swallowed it down.

'My life is quite complicated.'

'Everyone's life is complicated, Susan. That's life.'

Amelia stood and walked the dirty plates to the sink. She placed them on the sideboard and turned back to Susan, leaning against the counter.

'I need to go. The students are leaving today, and I have some bits to sign off for them.'

'Are you leaving as well?'

'No ... you're stuck with me for another few weeks.'

'That's not what I meant.'

'I know.'

Amelia gave a sad laugh, then made for the bedroom. She paused as she passed Susan, leant down and left a gentle kiss on her lips. Susan pulled away reluctantly.

'Thank you for getting me home.'

Amelia shrugged and walked off. Susan waited in the sitting-room, hearing the clock tick, while the younger woman pulled on her clothes and left.

Susan had gone back to bed, lying in the stink and misery of her hangover until the heat went out of the sun over the island. She wasn't sure if she had slept or just drifted through time on the cloud of booze seeping out through her pores. When she fully woke, she instinctively reached her arm across the other side of the bed, then remembered she slept alone now. The night before had been an aberration since blowing up her life.

The food had settled her sickness, and the sleep had lifted

her headache, but her brain was still slow. A glance at her watch, – 4 p.m. She was lying naked on top of the duvet, her unconscious self having stripped and manoeuvred to find the comfort her subconscious needed. She rubbed her forehead with the heel of her hand and pushed herself up on her elbows with a groan. Sore. Raw and fiery from getting sick. Her teeth would never be clean again. The shame and embarrassment had no bottom today.

Still groggy, but sleep was finished – she would be awake for the night. She waited for the moon to join her, a companion on so many long sleepless nights, radiating peacefully through her window.

Was she hungry? Thirsty? An unwelcome thought flashed across her mind: was she even still alive? She remembered a homemade weed brownie incident in her youth – lying on the bathroom floor of her first rented house with Jen, eyes squeezed shut, convinced she had died and was trapped in her dead body, unmoving and unable to move, for the rest of time. There had been someone to rescue her then too. Lift her up, run a gentle hand through her hair, reassure her.

'You're not dead, you fucking eejit.'

She remembered Jen's soft kiss on her lips and her strong hands guiding her into the bedroom, her warm body lying with her, talking soothing words and rubbing her hair gently; sporadically reassuring her she didn't need an ambulance and yes, she was definitely still alive.

That was a long time ago now.

She pulled herself out of bed and staggered into the sitting room where Walter glared at her from the couch.

'Oh fuck. You've not had your dinner.'

At the word dinner, his ears perked up; he gave a yip and threw himself down, tapping his way to her with a bounce.

'I'm so sorry, Walter.'

She bent down, his wet nose and flicky tongue touching off her face as he wagged his tail into her leg.

'I'm so sorry.'

He yipped again.

She filled his bowl with nuts and piled some chicken from the fridge on top. She had already earned his forgiveness, but thought it was no harm to go overboard. For herself, the old reliable: tea and toast. It had never failed her before, and in the heavy quietness of the late evening sliding into night, it brought a comfort she hadn't realised she needed. Her mother used to bring her tea and toast when she were home sick from school, the bread buttered all the way to the edges, gleaming and dripping with gold. Thinking of her mother made her think of her father, and her small aunt Fiona haunted her thoughts. She glanced at the journals piled on the dresser and grabbed one.

This was from recent years. Small snippets of Frank alongside details of marts and cows and sales. She turned to a full-page sketch of Walter, his tongue lolling to one side, ears perky and waiting for a treat. Frank's pencil work was incredible, the lines and strokes and shading brought the dog's friendly face to life; even Susan, with as much artistic skill as a rock, could see the artistry. She showed Walter the drawing, as one would a small child.

'Who's that? Is that you?'

He sniffed the page, seemed to recognise something

in the scent, but went back to farting in his sleep. She turned to the next page, another text entry.

Went to mart. Sold heifer 46 – got a good price for her despite not being a great milker anymore. JP not happy. Loved that one, he said. Softie.

Susan laughed. She could believe this; JP's only warmth in her meeting with him came from his inter-action with the cows – or Walter. She turned a page and gasped. A full-page sketch of JP's face, captured with perfection – his mad, expressive eyebrows; his wavy hair; that shy half-smile Susan had seen when he talked about the herbs around the distillery; or when he let Minnie scratch her beefy head off his hand, or when his plans for a whiskey distillery landed on her open ears. Frank's sketch had him staring directly at the artist, a challenge. Underneath a caption:

JP being more stubborn than me.

The page was dated September 2018. She turned to the next one, her curiosity piqued. She spotted the words 'wedding invitation' and slammed the journal shut with a bang.

CHAPTER THIRTEEN

'I never knew Frank was such a good artist,' Susan said, performing off-handedness as best she could.

'What do you mean?' JP said.

She had spent this afternoon learning to make gin, drawing sub-par sketches of the flowers, writing notes and looking over the book on herbs and botanicals that JP had given her when she arrived; a gesture she considered a firm win in her JP charm offensive. He had made himself scarce as soon as possible – but hadn't told her to fuck off, and insisted she do some taste-testing of the different flavoured gins. She felt the flush of the alcohol across her cheeks, wondering if maybe she had been over-generous with the measures of her tasting shots. She hadn't thought about home, or vomiting in front of Amelia, or the warm, soft snoozes of the younger woman for most of the day. JP had returned to the office, his face red from the sun. He was pottering about, placing his tools back in their correct places, but had paused with surprise at the mention of Frank's artistry.

'Oh, I found some sketches.'

'Where?'

'Around the house.'

JP narrowed his eyes at her and shrugged.

'Yeah, he was always drawing something.'

'He had some great pictures of Walter.'

There was the half-smile again.

'He loved that dog.'

JP wandered to a sink in the corner of the shed and sluiced the mud and dirt off his hands as he spoke. He scrubbed his skin with a nailbrush, checking each finger for traces of muck. Susan waited for him to turn back around.

'He had some drawings of you, too.'

His face blushed a deep red. He made some noises that sounded like choked disagreement or dismissal, sputtering around the shed. Susan stepped in.

'They're very good actually. I can bring them for you.'

'No, that's grand.'

His voice was flat.

'Are you sure?'

'Yes.'

He turned away again, grabbed a towel from the sideboard and dried his hands. He threw it into a pile of towels in a basket under the sink labelled 'washing' in what Susan recognised as Frank's handwriting.

'You guys had a nice setup here?'

JP narrowed his eyes, shoulders pulling back.

'What do you mean?'

'Just this place; out here in the hills, looking over the sea. It's gorgeous.'

'It's perfect.'

The wistfulness in JP's tone took her by surprise. He went to the small fridge and opened it – brown glass glinted inside. She leant around him to see what was on offer. The gin had warmed her up for the evening.

'Are we having a beer?'

He seemed annoyed by this request but handed one over. She cracked it open on the desk and knocked some back. JP opened his own and leant against the fridge.

'How's the house clearing going?'

'Frank didn't have much.'

'He didn't need much.'

'It's mostly just photos, journals, etc.'

JP's face lit up.

'You've been reading his journals.'

'No. No.'

'That's where he did his drawing, so you're lying to me.'

The direct call-out caught her off guard. She shrugged but dropped her gaze.

'Not in detail, just skimming through.'

'They're not yours to skim through.'

'I don't think Frank cares at this stage.'

JP slammed his beer on the table, and the glass broke in his hand.

'It's still none of your fucking business.'

Susan sprang to her feet, scared and ready to flee. Walter had been dozing in his bed under the desk and jumped up too, ears flattened in fear.

'JP, what the fuck?'

He shook his hand. There was blood running down his palm onto his wrist, sticking in the sandy hairs of his arm. Everything seemed drained from his face in that moment: anger, fear, sorrow. He stood like a stretched canvas, muttering.

'I'm ... I'm sorry. I think it's time for you to go, Susan. And stop reading those fucking journals.'

Exasperated, she packed up her new books and

drawings and walked out. She glanced back when she pushed through the door. JP sat in his chair, head in his hands, deep breaths lifting his shoulders in quick bursts. She thought about going back in but remembered his shouting and turned again.

CHAPTER FOURTEEN

---∞◇◇∞---

Frank

Frank stood to attention by the coffin, mourners filing past, his black suit and tie squeezing him into an acceptable shape. They shook his hand, went to Derek and then onward to press their hands against the cold flesh of his father's dead body. Some of the women were weeping. Some kissed his dad's waxen forehead, and he turned away, his face contorting with disgust.

Pat Quinlan was before him.

'Jesus Frankie, the size of you these days. You're as handsome in that suit.'

He blushed. He had grown upwards and outwards as his teens and early twenties marched on, the army building him up from the small, useless creature he had been.

'Ah, thanks for coming, Mrs Quinlan.'

Peggy came after her, in her late teens but already as steely and determined as her mother.

'Are you home now for good, is it Frank?'

He stuttered and shrugged.

'He is, yeah.'

He threw Derek a look. Derek hijacked Peggy and dragged her towards him.

'How are you doing, Peggy? Thanks so much for coming.'

He shook her hand and gave her a wink. She scowled and looked back to Frank.

'Come see me tomorrow for a pint.'

She laid her hand against the coffin, muttered something under her breath, and walked on. Frank watched her, wishing he could join her for the pint now, but he had a job to do. Hands to shake. He blew out his lips and turned back to the line.

The next person was tall. Eyebrows bushy, his grey eyes watery with emotion. His face was soft. Frank reached out a hand to the stranger, waiting for the customary words of sympathy. When the man spoke, his accent was from the mainland. His voice was kind and his hand strong – the hand of a man who worked the land.

'I'm so sorry for your trouble. You must be Frank?'

The tall man continued, sounding shy and embarrassed by his own presence.

'I'm … JP … I've eh … I was helping your dad out with the farm.'

JP. turned to Derek.

'Derek. Sorry for your troubles.'

'I'll keep things ticking over for you while ye're sorting everything out.'

Derek shrugged and glanced at Frank.

'Thanks, JP, that's appreciated.'

JP shuffled on. He stopped by their dad's body, his face a mix of all the emotions Frank knew he should be feeling right now. Frank felt none of it – only a sinking, clawing creep of a lasso tightening around his chest..

Since his return, there hadn't been a moment to think, a moment to mourn. There were suits to acquire, coffins to choose, sandwiches to arrange and houses to clean.

The Quinlans, as always, had been the chief organisers of all events. The wake in the tiny cottage, Derek and his family staying in the old farmhouse, damp and neglected as it was. Frank opted to stay in the cottage, the small bedroom a wall away from the corpse laid out in the sitting room.

The little one, Susan, named for her grandmother, toddled about the wake, bashing her head off coffee tables and getting rewarded with sweets and passed around from mourner to mourner.

Another hour of mourners streamed past. Frank's hand went numb, and his voice became raspy, dropping to a whisper. As the final trickle went through, he reduced himself to nodding, accompanied by what he hoped was a grateful look on his tired face. Derek spoke to him once, despite the prompting from mourners.

'This fucking place. Who the fuck are all these people?'

Islanders, mostly, he guessed. And mainlanders, his father had worked with. Derek seemed to recognise some from his job in Dublin; Frank watched them shuffle in, uncomfortable, shake hands, then slink off. The hostel would do well out of the funeral. And any other corner they could shove visitors into would be full. The pub would be out the door, the taps flowing. Everything would function, and the island would be ironically, heaving with life and sound and noise for a few days. Then it would end. And Frank and Derek would be here, looking at each other, figuring out who they are without a mother or father to bind them together.

'Why don't we sell it?'

Derek was pragmatic as always and right, of course.

Why didn't they sell it? The unproductive farm with the few scraggly cows, the tumbledown farmhouse, the cottage with one bedroom – what was it needed for?

Frank looked across his life, a helicopter view of his years so far. He was twenty-three, and he was a terrible soldier. He was bored. He didn't fit in. Why go back? He thought of Rúairí and his fiancée. He thought of Martin and his suspicious, sneering looks. The boots to the head.

Where else could he go? What could he do?

All this he pondered as Derek sat across the table in the cottage, baby Susan balancing on his knee, staring around her. She looked unnervingly like Fiona. He wished she'd leave along with her father.

'I want to think about it.'

Frank stood and walked out the door – days since he had stripped himself of the funeral suit, but the tightness of the white starched collar and tie still grasped at his neck, squeezing him. He turned left out the red gate of the cottage and walked on, up the hill, past the ditches and birds and wild fields of heather he'd known all his childhood and teenage years. The greenery was a waterfall after months in the desert. He walked up the hill, pausing at the stone wall of the graveyard. Fiona and his mother's graves were overgrown, his father not well enough to maintain them over the last few months. All buried in separate plots, the ground too hard to go deep enough for multiple occupants. He sat next to Fiona's and tears – for his father, his mother, and his lost little sister – spilled down his face. He sat and mourned them all at once.

I don't want to leave you again.

He grabbed at the weeds and moss, peeling them away with his hands, until at last the plot looked, perhaps not loved, but certainly not forgotten.

He rose to leave when he spotted a large presence at the other exit of the cemetery, standing awkwardly, as though waiting for him to leave.

'JP?' he called out.

JP waved stiffly, walking towards him with a look of relief.

'Ah, sorry Frank, I didn't want to be, eh … disturbing you. I just … I just wanted to pop over and tidy the place up a bit.'

JP glanced behind Frank, his face brightening.

'Oh, you've done a great job. I'll put a few of these down now.'

Frank noticed JP had some flowers in his hands. Sprigs of daisies and other wildflowers. He laid them against each of the three graves.

'There now.'

He seemed pleased. He noticed Frank watching him and reddened.

'Sorry. I hope you don't mind.'

'No … no … not at all.'

'Your dad … he was very good to me.'

'He was a good man.'

JP coughed.

'Right, I'll head on so.'

He tipped his forehead and went to move.

'JP …'

JP turned back, his face bright. Frank's voice rasped, nervous.

'Would you like to grab a pint sometime?'

CHAPTER FIFTEEN

Susan arrived at the pub that evening pissed off and reckless, still boiling from the argument with JP, gin still swirling around her veins, her senses on edge from his anger. She needed noise. She needed distraction.

There was a céilí on. She finished her burger and chips, washed down with a G&T, while the gentle strum of instruments grew into a pulsing, banging rhythm. The band tucked into a corner, almost piled on top of each other. She was glad she had dropped Walter off at home to miss the chaos. Tables and chairs had been pushed back, and every inch of the tiny pub was swarming with locals and visitors alike, whooping amid their bad Irish dancing.

Mick was at the bar in the middle of it all, tapping his foot along with the jigs and reels. His face had a look Susan didn't quite recognise when she stomped up to order a drink. A double G&T. She sipped it when it arrived, the sweetness of the tonic, the slight sourness of the alcohol. Mick kept watching her.

'No pints this evening?'

'Nah, you can't be drinking pints when it's time to dance, Mick!'

Pints didn't suit her mood – too leisurely, too relaxing. Mick pulled himself up, reaching over the bar to grab some envelopes. He handed them to her with that same strange look.

'Maureen had these for you at the post office.'

One was formal, an estate agent's details on the return address. The other two were handwritten. Susan turned them over and recognised the writing with a pull in her heart.

'Thanks.'

'She was going to wait until you called in yourself, but I told her I'd be seeing you.'

Susan traced a finger over the return address in Dublin, written in fountain pen. Its familiar Eircode.

'Someone's keen to get a hold of you.'

Mick stared her down. The usual warmth was there, but underneath it – disappointment. She recognised it now.

'Probably one of my pals,' she lied.

'Probably,' he agreed.

He seemed about to say more when a group of teenagers jigged past, knocking into his pint and making him swear.

'Sorry, Mick!'

Susan grabbed the moment and disappeared into the crowd, scanning for somewhere to sit and drink. Her hands were sweaty around the letters – Mick's disapproval clinging to her.

Amelia was sitting on her own in the corner. No gaggle of students hung on her words this evening – just her and her pint, looking out over the dancing and the noise. She spotted Susan and looked away. Susan took another sip of her drink and marched over. Shove it down, Susan. Just shove it down.

'Heya.'

'Oh, hey.'

Amelia pretended to have just noticed her. Susan placed her hand on the table, angling her body towards her.

'Can I sit with you?'

Amelia's face was unimpressed.

'How's your complicated life coming along?'

Susan resisted the urge to look at the letters in her hand. Instead, she laughed.

'A mess, as always. Yours?'

Amelia fixed her with a stare but moved over on the chair. Susan sat down, stuffing the letters into her bag.

'What are those?'

'Stuff about the house.'

Amelia accepted this and returned to her pint.

'You're not joining the dancing?'

'Not really feeling it.'

'How come?'

'Do you even actually care?'

Amelia's voice was thick with exasperation. The box of guilt leapt up in Susan's chest, then fell back into the pit. She placed her hand on Amelia's forearm, resting on the dark wood, and gave it a squeeze – willing the sincerity trapped beneath her layers of gin and rage, to travel through her fingertips into Amelia's bare skin.

'I wouldn't be asking if I didn't care.'

And she did – she cared about everything. Too much. All the time. She was soaked in it. She gulped more of her drink and hardened herself against the world. Amelia took a quick sip of her stout before continuing, some warmth seeping back into her weary voice.

'I'm just a bit wrecked from other people's bullshit to be honest, Susan.'

'Sorry.'

'It's not only you.'

They sat in their own bubble amongst the chaos of the pub. Amelia continued in a blurt.

'My ex still lives in our flat. She was supposed to be taking the summer to figure out where she wants to live next – hence, me staying here and not going home at all. But she messaged me earlier to say she's not leaving after all.'

'Ah, that's shite … lesbians, eh?'

'I told you I'm not a lesbian,' Amelia snapped. After a moment, more softly: 'She is though. Maybe that was my mistake.' A quiet laugh, sadder than Susan had heard from her before.

'See? I'm complicated too.'

'How long ago did you break up?'

'Two months. About two weeks before I came here. So I just told her to take the summer to get sorted with a new place.'

'You don't want to move out?'

'Absolutely not, it was my place first. And it's her problem to find somewhere new. She's the one –'

She stopped herself and shook her head. They sat in silence, Susan's hand still resting on Amelia's arm.

'Anyway, it's not really a big deal, it's just annoying.'

'Now,' Amelia pulled her arm away and turned to face Susan directly. 'it's your turn. What's going on in your complicated life?'

Susan shook her head and took Amelia's hand again, stroking her palm with her thumb. The light hairs on

Amelia's arm rose to her touch. Amelia's blue eyes searched hers – sceptical, yet hopeful.

'You're not going to distract me this easily.'

'Aren't I?'

Amelia's eyebrows twitched.

'You're drunk again.'

'No, I'm not,' Susan lied.

'Oh yeah, me neither.' Amelia grinned. Susan felt Amelia's hand grip hers in return.

'I feel like I should apologise to you properly for the other night.'

'Which part? Running away after kissing me – twice – or being rude to me for making sure you didn't Attila the Hun yourself?'

'All of it. You've been so kind to me.'

Amelia licked her lips, gaze darting towards Susan.

'You could make it up to me?'

'Oh yeah? How exactly?'

'Let's start with a drink.'

'Is that all?'

Her other problems faded to background noise, the sizzle between them turning everything else to a mild static. Amelia leant in, close enough for her hot breath to graze Susan's cheek.

'The night is young, right?'

A thrum ran through her. She peeled her hands away.

'Same again?'

'You bet.'

Susan pushed through the crowd to the bar, where Daniel was skipping between the taps, keeping up with the heave of the crowd.

'A pint of Murphy's and a double G&T, Danny.'

'How was the head after the other night?'

Susan's face said enough and he let out a loud cackle. His dad was still at the bar, eyes a bit glassy. Well oiled, as her mother would have said. No doubt a long week out at sea, ferrying tourists around in between fishing trips. He glanced at Susan, then over to Amelia.

'Y'all right, Mick?'

'She's a nice kid,' he said gruffly.

Susan bit her lip. The gin haze cleared for a second.

'She's not a kid, Mick.'

He looked her dead in the eye, and she shrank two feet.

'Neither are you.'

Daniel set the drinks in front of her. She placed cash on the bar and got out of there. Behind her, Peggy was giving Mick a scolding. He shook her off and kept staring, his normally open brow furrowed.

Susan forgot all about Mick's mood when she returned to Amelia. The booze warmed her, made her tongue fuzzy and carefree. They whispered in the corner of the pub, thighs touching as they giggled.

When the band took a break, Mick careened towards them and sidled up alongside.

'It's myself and herself's anniversary next week.'

'No way,' Susan replied.

She was annoyed at the interruption, but cautious. She had a sense of unease fingering its way up her neck.

'I know. Twenty-five years! 'Tis a long oul time, but you know marriage, it's a commitment, isn't it?'

He looked Susan in the eye again. Her sense of unease

grew as his face glowed with drunken determination.

'Frank was telling us you got married yourself a few years ago?'

What the fuck, Mick?

All the air left the room. Susan felt it leave her own lungs first. Amelia let go of her hand, bit her lip, wide-eyed, and turned her head towards her, cheeks reddening.

Susan puffed out her cheeks, attempting to gather herself. 'Yeah, feels like forever ago now.'

Mick's mischief engine revved up. He pulled up a stool, pulling himself closer to Susan.

'Sure, we all voted yes on the island. Well … most of us anyway.' He cocked his head towards a tall, thin woman with round glasses and a tight bun sitting primly at the next table.

'But sure, some people just love everyone being as miserable as them. Isn't that right, Agnes?'

Agnes threw him a filthy look and sipped her sherry through pursed lips. Mick gave a hearty laugh then his face turned serious. Susan felt his disappointment in her rolling off him, and her heart sank.

'Anyway, hopefully you'll be about next week for the party … sorry for disturbing you ladies.'

He dragged himself off the stool and weaved his way back to the bar. He passed Peggy on his journey, giving her a cheeky pinch in the ribs. Peggy swatted him away and offered Susan an apologetic glance. She returned it with a nod that seemed to come from a disembodied part of her. *Shove it down shove it down.*

Amelia was still looking at Susan with one eyebrow

raised. Susan's mouth was dry; she sipped her drink, staring into it. Her hands and limbs were disconnected, inhuman. She knew Amelia had said something, but it bobbed like a boat through fog.

'What?'

'You're married?'

Susan coughed.

'Yeah … I mean … sort of, yeah.'

Amelia squinted, dubious.

'To a woman, presumably?'

'He didn't vote yes to let me marry a man, Amelia.'

Susan thought of herself slamming shut Frank's journal the other day. She remembered Frank at the wedding – silent, glum, awkward. It had been Jen's idea to invite him – to help Susan reconnect with her family and herself, she'd said. Jen knew how Susan got, how she felt so alone in the world at times: her parents' deaths, her lack of siblings. Frank was the last blood she had left. He spoke to Susan only once during the entire day. He had shuffled up to Susan and Jen, their hands entwined as they beamed at each other. He was awkward, coughing his words at them.

'Ah … ye … ah ye look gorgeous. You're the image of … my mam.'

He shook their hands, stuffed an envelope full of cash into her hand, and disappeared back into the crowd. He sat at a table with some of Jen's friends, got pissed on red wine and staggered off to bed at eleven o'clock. Her last memory of him was at the breakfast buffet the following morning, rashers and sausages piled high on his plate as he tucked in, oblivious to the noise and chats around him.

He left without a goodbye. To hear he'd been talking about the day at all was a surprise.

Amelia had been quieter for longer than Susan had ever observed in their short time together. Finally, she spoke, her voice quiet and trembling.

'I wish you'd told me that sooner. I don't like being part of something like this.'

Susan didn't even know where to begin.

'I told you … my life is complicated.'

'This is a level above complicated.'

'I did try …'

She bit her lip before finishing the sentence. They both fell silent, the sounds of the pub filling the sudden gulf between them. Susan was almost relieved when Amelia broke the awkwardness.

'Are you two separated?'

Susan paused.

'Yeah.'

Amelia narrowed her gaze.

'More or less.'

'What does that mean? Did you end it or did she?'

Susan sucked her gums.

'It's not really your business, Amelia. And it's not Mick's fucking business either.'

Susan felt raw fury bubbling at Mick, sipping on his pint across the bar. Amelia raised her eyebrows again.

'And you can fuck off with the dancing eyebrows.' Susan tried to sound light-hearted. Amelia's face darkened.

'All right, you know what – figure your shit out, Susan. I'm not your midlife fucking crisis.' She jerked to her feet. Susan grabbed her hand.

'Hey, please. Sit down. Please.'

Amelia paused, gazing at their hands entwined. Susan took a breath and spoke quietly, 'I left my wife. And now I'm here.'

Jen at the kitchen table, head in her hands. A suitcase grabbed and filled amid torment. Her car screeching out of the driveway. Susan blinked it away and came back to Peggy's pub, her hand grasping another's.

Amelia looked uncertain – heart, head, and other body parts wrestling with each other. Susan needed this. Not just Amelia – warmth, a body, comfort, the wildness of forgetting.

'I'm here with you.'

CHAPTER SIXTEEN

---∞∞∞---

Frank

JP was a couple of years older than Frank. A distant cousin of the Quinlans sent to the island to be less of a nuisance to his family on the mainland.

'How were you a nuisance?'

'Well ...' Frank had learned over the past couple of weeks that JP was more talkative with four pints of Murphy's on board. 'I have six older brothers, and I'm not sure any of them like me.'

He gave a shy laugh. Frank raised his eyebrows at Peggy behind the bar for another pint.

'I think ... I think they thought I was a bit soft.'

'I know that one.'

JP took him in. There was nothing soft about Frank now. A strange, buzzy lightness moved through him as JP's gaze lingered. He lifted his pint, took a slow sip. JP looked away first and changed the subject.

'Am I out of a job so or what?'

'Eh?'

'Are ye selling up?'

Frank exhaled. Derek and his family had returned home without having settled on a decision. Frank had asked for more leave, but he'd have to make up his mind about that soon, too.

'We don't know,' he said.

'Are you going back to the army?'

Frank was sick at the thought.

'I don't know.'

'Derek didn't seem like the island type.'

They both laughed.

'No … I don't think he ever thought it was good enough for him. Sorry … that was …'

'Honest?'

Frank shrugged.

'I don't think either of us ever felt like we belonged here.'

They sat in silence, contemplating the fresh pints placed before them. The black ink and milky clouds settled in their glasses. JP sipped.

'Well, Frank … there are worse places to feel like you don't belong.'

CHAPTER SEVENTEEN

———◇◇◇◇———

Neither of them raised Susan's marital status again. Amelia sat with her in the snug, her resolve seemed to melt as she lay against Susan's shoulders, gripping her hand under the table. She told Susan stories of years of bringing clueless students to an island in the middle of the Atlantic – falling into bogs and rolling down dunes. She told Susan of her plans to travel to the far reaches of the earth, to see flora and fauna Susan had never even heard of. Susan listened intently as she spoke, laughing at her jokes, following the pulse in her neck, the smooth arc of her skin down from her mouth, over her throat and into her body. Amelia stopped mid-sentence. Susan kissed her.

'We should go.' Amelia had whispered. Susan agreed, silent and breathless.

They walked home together, her face sore from laughing. She thought about when she'd last felt like that, remembered a night with Jen when Indian food spilt all over the hotel sheets – and guilt shifted in her chest. She shoved it down and returned to the moment, bathed in moonlight and flushed from booze.

Amelia was watching her. A hand slid into hers. Susan glanced coyly at Amelia – her breath shook, her heartbeat quickened. A pulsing grew within her, warmth spreading from her centre.

The island shone; the moonbeams carved shadows and pits into the rocky, sleeping surface. Shapes and forms littered the landscape in front of them as they strolled, almost liquid, flowing into each other as they meandered down the narrow, stony roads.

The only sounds were their footsteps on the gravel and the quiet hoot of a hunting owl. Occasionally, cattle lowed in the distance, enjoying the balmy evening under the stars. A beam of moonlight caught the nape of Amelia's long neck. Susan stopped, transfixed. Amelia's stare was powerful and pleading. The silence between them was heavy and hungry – the gin and an old spark burning in Susan. She moved towards Amelia, fingertips resting gently on the young woman's elbow, pulling her a few millimetres closer. A mischievous smirk crossed her face as Amelia raised her eyebrows, unsure. Susan tilted her head towards the beach.

'Fancy a swim?'

It had seemed only a few seconds before they were down on the sand, the sea an abyss before them. Susan blamed the moonlight, the gin, and especially the mad woman standing beside her. Amelia had fully embraced the insanity of Susan's suggestion, gesturing towards the water, her face a picture of glee.

'Are you ready?'

Susan made a face. The ocean crashed against the sand a few feet away from them in the dark. The wind had picked up – Susan could feel water on her lips, but couldn't swear if it was rain or sea spray. Susan shook her head. Amelia's eyes grew wide with indignation.

'This was your idea!'

'Yeah, that was a mistake. We could actually die, you know.'

Susan was soft from years of living on the East Coast. The Irish Sea was calm and forgiving. The Atlantic roared and threatened – it could and would swallow them whole. Amelia laughed and squeezed Susan's hand again.

'Too late now!' Amelia's voice was as soothing and kind as the ocean was violent. 'Come on, I have you.'

Another moment's pause, and they started to strip, laughter stolen on the breeze as skin goose-bumped, hairs on end. Pants, tops, watches and wallets abandoned on the sand. Amelia stood naked and wild, the moonlight contouring her curves – toned, muscles rippling down her legs. The springy mound of hair between her legs shimmered in the light. Susan could barely breathe. She covered her breasts with her hands. Amelia pulled them away and a rush of giddy excitement flooded through her. Amelia's skin was a balm. Susan's hands had carried too much, wiped too many tears, held her own sobbing face too often. Amelia's hands knew none of this – strong, warm and silky, her palms pressed against Susan's and she steered Susan gently towards the sea, giggling.

Hands entwined, they ran screaming into the water.

The cold hit her and she let out a cry, then submitted to it. Her body waking up, its parts coming back together.

The sea beyond the swell was black, moonlight sketched across its surface. Amelia dived under, fearless, slicking her hair back and grinning as she resurfaced. Eyes wide and alight, soft lips shiny pink, moist from the sea spray. Their limbs entangled as they floated together, and those warm strong hands found Susan's body again. Amelia moved behind her, pressing Susan's back against her. Susan turned her head – the laughter and screaming had stopped. Silent now, holding each other's gaze. Susan's breath quickened towards Amelia's lips, fingertips moving across her stomach, pulling her closer. Amelia's heat radiated even in the cold water, the press of her breasts against Susan's shoulder blades.

Amelia's open mouth was gentle but certain – reassuring, guiding. Fingertips resting on Susan's hips, pressing their bodies together. The tip of her tongue traced the inside of Susan's mouth. Pleasure spread through her and her legs wrapped around the younger woman's solid calves, planted on the sand. Lips on her neck, tracing kisses up her skin, tongue sketching slow patterns. One hand cupped her breast, fingers lightly pinching her nipple. Susan gasped – Amelia's fingers moving more quickly now, down past her belly button, dancing over the soft wet hairs between her legs. Under the water, Amelia touched her where she longed for it and a soft moan, long lost, escaped Susan's lips. More moans while Amelia's hand worked, their lips finding each other again. A slight sharp surprise that quickly gave way to a need for more.

'Oh wow,' Susan gasped.

Amelia paused, panting.

'Is this all right?'

'Yes … yes.'

Susan pulled Amelia's lips back to hers, their mouths open wide, consuming each other in the cold water – the pressure building, Amelia's hand setting the nerves in her legs on exquisite fire. Her head began to swim, thoughts scrambled and stretched and finally pushed out entirely as she came. Amelia's fingers stayed inside her as she rocked, her other hand holding Susan close, keeping her safe and above water. Susan kissed Amelia's neck as the final spasms moved through her, as the soothing calm spread throughout her body.

They stumbled out of the water, still wrapped in each other, landing with a thud on the wet sand. They stared at each other, breathing in sync, waiting for the next impulse.

Amelia kissed her again, tongue caressing the inside of her lips – Susan bit it gently and they smirked hungrily at each other.

'You're so fucking hot,' Amelia muttered, breathless.

Susan kissed her in response, revelling in the worship. Pressing her lover back down into the sand, Amelia climbed on top of her, naked form resting on her hips. Her lips traced the outline of Susan's nipples. They hardened beneath her tongue, and a shiver moved down through Susan's body. The lips travelled lower, across her ribs, licks and kisses and sighs mapping their way across her skin. Amelia's fingernails traced up her inner thigh as Susan grabbed her hair, arching her back to guide Amelia's lips to where she needed her. Amelia cast her eyes upwards, and the unfamiliar startled Susan. She sat up with a jolt, Amelia losing her balance and falling into the sand with a yelp.

'What the fuck?' She laughed.

'What if someone sees us? What the fuck are we doing?'

Amelia stretched her leg over Susan again, pushing her back down. She bit her own lip.

'I don't give a single shit if someone sees us.'

The shiver again – Susan pulled Amelia down on top of her and they kissed as the waves roared. Susan pushed her off again with a groan.

'No, no, no. We are not fucking on the sand.'

She kissed Amelia's fallen face, already sandy from their antics.

'Come home with me.'

Amelia's pupils were dark, her breath catching as she spoke. She kissed Susan, lips swollen with arousal.

'Will I be sleeping on the couch again?'

Susan took Amelia's fingers, kissing them gently, sucking the tips, her eyes lasered on the redhead's. Amelia moaned softly. Susan growled.

'Absolutely not.'

They dragged their tops on, staying naked from the waist down, hoping no one would see them on the short walk home. Progress was slow, interrupted by the need to wrap their lips around each other every few paces. They finally reached the house, Amelia dragging Susan into the bedroom, crashing through the door, pushing her onto the bed and climbing over her, straddling her wet, hot centre over Susan's leg. Susan couldn't contain herself any longer – she sat up and rolled Amelia onto her back. The redhead gasped with surprise and pleasure. Susan moved down her body with her lips, tracing shapes across the salty skin, the body beneath her arching and swaying with each kiss. She reached her hips and inner thigh, working inward with small nibbles and kisses, Amelia's appreciative moans sending shocks of pleasure through her. Amelia was swollen and pulsing. Susan licked and sucked as the redhead rocked, hips in the air, hands in Susan's hair, pushing her, begging her to keep going.

Susan's tongue and fingers searched, pushed, and massaged. Her head swam, her own moans smothered by Amelia's thighs and hands pressing against her head as Susan fucked her. Amelia contracted around her and Susan's mind went blank – the world fell away, her sight zooming out like a camera lens. She saw herself lying in the white light of the moon through her bedroom window, face between the legs of this young woman, the sheets bunching at her feet. As the world came back into focus, Amelia fell back onto the bed with a satisfied thud, gazing down at Susan, sleepy and satisfied, one question roared at her from the box she had buried deep in her brain.

What the fuck am I doing?

CHAPTER EIGHTEEN

The Irish summer broke the next morning. The sun hid behind heavy clouds, threatening a downpour. A sticky overcast heat clung to the island, suffocating the greenery, but a breeze from the sea offered some relief.

Susan and Amelia knew nothing of this yet. They lay tangled together in sand-covered sheets, their bodies worn out and stretched clean. Sometime around midnight Susan had lost count of how many times they'd fucked, how many times she had pushed the doubts out and Amelia inside her, physically, metaphorically – how many times she had made Amelia's back arch and desperate cries burst out of her perfect mouth. The room reeked of sex and sweat and salt. She couldn't open the window for the sounds and scents that would drift out to the rest of the island. That sick feeling returned, a rebellion against the sourness she swallowed down each time she forced her brain to reset and forget.

Susan's eye wandered to her handbag on the floor next to her side of the bed, the letters searing a hole through its fabric and into the back of her brain – the part untouched and unsoothed by the pleasures of the night. She bent down and rifled through the bag like a cat burglar, watching the sleeping form in her bed. The envelope with the oldest stamp fell into her hands almost too perfectly. She lay back, propped against the pillows, and unfolded the letter. Short. Jen's handwriting so neat and exact as always. The paper smelled like their house – Italian cooking, lavender from the garden. She inhaled it, her heart thumping.

Dear Susan,

I feel like a gentleman in a Jane Austen novel, writing to my wife from a distance – but all I have for you is an address and no number. I've been trying your phone, but maybe it's off? Or maybe you've blocked me?

It's only been a few days since you've gone and I miss you. Although I think we both know you've been gone for a while.

I've been thinking a lot about the night we first met, me trying to look cool, you just being cool, and flirty and fun. Our kisses in the corner of the nightclub, how we talked for hours. When did we stop talking like that? When did we stop kissing like that? I miss the days when our only problems were finding enough money for booze and staying at the right level of hangover that wouldn't get us fired.

I remember how confident you were. Do you remember what you were like then? So bold and flirty.

Sorry, I'm broken from all this.

From our first kiss, you felt like home. My whole life I've never felt so safe and so minded. And now here we are.

I know that we can't capture the past or go back there. I know it's a foreign country. I felt you slipping away for such a long time. When you sat silently on the couch beside me, when we lay in bed together, you on your back, staring at the ceiling, hands on your belly. And now you're gone entirely and I don't know if you'll be back, or what version of you will return. I sit in the house we built and decorated, the house we made our dreams in together, the house where we loved and shared and fucked and cuddled and needed each other, and I miss my home.

Please come back to me.

Jen

A vomit-like sensation rose through her. It emerged as a choked cry, a sob she forced into a cough. Her brain fired images, sounds and smells at her faster than she could process them. Jen's chestnut hair glinting in disco lights. Her lips for the first time. Watching her stumble through a crowded foam party, the music sounding like they were underwater, surrounded by sudsy half-naked bodies. Susan had one night of the year where she pretended she wasn't getting older, living in houses just on the right side of student dinginess. She still binged on cheap booze and good vibes, but the following morning slinked off to a semi-respectable job with a quasi-acceptable hangover. The beer fear still worth it.

Susan remembered leaning against a pillar, trying to look cool, surveying the crowd. Her friends were in there, covered in bubbles somewhere, but beyond the line where the wooden floors met the tile of the dance floor, the crowd moved as one congealed wild melee.

That's when she spotted Jen, queuing at the bar, looking like she had also just realised she was getting a bit old for it all. Jen caught her watching from across the purple haze of the heavy, soaking club, and Susan knew she had liked what she saw.

Susan gave her best flirty nod of acknowledgement and strode towards Jen, not knowing the future she was teeing up, the love she was about to let into her life, and the heartbreak that would come with it.

Someone bought the other a beer. They could never quite agree who paid, but they both remembered the bottles were warm and slightly tacky – residue from the cheap shots the barman had been serving all night directly into the mouths of patrons. Susan remembered Jen's tongue moistening her bottom lip, shiny and pink and slightly swollen with something – lust? excitement? confidence? Both with pale skin, slight sheens of sweat across their brows from the warmth of the club.

The rest of the evening came back only in flashes. Susan taking Jen's hand and steering her into a corner so she could 'hear their conversation better'. They sat, one leg on the couch each, turned to each other, sipping their beers. Their knees touched. They'd pause and look at each other. Jen's deep, full-faced blushes warmed Susan as she considered Jen's lips, her teeth slowly tugging at her own.

They covered every topic they could, from family to college to work to dreams to pets to hobbies to fears and hopes. Every sentence brought their faces a millimetre closer, until they were so close Susan knew Jen could feel the heat of her breath on her lips. Susan bit her cheek.

'What are you smirking about?' Jen grunted, throwing Susan a light-hearted side-eye.

That had tipped Susan over the edge. She'd pressed her lips against Jen, the softest lips she'd ever kissed. They'd sucked and pulled against each other, the slight tip of Susan's tongue flicking, exploring, licking. Jen had melted into her, with all her softness, her fun, her laughter. Susan's long fingers had laced with Jen's, her thumb stroking the back of Jen's hand, pulling her closer into an embrace, the soft shell of Susan's body wrapping around Jen's as they kissed.

Amelia stirred, and a small yawn slipped out, yanking Susan back to the present day. She dropped the letter off the side of the bed, the indecency of the moment shocking her. Amelia blinked herself awake. Susan thought about how young she looked in this light, naked and tender from a night of intimacy. She rubbed Amelia's cheek with her thumb, enjoying the peachy feel of her skin. Amelia smiled into her hand, groaning a greeting as she awoke.

'Morning.'

'Morning.'

The shyness between them didn't fit all the things they'd done to each other during the night and through much of the early hours of the morning.

'What the fuck am I doing?' Susan asked herself again.

Her fingertips rested lightly on Amelia's skin as they pulled each other close. She kissed the top of Amelia's head, smelling her own scents and sweat from her hair as she whispered into it.

'Are you hungry?'

'Starving.'

'I'll make us some brekkie.'

Amelia pulled away.

'No, I'll make it. You did it the last time. It's definitely my turn.'

The word 'turn' suggested a pattern, and Susan's sickness returned. *Shove it down.*

Susan lay back, stretching out across the sheets. In the sitting room, Amelia said hello to Walter and set about making breakfast from whatever the cupboards had to offer. Susan must have dozed off in the half-light of the grey morning, because when she woke Amelia was there with a tray.

'I own a tray?'

'You do!'

Amelia stepped around the side of the bed, her feet brushing against the pile of papers and letters falling from the handbag. She plopped the tray on Susan's legs, two plates of scrambled eggs and toast, with coffee that smelled like heaven. She glanced down.

'What's that?'

She bent down before Susan could stop her.

'Is this from your wife?'

Amelia was pointing to the line, 'Please come back to me.' Susan swallowed. Amelia looked down at the other envelope on the floor, with matching neat handwriting.

'She's been looking for you.'

'I haven't read the other one yet, I'm not sure …'

Amelia dropped the letter and slid into the bed, taking a plate and fork from the tray. Her face was unreadable, for once, and dread settled in Susan's veins..

'Is Walter all right?'

'I let him out for a wee and gave him his breakfast.'

'Thank you.'

'Sure.'

They ate in silence until Susan couldn't bear it any more.

'We don't have much luck with breakfast conversation, do we?'

'I guess actions have consequences, eh?'

Amelia's tone was uncharacteristically harsh and devoid of her humour. She finished her food, slid the tray off the bed and set it gently on the floor. She was still silent, but not leaving yet; just thinking. Susan could see the turmoil in her face, the furrowed eyebrows and the clouds gathering in her expression.

Susan lay down. She turned over and pulled Amelia down with her, placing her arm over her body. Amelia was stiff. Susan kissed her hand. They lay together, Amelia's warmth wrapped around her. Amelia took a deep breath and blurted.

'Why did you leave your wife?'

The question sucked the air out of the room. Susan tensed and pursed her lips. She swallowed more acid into her gut.

'Again, I don't think that's any of your business.'

Amelia rolled to the side and sat back.

'I think it is my business right now.'

Susan sat up too, scooching her bum back along the bed until she was leaning against the headboard. Amelia's shoulders were inches from hers. Amelia surprised her by lacing their fingers together.

The silence engulfed them both. Susan let go of Amelia's hand, moving slightly away from her in the tiny bed. She pulled at the small hairs at the front of her scalp.

'Did she cheat on you or something?'

The oddly hopeful tone in Amelia's voice broke something in her.

'No. No, she'd never do that.'

Susan felt a wave of suffocating guilt rise. The words bubbled up that she couldn't stop.

'She's ... um ... she's wonderful, actually. She's kind and smart and ... But ... there's only so many times you can tell your wife to fuck off before you take your own advice ... you know?'

Amelia looked like a kicked puppy as she slowly unravelled the reality of the situation before her.

'You still love her?'

The corners of her eyes stung. She glanced sadly at Amelia. This conversation had seemed inevitable from the start, but here it was now, the elephant in the room trumpeting loudly.

'She's the love of my life, Amelia.' Her voice sounded drained and strained. She raised her palms, a casual gesture to try and pull her back from this emotional cliff.

Amelia's face changed and her voice took on an unfamiliar edge. 'Then why are you here fucking me?'

It was a reasonable question. Susan paused, trying to choose her words carefully, but at this stage – what was the point? How much is appropriate to reveal to a naked twenty-seven-year-old you've spent the night fucking behind your wife's back? Where is the line? Does the line still exist?

'I don't know if I want my life anymore.'

She'd said it. The doors blew off her emotional bunker, and Amelia surveyed the broken shell within. The silence fell again. It settled in her chest. There was nothing more she could or would say; she was empty. Amelia moved like a cat, gliding out of bed, picking her way through the abandoned clothing. The sunlight pierced through the dust motes, picking up the red and auburn notes throughout Amelia's hair as she moved.

'I'm sorry, I didn't mean to hurt you.'

Amelia sat on the edge of the bed and rested her hand on Susan's foot. Her shoulders dropped.

'It's my fault. I knew you were married ... but I should go.'

Susan didn't have the energy to stop her. Amelia

dressed herself and left. Susan lay in bed with the pieces of her life around her.

CHAPTER NINETEEN

——⋄⋄⋄⋄——

Dear Susan,

How am I supposed to just keep moving through my days as if everything is normal?

Karen and Tracey called for lunch the other day, full of fake smiles. Isaac is six months now. They seem almost embarrassed to talk about him. They didn't even bring him over. I think they thought I'd find it upsetting? I don't even care about babies any more. I just want you to come home and we can talk through whatever is going on.

I think they think I murdered you. Mostly because Karen said 'It's not like we think you murdered her or anything!' Tracey was mortified. I suppose they just want to know if you're all right. They can join the club.

We talked about our trip to Croatia. Parts of you, some of the best parts, never came back from that trip, did they?

I wish you could have seen how broken we both were, how broken I was. But it was only ever about you.

I think back to our moments of optimism, when things didn't seem so bleak, lying in bed together, whispering, spooning, loving.

And now I'm alone in my sadness, and you're there alone in yours. What is this achieving? What are you doing on that island? Why is being sad on your own better than being sad with me?

I'm sorry to tell you the back garden is starting to look a bit ramshackle, despite my efforts to keep it how you like it. Weeds sprouting up from every corner, your dahlias are in a shocking state. I'm doing my best, but nothing seems to be working. The slats in the garden bench collapsed yesterday. The paint is peeling off every surface … the place is disintegrating without you, including me.

I keep going to make some stupid joke that only you would understand, and then remember you've left.

My mother rang me yesterday, asking for an update on 'that wild woman you married'. If you can't come home yet, some other proof of life would be great.

I miss your shepherd's pie.

Love, Jen X

Susan read the other letter in her empty bed. Her eyes stung, and a burning, clenching, clawing feeling was within her. The trip to Croatia. She remembered it like one remembers a dream.

They had splurged on a trip away with their friends – the one luxury they'd allowed themselves since IVF had begun to drain their savings and spare cash. And then delays with the clinic resulted in tight timelines, the egg retrieval the day before flying, and then waiting, waiting, waiting for the clinic to call with the result of the process. When Susan should have been basking in the sunshine, sipping light beers and enjoying the warmth on her face, she was lit up with stress, waiting for the phone to ring. Waiting to hear the number of fertilised eggs, the number of embryos progressing, and the number of blastocysts ready to freeze. Numbers, numbers, numbers.

She knew she was on edge. She knew everyone else felt something churning underneath her surface. Like attending a play, she was in the audience of her life, only speaking to snap at Jen or speak tight words to everyone else. Every moment she got, she slunk into a corner with a book she couldn't seem to read. Her abdomen ached from the egg collection. Jen watching her, laughing a forced laugh with Tracey and Karen. All four of them on the precipice of parenthood. Or so they'd thought.

Susan would read for a few seconds, pause, stare into space, then read again before pausing for another look around. For the first five days of that trip, she was on page thirty. She caught Jen checking her progress when the book was unattended and gave her a snarl. That day, near Šibenik,, the phone call came; she slipped down into the cabin and got the news no one wanted. Not a single blastocyst had developed beyond day four. The embryologist had been kind but brutal.

'We can monitor for another day, but I think it's very unlikely to make a difference.'

She couldn't remember a lot after that phone call, just floating back on deck and walking, zombie-like, towards the front of the boat.

She stopped before the deck ran out, leaning against the railings, the wind blowing her hair – thinner now from all the medications. She rocked back and forth. The Adriatic was crystal blue that day, stretching out far ahead, broken by dots of islands and clouds hanging low, touching the sea. She looked into the horizon and let the wind blow away what was left of her. She shook herself, set her jaw, wound up her smile. Jen would see through it – there was no charm in that smile. Less discerning viewers might be fooled, but the light was gone. The armour pieced itself together, creaking at its hinges. She stomped back towards the gang, rubbing her hands mechanically.

'All right, enough of this crap Croatian beer shit, where's the real stuff?'

She grabbed a bottle of the moonshine the captain had

procured from an island farmer. Karen, shocked at first, shrugged and joined her. Tracey protested and grabbed some glasses.

'We can AT LEAST not be total animals.'

Jen drank slowly and watched her. Susan knew her dead eyes were getting watery and glazed as she drank, and drank, and drank. Jen tried to talk to her, but she pushed her away and shushed her in front of the others.

'What did the clinic say?' Jen whispered in a rare moment when the others were elsewhere on the tiny boat. They had been boozing for hours at this stage, the sun sending golden lace across the sky as it started to set.

'It wasn't good news, what more do you need to know?' Susan spat at her; her venom was hot and pointed.

'Did we get any embryos?'

Susan's lip trembled and, for a brief moment, the tears were right there. Perhaps that would have changed things. Perhaps if she had leaned into the gnawing, gaping agony instead of drinking it or snarling it away, things would have been different. Instead, she leaned towards Jen. A dark pain had settled over her.

'What do you fucking think?'

Jen recoiled, horrified. Susan felt like a monster. She opened her mouth, but Karen arrived back, sloshed and wobbly, landing down next to them.

'Fuck it, we're out of the good booze.'

The chance to take things back was gone. Susan pulled herself to her feet.

'I'm off to bed anyway. See you guys in the morning.'

'It's only nine p.m.!'

She shrugged and sauntered off to their cabin, leaving

Jen to watch her, shell-shocked.

Susan's self-hatred still lurked inside her as she lay in the white-walled bedroom in the cottage. The rain was battering the cottage. It was a perfect day to remember her wrongs and her pain.

She thought of how they had swum off the yacht, the others screaming and laughing, Susan quiet, contemplating the salt on her lips. She had dived deeper than the others, seeing the bed of the ocean almost in reach, but too far. Fish swam out of grasp from her fingertips, shafts of sunlight spearing through the water as the joy of the others muffled its way to her ears. *If I had only stayed there underwater and let the sea take me, what difference would it have made? If I had died that week, would I have missed anything except pain?*

The thought scared her. She pulled herself out of bed and shook it off.

Jen's letter had awoken some part of her and her brain flooded, its mechanisms jammed with past failings. Her stupidity, her selfishness – all there, prising apart her well-constructed shell of repression. She paced the sitting room, Walter dozing on the couch.

She stopped at the window. The island stretched out in front of her, grey and green under the clouds. She had talked about this place once, back when the future still had a shape.

'Someday, when we have a tiny beggar …' Susan's voice had been dreamy and calm. They had stopped using the word baby sometime after the first cycle and before the second. It made the gap, the loss, the heartbreak too real.

'… I want us to visit the island.'

That morning came back to her now. A different bed, a different life.

Susan was half-awake and still dozy in the summer morning light, enveloped in cool cotton sheets and duvets. As always, Jen was watching her, one eye open. Susan was starry with potential happiness. The dull threat of anxiety and fear lived at the edges, but somehow, for this moment, she had forgotten it.

'Yeah?'

Jen's word was a string to pull Susan closer. She rolled over and flopped her arm around Susan's belly, gentle to avoid the bruises and puckered flesh from the injections. She kissed her shoulder as Susan lifted the back of her hand to her lips for a quick morning hello.

'Yeah,' she whispered, starting to fall back to sleep. 'I'd like her to meet her family.'

'Frank?'

Jen sounded sceptical. Susan pinched her hand with reproach.

'Not just Frank. All of them, ancestors and all.'

'Oh, right. That'll be nice for a toddler, saying cheerio to a bunch of headstones.'

Susan giggled.

'You're the pits! You've no soul.'

Jen snuggled close, kissing her neck again, breathing into the folds of Susan's shoulder.

'It's just …' Susan paused, choosing her words carefully as always. 'I want her to know where she came from.'

'What if it's a boy?'

'Shhhh.'

'You might have a tiny penis inside you in a few months.'

'Gross, Jen.'

Susan cupped her tummy, flat now but swollen with potential.

'He'll be waving it around the house, pissing in all of our faces.'

'Stop!'

A moment of laughter and warmth and cosiness – and then it was gone again. Susan bit her lip, her mind somewhere else, even as Jen pulled towards her.

'What's up?'

'I really hope it works this time.'

'I think it will.'

Susan chewed her lip.

'I just …'

Susan knew Jen saw her pushing it down, locking it tight, swallowing the key. Susan wanted to tell her she couldn't take another disappointment, that her heart and body were already broken from it. Jen tried to nuzzle her back to hope.

'I know, my love. I know.'

No, you don't. The thought darted across Susan's mind. She shook her head and turned over again, drawing Jen close to her back, Jen's palm resting on her soft, bare breast. Susan's heart beat into Jen's hand as they both drifted back to sleep.

CHAPTER TWENTY

———◦◦◦◦◦———

Susan cleaned the house in a whirlwind, washing sheets and purging the small cottage of the scents and evidence of her bad decisions. Walter snoozed on, lifting his head on occasion to cast a curious eye at Susan's mania. The weather outside made it easier – an angry Atlantic wind had whipped up, sending the island's vegetation into disarray. The wind sent the rain splattering against the small windows of the cottage. She sloshed water and bleach around with a mop on the kitchen tiles. The house reeked of disinfectant.

When the night came, she returned to the journals, dipping back into the mundane life of Frank on Dune Island, hoping to fill in the gaps in her family tree and her uncle's life. Sketches of JP and Walter watching the cows together. An owl perched in a hedgerow. Written entries such as:

Won that award today. Great stuff.

She was moving through the years. The journals were less dusty and creased around the edges, and with a sudden increase in detail. The drawings here were elaborate, detailed sketches of herbs and flowers, snatches of close studies of Walter sleeping or JP tasting gin; the lighthouse beams casting their light across the ocean at night, a full moon offering its assistance. Some of the entries offered more insights.

JP on about whiskey again. Told him to get his own distillery if he wanted to. Not talking to me now.

Brought JP some macarons from the place in Skibb. He's talking to me again.

Her energy was starting to dip, eyelids closing when her attention was drawn by an entry on the page in front of her, just turned by her sleepy hand.

Went to the wedding. Went well. JP not happy with me.

That was her wedding – the one that went well. And it had – but what did it have to do with JP? She flicked through the journal, but there were no more sketches, no more personal entries. Only the robotic farm and distillery journals remained, detailing liquor sales, farm work, customer queries, and cattle yields. Whatever happened with JP, Frank shoved all his personality back inside and away from this journal.

Shove it down. The thought arrived and with it a flame of connection to her long-dead uncle. She put the books back for now, slipping off to bed with Walter following behind. The bedroom smelled like bleach and fresh sheets – a forensic team couldn't find a trace of Amelia in there. She opened the window to let in some fresh air and the sound of rain. No moon tonight. Only clouds and wind filling the empty space across the island.

By morning, the rain had left, leaving a wet sheen over the roads and paths – the hedgerows and grasses were springy and shining – the heat of the summer had left them parched. Susan and Walter walked up into the heart of the island; she puzzled over the journal entries and the stories of the people who had lived in her new home. The wall of the graveyard, chest-height, followed along beside her on her stroll, her hand scratching along its rough stone. The gate appeared; she thought for a second, then pushed inside, unsure what she was looking for but hoping answers could be found within.

The Shaw family plots were quite easy to find if you were looking for them – they all rested in the same area of the graveyard, containing multitudes of old names she recognised, great-aunts and great-uncles, grandfathers and great-grandfathers. Lichen and moss had taken over the older generations, but the newer ones, Nanny and Granda Shaw and Fiona, were taken care of. They were clean and tidy, the weeds and grass kept well-behaved, the lettering still shining gold in the black marble. Pots of purple lavender at each corner, the scent filling the quiet air, the buzzing of the bees breaking the solitude. Frank's grave was a separate headstone, but the same stone and design, and the same loving upkeep.

'Frank Shaw – 1965–2021. Beloved son, brother and friend.'

Frank's whole life reduced to one line on a marble headstone. She sat, pressing herself against the wet grass, not caring that it soaked the seat of her pants. She took in the entire plot, surrounded by history. Only her parents were missing, buried on the mainland with each other. Their deaths from illnesses 'bravely borne' ten and twelve years ago, respectively. She was young at the time, but not so young that she hadn't known them, hadn't grown up without them. When they died, the overwhelming feeling was disconnection – what was her place in the world with no biological ties to anyone around her? Her mother was an only child, her father had effectively chosen to be one.

She floated untethered through life, until Jen.

Oh god. Jen.

She sat in the graveyard and willed the grass to grow up through her skin, twist around her and drag her into the earth. A large pot of bright yellow flowers lit up Frank's plot – like big daisies, she thought. She recognised the smell. Chamomile. Frank's favourite.

JP stood inside the office, pulling himself up to his full height as she approached. His face was flushed, jaw tight. He rubbed his lower back as though it pained him, and Susan noticed his lips pressed thin, barely holding something in.

'All right, JP?'

She was cautious, his silence filling the space between them. He stepped towards her – his grey eyebrows knitted together, something working behind his eyes. Not just anger. Fear, maybe.

'Just like that, then?' His voice was low and strained.

His breath smelled sweet; something sour beneath it.

'What?' Susan started to bristle. She kept her back to the open door, ready to leave if she needed to. Perhaps today wasn't the day to bring up Frank, the chamomile, and the wedding that made JP unhappy.

'Selling up? Just like that?'

She bit her lip.

'The estate agent rang. Trying to set up a time to visit and evaluate. Talking about getting the place tidy and ready for viewers.'

His voice was shaking. Susan stayed silent, feeling a deep ache.

'He was trying to get a hold of you to confirm a few details.'

JP affected a Dublin 4 drawl, waving his hand in a mock flamboyant flourish. Susan bit the inside of her lip to stop herself snapping.

'JP, I was going to –'

'What? Give me a ten-minute warning? Let me know before they dragged me out by my boots?'

'No one's getting dragged out by their boots, for fuck's sake. I don't even know if I'm going to sell; I'm looking at options. Frank's solicitor recommended I get it valued.'

JP sniffed, rocking back and forth on his feet. He swallowed hard, not looking at her. She continued, carefully.

'If I sell it – IF – I sell … I'm sure whoever buys it will need you to run it anyway.'

JP slammed his fist into the desk.

'How fucking dare you? Do you have any idea what you're doing?'

Susan snapped.

'Do I look like I have the first clue about what I'm doing, JP?' Her voice was verging on hysterical. 'I have no fucking idea what I'm doing!'

JP squared up to her, his eyes boring into hers as he pressed against her smaller body.

'If Frank was still here …'

He paused, the fight leaving him. His face collapsed in on its own anger, and he folded himself onto the chair, timber creaking as his dead weight landed. He put his hands to his face, running his fingers through the front of his hair.

Susan stepped back, confused. She had unleashed something unexpected in both of them. She placed a hand on his shoulder.

'He's not here, though, JP. And … we have to find a way forward.'

JP whipped his head up and stared at her. He pulled himself to his feet again.

'Frank wouldn't want it to be sold … he wouldn't want … this.'

He shuffled off, pausing at the door.

'This was ours … even if he … it was ours.'

JP left. Her fear was gone, her ribs still tight. JP's anger and misery hung in the air of the small dusty office. It clung to the papers and the folders that lay about. The smell of stale beer and gin clung like petrol in her nostrils. She cursed the estate agent for calling before checking with her, then cursed herself when she thought of her phone lying at the bottom of a drawer in the bedroom, the email she had ignored, and the letter she hadn't opened. Walter gave a yip to remind her he was still here and shook himself off. His ears were flat against his head.

'I know, pal, I know.'

She bent to give him a pet and a nuzzle. As she crouched, she noticed a small box on the floor, tucked underneath the drawers of the desk. Shiny, polished and crafted, it stood out from its worn surroundings. The word 'Cross' raised from the chestnut-coloured wood in gold lettering. She looked towards the empty doorway where JP had left. He had gone elsewhere. She stretched her arm under the desk, flattening herself to fit. Her fingertips grasped, and she felt the box's firm, smooth grain under her skin. As she pulled it out of its nook, footsteps echoed outside the office and paused. They left again; JP on his way to a far corner of the distillery to 'test' some product. She pulled the box out and examined it. It was old but well kept; she found no scratches on any part of it, golden hinges still shining as she opened it – they slid open with a slight click.

A silver fountain pen lay on a cloth bed, small blots of ink across its nib. The pen itself, though elegant, soon lost Susan's attention. A carving of gilded lettering across the inside of the case caught her eye.

To JP, my island in the storm. F

Walter yipped as another flurry of footsteps outside the door brought JP rushing back into the office. He looked surprised to see her still there, then he noticed the box in her hand. He stormed across the room, knocking her aside as he grabbed it. He opened a drawer in the desk, tossed it in, and slammed it shut. He stood for a moment, his back to her, his breathing heavy as he gripped the drawer closed with white fingers. His shoulders rose up and down.

'JP ...'

'Get out.'

His voice was a growl.

'Can we just ...'

He turned, red and feral.

'GET OUT.'

CHAPTER TWENTY-ONE

Frank

They'd been working together on Frank's father's farm for a few months, slowly adjusting to each other's presence while Frank figured out his place as the bearer of responsibility for the family business.

'Why did you join the army?' JP asked.

His question would seem out of the blue to anyone else, but Frank was getting to know JP's workings, his moods, his thoughts, how the wheels in his head turned, how statements and thoughts fermented there for days before finally being released into the space between them. Frank had mentioned the army days before, when JP remarked on how precisely he shone his shoes and boots.

'Sure 'twas the only good thing they taught me in there.'

JP sank back into his own thoughts.

Now, mending fences together, Frank pondered the question. Why had he joined the army? He wanted to draw himself close to this relative stranger. He resisted.

'Ah, you know, sure there was nothing else to be doing.'

JP consumed this sentence. Frank could see he didn't believe it. He leaned into the spark that seemed to burn and taunt him.

'… I thought it might toughen me up.'

JP's face softened.

'Did it?'

Frank thought of the stories he could spin, the tales he could tell. He resisted.

'No.'

CHAPTER TWENTY-TWO

During Susan's walk home from the distillery, the rain returned and the wind pushed her along the path as she tried to make sense of her encounter with JP. Walter's ears stayed flat against his head, bent low against the storm, tail between his legs. She picked him up, opening her jacket and hiding him from the elements. He gave her a gentle lick on her chin, and she surprised herself with a soft kiss against his ear.

'It's ok, love, we'll be home soon.'

She thought of the house, cold and empty. She had ploughed through her meagre supplies, snacking her way through her fear and hangover. She checked her watch and remembered Maureen was closed today for a visit to the mainland. There was no good choice left; it was Peggy's or hunger. She pressed the heat of Walter's body close to her, his nose tucked under her collar away from the driving rain. She walked past her little house, down the hill towards the pub and braced herself against the wind and what awaited her in there.

The pub was busy as always, the new flock of students making themselves at home. Somehow, they looked the same as the previous gang, all awkward limbs and daft confident opinions on things that never seemed to matter once you left college. She set Walter down on the mat inside the door. He shook himself and took off in the direction of the snug's glowing stove, squeezing his way past legs and bags and hands trying to grasp him. He curled his tail across his nose ignoring the human occupants of the snug as they looked around for his owner.

There was an odd tension as she took a seat at the bar. Peggy took her order for lasagne with no other chat. She sat in her wet clothes in the warmth, water dripping from her coat, which hung on the hook under the bar. She was relieved when Daniel emerged from the back. He gave a grin when he spotted her.

'Danny, please give me a pint, it's badly needed.'

He slid up to the Murphy's tap. He watched her under his eyebrows as he poured.

'How's it going anyway?'

'Ah, sure look. Yourself?'

'Ah yeah, sure.'

He paused for a bit after this non-exchange, then nodded towards her, full of mischief.

'Is it true?'

She furrowed her eyebrows together.

'Is what true?'

'That you're having an affair with herself.'

He indicated with his chin towards the back of the pub, where Susan realised Amelia sat amongst some of her fellow lecturers. The colour drained from her face. He gave another grin.

'That's a yes, so.'

'I'd hardly call it an affair.'

'Oh? What would you call it so?'

'Just pour my pint, ya little bollocks.'

He snorted and put his head down. Susan sank into the bar stool, feeling her spine press into itself as the tension and scrutiny she thought hung in the pub seeped in through her skin. Mick walked through from the back of the bar, a crate of beer in his big arms. He caught her eye. She thought he looked sheepish. She ignored him. He grunted and walked off, the sweat on his brow glinting in the lights of the pub.

Daniel had a serious look on his face – an unfamiliar sight for Susan. He looked her in the eye as he handed the pint over.

'He meant well the other night.'

Susan dropped her gaze, cheeks burning with shame. Daniel continued, lifting her pint to slide a beermat under it.

'I think he kinda sees himself as dad to everyone.'

Susan's eyes stung.

'He's a good man.'

'He is.'

'I'm … I'm sorry I'm such a shit, Daniel.'

Daniel shook his head.

'Would you fuck off, you're not a shit. Just go and chat with him, he'll forget all about it.'

Maybe so, she thought. But I can't forget it. His face, disappointed. The way he tried to stop me and I swatted his warnings aside. How I pushed through that feeling and brought Amelia into my bed.

As though summoned, Amelia appeared at the other end of the bar – as far from Susan as possible in the tight space.

'Danny?'

She called to him, breaking his concentration on Susan's downcast face. He gave a wink to Susan.

'That one's on the house.'

'How will your mam feel about that?'

'What Peggy doesn't know won't hurt either of us.'

He wandered over to Amelia, greeting her with a grin. Susan cast an eye towards Walter, still snoozing in the heat. The cold crept in – a shiver down her back, a tingling in her fingers as the feeling returned. Peggy set a steaming plate of food in front of her with a small 'now', giving her a fright.

'Amazing, thanks, Peggy.'

Peggy's smile was flat, her nod perfunctory. She retreated without anything further. Susan's mouth was dry despite the drink. There was no room for food in her body – the anxiety and dread filled it up, squeezing everything together. Her organs had shrivelled.

'Daniel,' she called out to him, as though watching from a distance. 'Can I get a double Jameson when you've a chance?'

He looked surprised but gave a thumbs up. The whiskey wet her mouth, its fire burned through her.

She sat ordering whiskeys and reading an abandoned newspaper as her food went cold. Over time, the words started to make less sense on the page. The stool wobbled underneath her. She asked Daniel for another. He handed her something that tasted like water. She stuck her tongue out.

'What's this?'

'It's a glass of water. You might have heard of it.'

She grumbled at him as he walked towards the other

end of the bar, where Amelia had reappeared. Her red hair was damp, frizzing in the heat, small wild ends sticking up here and there. Susan thought of that hair on her pillow, her scent, the softness of her pale skin. Amelia's touch. She took a deep breath and shook her head – dizziness washed through her brain. She drank her water, leaning one elbow on the bar to steady herself.

Daniel and Amelia exchanged a quick glance and the tightness in Susan's chest became vice-like as Amelia walked towards her, face stern and bold.

'Heya.'

Susan lifted an eyebrow.

'Hello?'

'Are you ok?'

'Dandy.'

Susan swallowed, her tongue thick with apology.

'Sorry.'

'Hmm …'

'I don't know why I'm like this.'

She held her hands out in a drunken shrug; Amelia laughed.

'I wonder that also.'

They stared at each other, Susan unsure of how she felt, or how Amelia felt. She knew Mick and Peggy were watching. She knew Daniel was peeking at them as he spoke to other customers.

'Amelia, I have had a really bad day …'

'I can see that.'

'What's that supposed to mean?'

'It means it's barely eight o'clock and you're sitting here on your own, locked.'

'I'm not … I'm not … I'm not LOCKED.'

Susan blinked one eye at a time, thinking to herself.

'OK, maybe … and sure … aren't we all alone really, in the end.'

She sounded sad and angry and spiteful.

'Do you want to go home?'

'With you? That is a bad idea.'

'You know I didn't mean it like that.'

Susan scoffed. The other customers had gone quiet around them. Amelia placed a gentle hand on her shoulder and reached for her coat.

'Look, come on, let me help you home.'

'Fuck off and just mind your own fucking business for once.'

Amelia stepped back, hurt.

'I'm just trying to help.'

'Everyone just wants to fucking help. Well, you can help by fucking off.'

'Susan!'

Amelia's tone was sharp. The dangerous edge jolted Susan out of her mood.

'Sorry. I just can't do this … here … now … with you.'

Amelia shook her head.

'What do you think we're doing?'

'I think it's pretty clear I have no fucking idea what I'm doing.'

Susan turned away and shouted to Daniel.

'Do I owe you anything Danny?'

'No, you're all settled up.'

'Right. Fuck this so.'

She slid off the stool, her legs shaky. Amelia helped

steady her as she dragged her coat on.

'Oh! The bloody dog!'

Walter appeared by her side. She bent to him, allowing him to lick her face.

She knew Amelia was watching her as she staggered out the door, bashing her elbow on the brass handles. She thought she heard footsteps following as she walked home through the hills; eyes on the road ahead, the rain still falling but somehow not seeming to land.

She fell in the door of the house, landing with a smack on the wooden floors of the hall. For a few moments, she considered staying there, the rain and wind pouring in the front door. Strong, soft hands under her arms, forcing her back to her feet. The hands guided her towards her bed. Amelia's voice was irritated but kind.

'Bed now, come on.'

'I'm so tired, I'm so tired.'

She cried pathetic tears.

'I'm sorry. Amelia, I'm sorry.'

'I know. Sleep now.'

Her head hit the pillow and darkness descended.

CHAPTER TWENTY-THREE

Even in her drunken stupor, Susan drifted in and out of dreams and memory – the edges of each blurring, one bleeding into the next. The cottage bedroom would swim into focus and then dissolve, replaced by somewhere warm and bright that no longer existed.

Their house had smelled of garlic and lemongrass. Susan was singing along to the radio as Jen arrived home, closing the front door on the darkness of her commute.

The kitchen was steamy from pots of rice and curry bubbling. Blobs of flour stuck in her hair and a fresh loaf of bread was perched precariously on the edge of the counter as it cooled. Jen peeled her wet jacket off and stared around at the chaos.

'What is going on here?'

'Oh. Ehm, I'm being domestic?'

Susan skipped towards Jen, planting a floury kiss on her lips. They were cold from the winter. Susan drew back then kissed them again.

'You need warming up. I'll put on the kettle.'

'You're feeling cheerful today.'

'Yes!' Susan declared. 'New month, new cycle, new leaf.'

'Did you have a session with Rena?'

'Yes.'

Susan's shoulders tightened and her lips clamped shut. Jen eyed her.

'What?'

'Nothing. Why?'

'I'm glad the sessions are helping.'

'It's not therapy I need, Jen, I need this fucking cycle to work.'

'OK. But I'm glad you're going.'

After the second cycle failed once again to produce any viable embryos, they had agreed that it was best for Susan to talk to someone, to help keep her on track when the rollercoaster started spinning off into space.

'How did the session go?'

'Grand.'

Susan's chopping had become more determined. Jen slid behind her, slipping her hands on her hips and nuzzling her neck. Susan relaxed beneath her touch, her shoulders releasing their tension. Her voice was sweet again.

'Hey, baby.'

'Hi, love.'

'I missed you today.'

Jen kissed her neck again.

'I'm here now.'

'Rena says I need to be kinder to myself.'

'Oh yeah?'

'Hmm ...'

'What does that look like?'

'She says my wife should treat me to massages, dinners out, spa days, etc.'

'Oh, right. Well, if Rena insists.'

Jen gave her another kiss, snatched a chopped carrot and retreated to the kitchen table.

'What's for dinner?'

'You have a choice: Thai curry, beef stroganoff or shepherd's pie.'

'Are we food prepping for the apocalypse?'

'You can go hungry if you'd prefer?'

Jen smirked. She seemed to be enjoying Susan's re-emergence again. Susan was enjoying it too. She floated around the kitchen, humming to herself. Her hips wiggled as she rode the post-therapy high.

'Did you do your injections today?'

'Yep.'

'Let me know if you need a hand with them.'

Susan fixed her with a quick, annoyed stare.

'I've been managing just fine up to now.'

'I know … I know … I just want to help, if I can.'

Susan took a deep breath.

'I love you.'

'I love you too.'

'I'm sorry. I don't mean to be such a …'

'Grump?'

'I was going to say a massive, massive bitch.'

Jen's face broke into a smirk.

'You're not a massive, massive bitch.'

'Just a normal-sized bitch then.'

Susan bit her lip.

'It's … it's not been the easiest with you lately,' Jen said.

Susan sat down on one of the kitchen chairs. They hated those chairs, inherited from the previous owners of the house, all fake beech and brown upholstery. There had been plans to replace them, but any spare money was going into the pit of meds, appointments, procedures, tests, therapy, and acupuncture.

'I just feel a bit … insane. A woman cut in front of me in the queue in Lidl and I called her a cunt.'

'Jesus, Susan.'

'I know! I don't feel … I don't feel like I'm in the driver's seat anymore.'

Susan's head was in her hands as she analysed and agonised over every misstep and outburst. Jen caught her hand gently and squeezed it.

'It's the hormones … and the stress. But maybe try and count to ten next time you want to call a random stranger a cunt in Lidl, yeah?'

They both laughed. Susan kissed her – those lips, still so soft after all these years.

Susan awoke from her half-dreams with a start the next morning, her head a wreck – pounding, crackling, deafening. *Shit.* The wave of fear dragged her back to the day before. JP's rage, Amelia jumping away from her anger, Mick's disappointment, Peggy's silence, Daniel cutting her off. Amelia putting her drunken carcass to bed – again – emerged through the blur. Her pile of bad decisions seemed to grow by the day. Maybe she had been right, back then. She was a massive, massive bitch.

She had slept late despite her early drunken night, it was light outside and Walter was up, stretching himself. She tidied herself, choking down tea and toast, showering to remove the stench of whiskey and rain-induced damp.

She sat on the bed in a hangover outfit, drying her hair, the heat and noise of the dryer temporarily blowing all thoughts away. When she turned it off, a knock on the front door. The pit of dread in her tummy gave a squeeze. Please don't be Amelia. Or Peggy. Or Mick. Or Daniel. Maybe Daniel would be all right, actually.

She came out of the bedroom. A woman-shaped silhouette stood behind the warped glass of the front door. Familiar yet strange. Comforting but entirely out of place. Susan's hand hovered on the latch. Her brain, still half-fogged, tried to place the shape. It couldn't be. She pulled open the red door and the ground shifted under her.

The woman on the doorstep looked tired, but she lit up with relief as she took Susan in. She stepped towards her.

'Hello, my love.'

PART TWO: CONSEQUENCE

CHAPTER TWENTY-FOUR

Jen

Jen had stepped off the boat and looked around. The island seemed dark despite the early hour – the sun's rays muffled through thick cloud on the eastern side, the little port oppressive. The smell of boat diesel, and salt and vinegar mixed in her nose and turned her stomach. Hot. Confused. Lost. Not sure at all that she was doing the right thing. But she was confused and lost at home, too, and at least here she was searching for a way not to be. Susan wasn't among the people at the pier – that would have been too easy. She had left no map or blueprint, only the names of an island and uncle. An island of fifty people was still as specific as one needed to get, especially in this part of the country where the islanders knew what each other had for breakfast.

It was quiet inside the post office when she pushed the door open. It smelled like penny sweets and Jeyes Fluid. The shopkeeper eyed her like a cobra.

'Can I help you?'

Jen still maintained her air of confidence despite the silver stare. Weathered hands leaned against the glass counter, casting shadows over the tubs of bonbons and cola bottles.

'Hi there. Yes. Thank you. I'm trying to find a house on the island.'

Jen's tone was polite but clipped. The older woman's stare remained unchanged as she drawled her words out.

'Oh right, to stay for the week, is it?'

'No ... no. It's my wife's uncle's house. Frank Shaw – she's Susan. Susan Shaw.'

A slight flash of something resembling surprise in the woman's eyes alarmed Jen. It disappeared in a split second, and she wondered whether she had seen it at all. The woman's voice remained almost casual.

'Oh yeah, I know the one all right.'

She paused there. Jen was impatient.

' ... Can you tell me where it is?'

'Sure, I suppose ... what's your own name?'

'Jen.'

'Jen ... Shaw is it?'

'No.'

Jen beamed serenely, enjoying the opportunity to withhold information. The woman remained unfazed.

'I have to take a note of who's asking around for these things, my dear.'

'Jen McCarthy.'

The lady softened; victory seemed to brighten her mood. She selected a tourist map from beside her till, grabbed a biro pen and circled something before handing it to Jen.

'Welcome to Dune Island, Jen McCarthy.'

'Thanks ... ah ...'

'Maureen. You'll have a cream cake.'

Jen left the shop with an overpriced cream doughnut,

deeply unsettled by her first encounter on the island.

The clouds were still oppressive, and the heat still hung in her limbs. A clawing, sticky heat that made the walk uphill towards the circle on the map feel like wading through warm treacle. A group of young people in their early twenties hung around at the turn-off towards the cottage. Their leader, a young redhead with a pixie nose, was trying to wrangle them into a functioning group. A woman with two little boys strolled past, clutching the children's hands as they babbled at her about their hopes for the day.

Jen's heart was in a vice. It squeezed out a beat between the stress and tension of her hopes and worries. She ran through the possibilities of what awaited her when she found her wife. Or which version of her wife she would find.

Would it be the version she married, the outrageous flirt that laughed and sang to herself while cooking? Or the quiet, lonely woman that she hid away, since the day they met? It could even be the angry Susan that would come spitting out of anguish, pushing her away and resenting every attempt Jen made to comfort her. Questions raced across her mind, like they had done since the day she arrived home from work to an empty house and a note that said: *I had to leave. I've gone to the island.*

Something else had been written but scratched out furiously. Was it love? Had the Susan, who wrote this note, hesitated, would the word love have been enough to claw her back to her life, to break the spell she was under?

When did we stop telling each other we loved each other?

How much Susan blamed her for their fertility

troubles, Jen was never sure. Jen's mother was more certain. She had slammed her mug of tea into the kitchen table when Jen called into home, crying and desperate after her missing wife.

'I said this to you, I said it to you when you started having the trouble. You can't keep pumping someone full of those hormones and not expect them to go mad.'

'Mam ...'

'Jen, I TOLD you. And why wouldn't you take a turn? Isn't that the great thing about being in a lesbian couple, you have a sub?'

'Susan wants to carry the baby.'

'But –'

'– and I don't.'

Am I the most selfish person alive? Jen wondered, not for the first time. She gave what she could: money, time, and love. She would take every other injection, every other hurt, every other pill and ounce of heartache from Susan if she could. She would love and care for that child from the day it was born; it would be her child from the moment it arrived in her life. She couldn't bear a pregnancy. She couldn't fathom handing her body over for nine months to another creature to swell and push and feed off. They had skirted around the topic once or twice, but Susan stayed vehement – despite the agony, the bruising, the weight gain and hair loss – that she wanted to carry. She wanted to feel it all, the baby inside her, a small cord bonding them for life. Would she still feel the same now, after everything?

Had they reached the end of it all?

Jen's unease, which had lived with her for several years,

continued to grow as she arrived at the circled spot on the map. The red front door sat waiting for her. Small birds swarmed around the front garden, the bird feeders full and fat with seeds and peanuts. The starlings watched her curiously, and somewhere in the distance, she heard the call of a lonely magpie waking up to the day.

Chapter Twenty-Five

Jen stepped towards her. The world narrowed to this doorstep, this woman, this impossibility. When Jen enveloped her in a hug, Susan's body went rigid. Her only thought was the need to leave – immediately, now, out the back door if she had to. She recoiled at the touch, warm and full of a love that landed on her like a weight. She didn't deserve this. She didn't deserve any of this. She pulled back and mumbled.

'What ... what are you doing here?'

Jen blinked.

'I could ask you that.'

'I ... I don't know what to do ... look I don't ... I can't ... I don't know.'

The panic rose, squeezing her chest, her throat, her jaw. Jen placed a hand to Susan's breast.

'Breathe, OK? Breathe.'

Susan looked into her wife's eyes. Her wife. Standing on the doorstep of her dead uncle's cottage on an island Jen had never been to, had only ever heard about in fragments and half-stories. She breathed. The anxiety left, the oxygen came in. Speech returned.

'Sorry. I just didn't expect to see you.'

'I know ... I know. I did write to you. I think we need to talk though, yeah?'

Susan held her hand over Jen's, rising and falling with her breath. The warmth of it was unbearable.

'OK. Can we go for a walk?'

She couldn't bring Jen into the house. She needed some where quiet, away from pub-goers, college students – and particularly their lecturers. The western path brought her by the hostel, the eastern cliffs by the beach where she and Amelia had been together. So they found themselves sitting in the graveyard, breathing in the quiet stillness, legs dangling on a tree stump, looking out over the Atlantic. The island and its edges lay before them, seagulls swooped from their nests towards the ocean. Jen fidgeted with her hands. Her fingernails were short and bitten, with red skin around the edges where nerves had nibbled them away. Susan noticed her plucking imaginary fibres from her coat before she finally turned.

'How's everything been … here?'

Susan shrugged, feeling shy.

'Fine … quiet.'

'What have you been doing with your time?'

Jen was never one for relaxation or pottering about; she loved to fill the quiet moments of her life with people, places, and activities. Susan knew she was baffled by weeks of empty hours on an island.

'Not much really. Visiting the distillery, learning the ropes … going for walks, cleaning out the house and Frank's stuff …'

Fucking another woman. She swallowed down the confession, shoving it below deck.

' … a lot of drinking.' She continued, feeling a blush sneak up her face. Jen's eyes were cloudy as they remained fixed on Susan – as if afraid Susan would disappear again.

'Really?'

Susan was sheepish. Jen tilted her head.

'That never goes well for you.'

'I don't think it agrees with me.'

The air was thick, Jen's sadness stretching across the divide.

' … have you had much pain, or you know … bleeding?' Jen almost whispered the last word. Susan felt her pushing her luck. The clamp in her chest tightened further.

'No. All settled.'

'Good. Good.'

Jen placed both hands on either side of her, gripping the tree stump until her knuckles went white. Out over the sea, channels of sunlight were piercing through the clouds, casting spotlights on patches of the dark, angry sea. Jen took a deep breath of sea air, relaxing her hands on the wood as she did.

'The light here is something else, isn't it?'

Susan blinked, relieved.

'Yeah. It blinds you sometimes in the morning. Like –' She paused and looked towards Jen, hopeful. 'I wake up and the whole room is white with it. The sun is blazing in through the window, filling me up.'

Susan noticed Jen's eyes seemed to shine, wet almost, as she looked back at her.

'Sounds beautiful.'

'It is.'

They looked away from each other, over the sea again. The breeze carried in from the ocean, stirring the sea grass poking into their boots, the pink fuzz of the sea thrift quivering at the precipice. Jen was gripping the stump again, looking straight ahead.

'The views are incredible.'

'Yeah. Next stop from here is America.'

Jen cast a sideways glance at Susan, her tone sharp.

'Is that where you're off to next?'

Susan sent a steely glance back to her.

'I don't really have any plans.'

'Clearly.'

'What?'

'Nothing.'

Susan bit the inside of her cheek and sucked the soft flesh, enjoying the pinch.

'What about you? How long are you staying?'

'Depends.'

On …? Susan considered asking, but didn't want the answer. They sat in silence as the seconds ticked by. Jen turned to Susan, her face set and serious.

'Do you still love me?'

Her voice cracked. The pause between them broke what was left of Susan's heart.

'I love you more than I can even think about …'

'But not more than this island?'

Susan murmured.

'It's not about the island, Jen.'

'Then what is it about?'

Susan shrugged and said nothing. They looked back out to sea. Jen's voice turned practical.

'Have you decided what you're going to do with the distillery?'

'Not really. The cash would be handy …'

'Yeah.'

'... but there are complications. I don't even fully understand them yet.'

Jen raised an eyebrow.

'JP.'

'The guy who worked for Frank?'

'Yeah, but ... I dunno, something went on with them.'

'Like what?'

'It sounds mad, but I think they were more than friends?'

'Really?'

'There's just something I'm missing, and I don't want to make any decisions until I know what the story is.'

'You'll figure it out.'

They both stared out across the sea, straining through the distant fog of the horizon.

'I'm sorry I left.'

'Are you?'

Susan looked out at the ocean.

'How's the house?'

'I'm not sure your herb garden will survive the summer.'

'You literally just need to water it once a week.'

Jen shrugged.

'I'm not good with that stuff.'

'Is this your way of trying to blackmail me to come home?'

'Is that what it will take?'

Susan didn't reply. Jen gave a little huff, folding her arms.

'I was worried you were dead.'

'No, you weren't.'

Susan continued.

'I'm still here. Mostly.'

'You're still here, and you still love me. That's a start, I suppose.'

'Yeah, maybe.'

Jen took her hand without warning. Soft, and so warm even in the breeze. Susan squeezed it. The comfort and familiarity travelled up through her hands, her wrist, into her chest, filling her lungs. Something loosened and a stifled whimper poured out of her.

'Why did you leave, Susan?'

Jen was staring at her again, looking scared and tired. Guilt began to bubble. She swallowed it down.

She thought about how to tell Jen that she could no longer see a way to continue living a normal life in her normal house with her normal wife, meeting up with their normal friends, feeling like she was silently burning to death. She couldn't live with the smell of her own singed skin, the memories of the losses, the day-to-day of everyone else's usual realities, as she felt her own organs melting inside her. The stink of her own grief, scatter-gunning all over her life. All this simmered inside her.

'I just had to leave.'

She left it at that, even as Jen gave a frustrated grunt. Walter chose that moment to return from his graveyard wandering, cocking his leg to piss on a slug-bitten sunflower struggling in the wind. Jen eyed him with amusement.

'I can't believe you replaced me with a dog.'

Amelia's face flashed before Susan's mind, the red hair across the pillow, those kiss-swollen lips open in a gasp of pleasure. Amelia sitting in her lap on the bed, Susan's mouth pressed against her breasts. Susan gasped and shook her head.

'Is he coming home with you?'

Susan didn't answer, the flashback sitting in her heart and her mind still. The squeezing within her, and the low throb deep in her centre, fought with each other. Her breath struggled through the mess as she felt another wave of nausea. She stood, pulling her hand away from Jen.

'Do you want to continue our walk?'

Jen's voice was cautious, like someone diffusing a bomb.

'OK.'

The rain interrupted their plans. It battered down from the clouds, forcing a reluctant retreat to the cottage. Susan combed the cottage in her mind, thinking of any possible trace of Amelia and her bad decisions. None existed; they had been bleached and scoured from its memory. Amelia's tracks lay only over her mind and her body; the house was a blank canvas to anyone but her. The door closed behind them, their hair wet, Walter soggy and miserable – the small house felt even smaller. Jen stood in the hallway, dripping onto the mat.

'Do you have any towels?'

'Oh, yes. Yes!'

Susan stripped off her jacket, tossing it onto the floor. She was aware of Jen picking it up after her and placing it with care on a hook in the hall. Jen called out to her.

'Can I have a shower?'

'Of course!'

'I won't ask if you want to join me.'

Jen tried to joke, but Susan felt a pang of anxiety and ignored it. She handed Jen a towel, took her coat and showed her to the bathroom.

'There are two knobs on the shower, one for the power and one for the temperature. You just—'

'I have used a shower before, Susan.'

Jen gave her a small kiss on the cheek; it seemed almost automatic. Susan recoiled, catching Jen's hurt reaction as she did.

'Sorry,' Jen muttered, but Susan shook her head.

'You don't need to be sorry.'

There was a time when all they did was joke together, pinching each other's bums, giving each other playful nips and kisses on the neck and shoulder and distracting each other when they were trying to work from home. Jen's hand briefly sliding inside Susan's pants at traffic lights. They felt like two different people standing awkwardly together for the first time in their lives.

Susan towelled Walter dry as Jen showered, then set about lighting the stove and warming the cottage. A small leak by the back door had revealed itself during the downpour; so she dispatched another towel to mop it up and block it up. The shower clicked off; footsteps, and Jen was there in the sitting room. She was wrapped in the snow-white towel, her hair wet and falling around her shoulders. Her skin was tanned; she was always darker than Susan, always laughing at her wife's pasty little sun-shy skin.

'Was the shower OK?'

'Glorious.'

'You can change in the bedroom.'

'Are you sure?'

'Of course.'

Susan found herself following her through.

'Do you need anything else?'

Jen turned to face her, all at once very close.

'... I need you.'

Jen leant towards her and Susan didn't pull away. Jen kissed her lips, soft at first. As Susan melted into her, Jen's arms wrapped around her, pulling at her clothes, tongue tracing the inside of her mouth. Susan needed this; needed to replace the memory of a naked, writhing Amelia with the reality of her wife. Jen pushed Susan back towards the bed, their bodies entwining.

Her body moved against Susan's, and they slid against each other, their convex and concave forms coming together. They formed a smooth if uncertain shape – Jen's brunette mixing with Susan's blond locks as their heads touched. Jen's breath smelled like sweet vanilla, and her still-damp skin was velvet under Susan's fingertips. Their lips sealed together, a slow swallowing of each other, Jen's hands guiding and pushing Susan as she stumbled backwards. They careened towards the bed and landed – Jen on top of Susan, lips still locked, hands grasping at belt buckles and zippers. Jen peeled Susan's rain-soaked jeans off her legs, pulled her panties over her knees. Kissed her again. Their tongues found each other's mouths as warm wetness spread between Susan's legs. She gripped Jen's towel and pulled it away. It flew across the room as she wrapped her naked legs around her wife, pulling her towards her with a startle. Jen paused, seeming unsure. Susan breathed heavily, hands and legs pulling Jen's body close. She rested her head against Jen's neck, her voice growling from deep within her.

'Fuck me.'

Jen tore off the remainder of Susan's clothes and lay her back down. She climbed on top, fingertips kittening their way up her legs. They danced inside Susan and she cried out, Jen moaning in sympathy. Susan's fingers searched for Jen's centre – warm and inviting. She cupped her hand around the mound of hair between Jen's legs, placed her thumb on the spot that made her moan. They fucked each other, eyes locked, moving in rhythm, their cries and moans mirroring each other. They came together, backs arching as the ripples of pleasure moved through them.

'I love you,' Jen cried in Susan's ear. 'I love you so much.'

Susan's response was barely a breath. Their lips found each other again, tongues intertwining, sucking the air from each other's lungs. They swelled and pulsed, pleasure bursting out from inside them as the sun disappeared from the island outside the window. Somewhere beneath the heat and the want, a small cold stone sat in Susan's stomach.

CHAPTER TWENTY-SIX

Frank

A trip to the mainland, to Dublin no less, always filled Frank with an electric current. Excitement and nerves swirled together in his body as JP and himself strolled down O'Connell Street, engines and shoppers and street-sellers mixing their noises and smells altogether. It was overwhelming. Dublin in the late eighties was the busiest, most glamorous place he'd ever been. He laughed to himself then, knowing how Derek would mock him. They sat across from each other in a coffee shop, a large window allowing them full view of the chaos on the main street.

Derek had lost all traces of the island, his accent ironed out of him after a few years living in the big smoke.

'But why is that man still living in OUR house? Couldn't he find his own place by now?'

He, being JP, of course, the farmhouse was still Derek's home, though none of them had lived in it for ten years.

'He's making a fine job of it. Mam would love all the flowers he has growing.'

That seemed to quiet Derek. He used to love mam's flowers too.

'And yourself? You're still in the cottage?'

'I am.'

'And the farm is going well?'

'Ah, tis struggling on all right.'

Frank was starting to tire of the constant struggle to make ends meet every month. He had grown to love the farm, the quiet days walking the land, fixing fences, milking cows and chatting to them about his day. He even loved mucking out the pigs, the feeling of accomplishment when sweat broke across his brow. The days when he and JP would meet each other at the farmhouse and have their lunchtime sandwiches together. He loved the quiet moments in the evening, when he and JP sat, sipping their whiskeys, staring into the flames of the stove until it was time for one of them to lope off home. Sometimes Frank would drift off and awake to JP wrapping a soft blanket around him. He wondered how JP was getting on in Dublin, left to his own devices to wander about Henry Street. Frank wondered what gadget he'd pick up for his house this time. The last time they came to Dublin, he bought an electric juicer. It sat in its box on the farmhouse kitchen table. He noticed Derek was leaning back in his chair, arms crossed, his cigarette dangling. The red flame ringed its way towards his mouth. He pulled at it, then spoke.

'Have you any romances on the go?'

Gossiping was an island pastime; it seemed to transport Derek home and bring his accent back, bubbling out of his carefully managed mouth.

'Ah no,' Frank muttered, 'sure there'd be no time for that.'

Derek's face was sceptical, but he probably didn't

really care anyway. Filling the time, pretending they were brothers who caught up with each other when they had the chance. Derek had coughed awkwardly on the phone when Frank called to say he was coming to the Farmer's Union conference in Dublin, and to ask if he wanted to meet for coffee.

'Oh … sure … sure … is everything all right?' Derek had asked.

'Yes. I just haven't seen you in a while,' Frank had replied, trying not to sound annoyed. It had been a year, in fact. Derek and his family had visited the island, the small one, four years old and in a phase where she only stomped and never walked. When he called her name, his mother's name too, she stopped and glowered at him from under her fringe, then promptly continued whatever she had been doing before he interrupted. He'd enjoyed her. They hadn't stayed long. Then radio silence until the awkward phone call. And now they sat sipping tea, watching a busker outside the window of the coffee shop.

'How's the small one getting on?'

Derek's face lit up.

'Oh, she's flying it, she started school last week.'

He rummaged in his wallet, pulling out a small photo of a little blonde girl in a navy school uniform, her chin up, face proud. Frank held the photo, his thumb smudging the edges.

'God, she's the image of Fiona.'

Derek took the photo back and put it away; the subject closed. They finished their tea, and no one suggested a second. An awkward nod of the head, and that was goodbye.

JP was in Arnott's looking at electric carving knives. He ran his fingers through his hair as the shop girl, barely to his elbows, described the wonders of the serrated blades and motors. Frank approached.

'Jaysis, is there something wrong with an ordinary knife?'

JP reddened, and the girl laughed.

'Sure he's up for the day, he's only treatin' himself!'

'This fella, he's only ever treating himself. Come on now, JP.'

JP smiled apologetically and placed the box back on the shelf. They left the shop, the sun glinting off the wet cobblestones.

'You're right, I know.'

Frank snorted.

'I'm always right.'

'You're always a pain in the hole.'

Frank nudged him in the ribs.

'Pint?'

'Only the one now.'

'Sure sure.'

They found a pub with a snug where they could hide from Dubs and planted themselves by the fire. Two pints of Guinness – no Murphy's in this godforsaken city – downed, followed by another two in quick succession. Frank found his flow, so they had two more followed by a few whiskeys. The fire blurred. He glanced across at JP, who always managed to hold his drink better.

'Derek was asking why you were living in the house.'

'I can get my own place if he's not happy with it.'

'He can feck off, it's none of his business anymore.'

Frank had saved up enough to have mostly bought out his older brother. Derek was in no rush. You could call Derek a lot of bad things, but money-grabbing wasn't one of them. As long as he didn't have to think about it, he was happy for the farm to struggle on without him. JP was gazing across at him.

'Why did you tell me so?'

'No reason. Just saying.'

Why did Derek's question bother him? He felt the suspicion beneath Derek's words, the question asking Frank something he hadn't dared to try and answer himself. He liked JP being in the house; he liked the idea of him being close, being on his land. The connection between them stayed alive, even when they each went home to the house or the cottage. JP was his best friend. He wanted him close.

They left the bar, darkness upon the city. Taxi lights flashed in the puddles by the kerbs. They waited for a cab to arrive at the rank, a crowd of locals huddling with them against the autumn cold. A young man bumped into JP, their shoulders clashing.

'Fucking watch it, bud,' the man spat as JP stumbled backwards, too tipsy to register the knock fully. He realised and started to apologise a split second too late. The man, or boy really, Frank realised, probably no more than eighteen, stuck his face up into JP's, the anger bursting out of him without warning.

'I SAID, FUCKING WATCH IT.'

This little twerp, Frank thought, I'll fucking kill him. He pulled his shoulders back and stepped forward, squaring up. The satisfaction of being bigger than this little shit.

He drew his arm back and his knuckles connected with bone as the young man's nose burst under his punch. Blood spattered as he spluttered, holding his face.

The crowd dispersed. Frank advanced on him. Now the shadows of his past pushed him onward. Fucking little bullying prick, he thought. I'll fucking teach you to pick on my friend. He readied his fists to go again, but felt a hand on his. JP was shaking his head.

'No, Frank, no.'

'I'll fucking kill him.'

'No, you won't, Frank, leave it, come on.'

JP was pulling at him, the teenager with his smashed face was considering his options. He didn't follow as JP dragged Frank away. They walked for an hour to their B&B. JP's usual silence felt oppressive. The landlady gave Frank a questioning look, seeming to spot the drops of blood on his T-shirt, the gash across his knuckles. Frank shivered, the adrenaline gone, the booze seeping out of his system and leaving him with a waking hangover slowly creeping across his brain.

They walked to their rooms. JP opened Frank's door and waved him in.

'Goodnight, Frank.'

Frank didn't want him to leave. He thought of that boy, spitting in JP's face, threatening him. He thought of the anger that hurled itself up inside him. He caught JP's hand, seeing the surprise register across JP's troubled face.

'Do you want to come in for a drink?'

'I think we've had enough.'

JP didn't pull his hand away, though. So this is what

it feels like, to hold hands with a lad. With JP. Frank's treacherous mind ran through all the thoughts he had hidden before. JP's hands were as soft as he had so often suspected they would be. He had watched him, mocked him, as he slathered on hand cream in the evenings. A birthday present from Peggy, apparently.

He saw himself pulling JP closer. They were just inside Frank's room, and JP smelled of Guinness and soap and, even in this dirty city still, of the sea and of the fields they called home and the cows and the grass and the way the Atlantic breeze would blow through you in the autumn. All he could hear was JP's breathing, usually so steady, but now heavy and quick. He brought his lips to his. And this is what it feels like to kiss JP, his skin smooth, the slightest hint of stubble brushing his own scruff. He pulled JP closer to him, one hand on the back of his neck. He pushed them together, their teeth banging, tongues getting braver as they consumed each other. They stopped suddenly, staring at one another. Frank knew it was the end of the before, and the start of something new. The years of friendship, of colleagues, of the companionable silence, their whiskeys by the fire. This would end it all. JP breathed heavy, and Frank knew he would never be the one to break any silence. What could he say? How could he save this? Stupid, useless Frank, fucking ruining everything again. Why couldn't he just keep shoving it all down? But JP wasn't leaving; he wasn't doing anything. He was standing there, panting, when he lifted his eyes and stared directly into Frank's, surprising him.

'Where did that come from?'

Frank was the one with no words. He tried to speak,

but his lips wobbled. JP's hand still clasped his. He glanced down at it. He remembered the only words he ever said to himself when he imagined moments like this, when they fluttered in his mind like a butterfly. No, a moth, banging their wings against his forehead.

'I'm not … I'm not a bender,' he cried, burying his face into JP's neck. JP ran his hand through Frank's hair, squeezing him closer. He whispered in Frank's ear.

'Of course you're not. You're my Frank.'

CHAPTER TWENTY-SEVEN

Susan and Jen lay deflated, dehydrated, drained. Susan's body was jelly – the sex and the situation had taken all the fight left in her. They lay on the bed, white sheets draped over their skin, pinkies entwined, eyes closed but not sleeping. Jen rolled over on her side. Susan opened one eye. Jen's voice low and sleepy.

'I'm hungry.'

'You're always hungry.'

'We've not eaten all day.'

Susan looked to the window and realised time had moved on without them, the light behind the house now, settling down for its western bedtime. Christ, what a day. Jen sat up and glanced at her watch.

'It's dinner time, my love, what have you got?'

A familiar irritation rose in her.

'Why am I expected to make dinner?'

'Because this is your midlife crisis, not mine.'

Susan gave Jen's shoulder a playful nip, then remembered her cupboards were bare.

'I can offer you toast, or tomatoes, or indeed tomatoes on toast. There may be some expired All-Bran in there somewhere.'

'Let's go to the pub – they do food, right? I saw something about stew on a sign earlier.'

'No.'

Susan's tone was sharp. The anxiety was sticking its barbs into her again.

'No?' Jen was incredulous.

'No.'

'Is there another place we can go?'

' ... No.'

'Is there a shop open?'

Susan glanced at the clock on the wall, which read six p.m.

'No.'

Jen's hangry eyes were laser-focused on her – Susan realised the situation was hopeless. No words passed between them for several seconds as Jen waited for Susan to accept it.

'OK, but I don't want to talk to anyone. And I don't think you should either.'

'That's a weird request to make.'

'Yeah, well, I'm a weird person these days.'

Jen shrugged in agreement. She kissed Susan – a soft kiss full of memory and love. Susan's body melted into her wife. She whispered,

'I do love you, you know.'

Jen sighed in response.

'Come on, let's get something to eat.'

Susan shooed a bemused Jen and a lazy Walter into the snug before anyone could talk to them. It was still quiet in the pub, the rain keeping most people off the island or indoors this evening. There was no sign of the college crowd yet. *Please, God, let them be partying in the hostel tonight.* Susan didn't pray much but issued a silent plea. Peggy appeared from the magic door and strode towards them with purpose – her little notebook and pen gripped in her hands.

'Now, girls, how are ye?'

'We're good, thanks, Peggy.'

'How's the head after last night?'

'I mean … it's been better.'

Jen eyed Susan, then turned to Peggy.

'Was she in here making a show of herself last night?'

'You could say that, all right. Who's this, Susan?'

Susan scowled at Peggy, who took no notice and kept her eyes locked on her.

'This is Jen, Peggy.'

Jen was watching her under her eyebrows.

'My wife.'

Susan suspected Peggy already knew this. Not much went on around here without her knowing. She made a little 'hmm' noise then shook hands with Jen.

'You're very welcome to the island, love. Can I get you anything?'

'I'll have a glass of white wine, please.'

Peggy's lips made an almost imperceptible purse of approval.

'And Susan?'

'Same, thanks.'

'Right. I'll be back to you with menus.'

'No need, we'll both have the stew.'

Susan didn't have time to peruse menus or dally over choices. Time was against her. Peggy glanced at Jen, who shrugged. The landlady spun round and retreated to her kitchen. Susan heard her hiss at Daniel to stop staring along the way. Jen turned to Susan.

'Heavy night last night then?'

'You could say that. Daniel's measures are quite generous.'

'Good to know.'

Susan knew she should feel guilty for blaming Daniel. Jen was oblivious, looking around the pub, her face lit up.

'This is nice ... it's almost like a date.' She beamed at Susan, who was weak with worry, still surveying the front door. *Please, please, please. Stay away for just one hour tonight, please, please, please.*

No such luck.

The steaming bowls of stew had just landed on their tables when the front door of the pub flew open. They all stumbled in, already half-drunk from pre-drinking and revved up for a rager. Susan started shovelling her stew into her mouth, ignoring her burning tongue.

'Jesus Christ, slow down.'

Jen laughed. Her face turned serious as Susan stayed silent. Amelia strode in last. Her bounce diminished as Susan lost her breath and started coughing on a lump of carrot. Amelia glanced over at them, then Peggy hooked her arm in Amelia's and led her away, whispering in her ear as she did. Amelia took a seat at the bar while Susan spluttered. Jen patted her back and soothed her.

'Sorry, love, sorry.' Susan muttered. 'I'm just a bit anxious.'

'That's OK ... no need to be anxious though. It's just stew and me.' Jen made a jokey face and Susan threw her a disgusted look. They laughed and Susan relaxed. Amelia was across the bar pretending not to know her. The relief outweighed the sting.

Walter, the traitor, was in no mood for Susan's games. He flashed her a treacherous look and waddled over to Amelia, rolling on his back for her to adore him. She laughed and obliged, smiling a shy hello at Susan as she did.

'Who is that?' Jen asked.

'That's … that's Amelia.'

Susan put her fork down and gulped her wine. Jen placed her forearms on the table.

'And who exactly is Amelia?'

The blood drained from Susan's face.

'She's a college lecturer, visits the island every year.'

'Oh right … She's cute.'

'Hmmm.'

'She's young.'

'She's not that young,' Susan replied, a little too quickly. Jen sat back and folded her arms.

'I'm getting another drink. Would you like anything?'

'Water …' She croaked. 'Sparkling,' she called after her as Jen pulled herself up and walked towards the bar. Susan realised too late Jen's true intentions. Amelia's wide smile froze as Susan's wife advanced on her like a bear. The noise of the student crowd made it impossible to make out anything other than Amelia's tipsy tones. Jen looked calm as she chatted but her shoulders were tense. Susan could see the clouds gathering.

'Jen, stop, leave her alone. It's not her fault.'

Jen grinned at her like a Barbie doll, the light never quite reaching beyond the cheekbones.

'What's not her fault? Amelia and I were just discussing her research, which sounds fascinating.'

Amelia looked sick. Susan sensed Peggy and Daniel watching from the corner, the landlady gripping her son's elbow. She moved close to Jen.

'Let's go back to the house.'

'Why? We're not finished our dinner.'

Jen's face was set and stubborn. Susan saw the hurt in her eyes.

'I want to go back to the house.'

Jen's exterior, calm and kind since arriving on the island, was starting to crack.

'Why, Susan? Do you not want me and Amelia to chat about how you've both been spending your time here on the island?'

'This has nothing to do with her.'

'Oh really?'

'Jen,' Amelia began, 'it is Jen, right?'

'Yes.'

'It's been lovely meeting you ...'

Jen sneered.

'... But I'm just going to let the two of you sort this out. Because frankly, as Susan has reminded me many times, this is none of my fucking business.'

With that, Amelia grabbed her G&T and ran out the back door of the pub. Walter stood up and shook himself, stretching and yawning as Susan and Jen glared at each other. Susan glowered at him. *I'll deal with you later, you little prick.* He seemed unbothered by the kerfuffle. Jen was still staring at Susan, her lips pressed together and distorted by rage and suppressed tears. Susan touched her wrist.

'I'm so sorry,' she whispered, feeling her own lips twist, hearing the quiver in her voice.

Jen was silent and walked away. She grabbed her bag from the snug and stormed out.

Jen's long legs had flung her halfway up the hill by the time Susan had burst out through the doors of the pub.

'Jen!'

Jen ignored her, power-walking back into the heart of the island.

'Jen, for fuck's sake, you know I can't walk as fast as you!'

'You do not want to catch up to me right now, Susan, I swear to fucking god, stay away from me!'

Susan took her advice and Walter, strolling behind, slowed down with her. They walked back to the cottage fifty metres apart. Jen reached the front gate first, and by the time Susan caught up she could see Jen's body shaking, hands gripping the iron. Jen made it to the front door and pressed her head against it, small sobs escaping. Susan knew talking wouldn't help, but she couldn't stop herself.

'I'm sorry.'

'Fuck off with your sorry!'

Not all the anger had left, but it lived side by side with a sorrow, grasping within Jen's voice, pulling Susan towards her out of habit and memory.

'Let me just open the door.'

Jen stood aside, fury radiating from her. Susan tiptoed past, the keys leaden in her hand. The door slid open into the darkness of the house. Jen pushed past her into the sitting room, gathering her belongings and shoving them into the grey backpack she'd carried with her across the sea. Susan stood still.

'What are you doing?'

'Leaving. Coming here was a mistake.'

'What are you going to do, swim home?'

'Don't be a smart hole with me, Susan, not now!'

Jen dropped onto the couch, hugging her backpack to her. Susan placed herself on a stool near the door and waited. They stared at their own feet, the only sound the crackle of the fire left in the hearth. Jen's breath was broken. Susan fought the urge to run to Jen's arms for comfort. A flash of Amelia's soft face and hurt expression shocked her, and she shook it off. Looking away from the floor, she spotted Jen watching her, her face a defiant mess of emotion.

'I can't believe you.'

Jen's voice was shell-shocked. Susan rubbed her eyelids.

'I'm sor – '

'Don't. Please. I can't.'

Susan shut her mouth.

'I didn't even get to eat my fucking dinner.'

'I'll make you some toast.'

Jen didn't argue. Susan pottered to the cooker, filling the kettle and keeping her mind occupied with the mundane task of filling the kettle and Walter's bowl, keeping them fed and watered for this nightmare. Jen took off her coat, folded it, and placed it on the table. Susan called to her.

'That'll get wrinkled.'

Jen responded with a dagger-filled look. They sat facing each other, chewing toast and sipping hot tea. Susan held on to a delusional hope that perhaps the worst of it was over. Jen swallowed a bite of toast and commenced round two.

'How old is she?'

'She's thirty,' Susan replied. Jen eyeballed her.

'OK, she's twenty-seven.'

'Fucking hell.'

Susan shrugged. What could she say? Amelia was mature for her age? That wasn't true. She had a wisdom and a confidence about her that isn't always found in her peers, but that wasn't maturity; it was probably just good parenting and luck. Jen's eyes filled with tears.

'What exactly happened?'

'I don't know what you think –'

'I KNOW something happened with her. I don't know what, but I know something did. I knew by your face the moment you saw her, I knew by her face when she saw me and realised who I was. So fucking tell me.'

'It wasn't anything, it was just …'

'STOP. Tell me.'

'It was one night.'

'In this house?'

'Yes.'

'Where we fucked?'

'Yes.'

'A little Irish college summer romance, is it? Is she going to add you on Snapchat?'

Jen stood and punched the wall, screaming. She wheeled around, furious.

'Is she … is she why you came here?'

'No, no. Jesus, no. I met her here. She was just … I dunno …'

Jen's voice went soft, bubbling out of her mouth as she slid back into the chair across from Susan.

'She was just what?'

'Fun.'

Jen gave a hollow chuckle, gesturing towards the fiery space between them.

'What? This isn't fun?'

Her tears were flowing. Susan wanted to say so much. She wanted to grab Jen, hold her, cry in her arms, and scream.

She doesn't know me. She wanted me. She didn't know the pain and the hurt and the scans and the injections and the loss. She didn't know what a failure I am.

Instead, she sat and breathed shallow as her wife sobbed across the room from her. A hole in Susan's chest sucked the breath from her lungs. She sat and let Jen wash the salty sorrow out of her body. When the moment seemed to have passed, she walked to Jen, placing her hand on hers, their skin reacting to each other's touch.

'I love you so much.'

'Please don't, please.'

Jen yanked her hand away, stood up and walked into the bedroom, closing the door behind her with a slam. Susan heard the key turn and stayed in the dim quiet of the sitting-room, the fire flickering, casting shadows of herself on the wall as she listened to the quiet keening of her wife on the other side.

CHAPTER TWENTY-EIGHT

Susan stood in the hall, morning light piercing the front door panels like javelins. Jen's backpack was on her shoulders. Both their faces lined with the bad sleep of the night before – Susan under one of Walter's blankets on the couch. She had lain staring at the ceiling, listening to Jen move in the next room. Jen emerged puffy-eyed and thirsty during the night. She made her way towards the kitchen and glanced at Susan lying like a pretzel trying to get comfortable. They looked at each other in silence. Jen seemed to consider a kindness, changed her mind and returned to the bedroom. The lock clicked and Susan blocked out the pain in her back, the springs of the couch sticking into her hip.

The first boat left the island at 10 a.m., and Susan knew Jen intended to be on it. She placed a hand on the front door, her arm blocking Jen's way.

'Stay, and we can talk.'

'What's there to say?'

'I don't know, I don't want you to leave.'

Jen rubbed her temples.

'Then come home with me and we can talk there.'

Susan folded her arms and shook her head.

'I can't stay here. I spent the night in that room, and I couldn't stop thinking about the two of you. And what you did together in there. I don't even fucking know you anymore.'

Susan's voice had a tremor she couldn't quite control.

'Please don't go.'

Tiredness pushed Jen back into anger. She sneered and shook her head.

'Oh, you want me around you now, is it!? You're done riding twenty-seven-year-olds behind my back?'

'I'm sorry, I'm so sorry.'

'No, you're fucking not!' Jen exploded; she looked like she could barely breathe with rage.

'I am –'

'Oh fuck off, Susan. Get your fucking shit together and stop acting like you're the only person in the world who's ever felt what we've felt. You're the one who left, you're the one who ran off like the fucking coward that you are!'

Susan 's heart tightened. Her jaw clenched and her head spun. Angry tears spilled down her cheeks.. How had this followed her here? It was never supposed to travel across the sea, never supposed to walk out of the ocean. She tasted metal in her mouth and realised she'd bitten her tongue and made it bleed. She swallowed the drops of blood, sending them down into the black pit in her gut. The darkness inside her spread, drowning her veins until silence filled the little cottage again. She and Jen stared down the hall at each other, only the dust motes in the shafts of sunlight filling the space between them. Jen stepped towards her.

'Look …'

Susan stepped back and crossed her arms. The draw-bridge was up. Jen pursed her lips.

'Ok … whenever you decide to wake up to yourself, let me know.'

Jen paused again with her hand on the front door. Susan held her breath for a second, waiting for the words that would fix it all.

They didn't come.

Jen walked out the door. The rage and pain drained away, and all that was left was the dark emptiness again.

CHAPTER TWENTY-NINE

Frank

The wedding invitation landed on the hallway mat with a smack. Frank paused, his coffee steaming his glasses.

Baby Susan was getting married. He read her partner's name twice, three times. Jen. A warmth washed over him with tendrils of sadness spidering out.

He'd seen Susan at her father's funeral over a decade ago. His brother's funeral, although that seemed moot at that stage. A strange older man in a suit, looking like their dad, with a waxen mask pressed into a peaceful expression. He was thinner than Frank had remembered, but that would be the cancer that stole him.

Susan was ashen.

The only word that kept coming to his mind when he saw her was, ashen.

He'd only heard at Derek's funeral about her mother's death the year before. She was barely older than him when he became an orphan. No one really cared about orphans once you were old enough to organise the funeral.

The house after the burial filled with Derek's friends. Susan sat in the middle of them, staring straight ahead. Her black blazer had a mayonnaise stain on it from a sandwich. She didn't seem to notice.

Every so often, a tall girl with a kind face and chestnut hair offered Susan a cup of tea. Warmth returned to her for a brief moment; she said no, and the girl retreated.

Susan lifted her head as he walked towards her. He could see her searching through her memories for him.

'I'm … I'm Frank. Your uncle.'

She stood and held out her arms; they hugged. She gave a small sob.

'Thanks for coming.'

She shook her head as if realising something.

'Oh … and sorry for your loss.'

'No, no … sorry for your loss.'

The kind-faced girl returned, and he noticed Susan blush.

'Eh … Frank, this is Jen, my … friend.'

JP returned from the back garden, Walter trotting after him. His hands were dirty from deadheading the perennials. Frank tried to hide the invitation under the paper, but JP was too quick, swiping it with a wink and examining it closely.

'Is this your niece?'

'Hmm …'

'Isn't that lovely?'

Frank snatched the invitation out of his hands, wiping the small smudge of garden muck off it. Walter hopped onto his lap, licking the crumbs from the kitchen table. Frank tapped his snout.

'Are you going?'

'I probably will, yeah.'

JP glanced again at the invite.

'It's a plus one.'

Frank returned to his coffee and felt JP's stare boring into him.

'We could both go, couldn't we?'

Frank was worried.

'I don't know, JP, I don't know who'll be there.'

'Sure, who'll be there? It'll only be us from the island.'

'I don't think it's a good idea.'

'Will you think about it?'

Frank gave a nod. JP washed his hands in silence.

A few weeks later, the topic emerged again. JP and Frank were on their usual daily walk on the beach, the wind blowing them along as the sea raged. Walter waddled after them, struggling to keep up with their long strides in the shifting sands. Frank paused, waiting for him to catch up. Frank knew JP was brewing something.

'Have you thought much more about the wedding?'

'Not really,' Frank lied.

He bent down to pet Walter's ears.

'Sure, there'd be no one to look after this fella.'

'Frank ...'

'You need to leave it, JP.'

They continued on, their usual easy silence clouded. JP's voice burst.

'I can't leave it, I don't know why we can't just go to a fucking wedding like any other couple!'

JP had used up all his words for the week with that sentence. Frank couldn't have this conversation again.

'You don't know who's going to be there, who'll see us. People will talk. Why would two lads go to a wedding together? Use your fucking loaf and think about it.'

'People already know, Frank, Peggy knows, Mick knows, of course they know! It's been nearly thirty years!'

'I don't think they know.'

Frank knew he was deluding himself, but he had dug himself in too deep. He kept digging.

'I don't want people knowing our business, is that too much to ask?'

JP stomped on ahead, shaking his head. Frank followed on, feeling his own anger stoked.

'Do you want people calling us the queers over the hill? Is that it?'

JP didn't reply; he just kept walking and muttering to himself. Frank was furious.

'What are you saying?'

JP whirled on him, pulled up to his full height, and he took Frank's breath with the fright. He had never seen JP look so angry.

'You're a fucking coward, Frank Shaw, and I'm sick shit of you!'

Frank stood as JP stormed away.

Chapter Thirty

Susan returned to the couch; the bedroom held too many memories that clashed against each other. Walter lay across her feet as she cupped her belly, tears leaking down her face, soaking her neck and the collar of her T-shirt. How had she got to this point? How had she become such a monster? She couldn't remember when everything had fallen apart. There was no moment she could point to when life as it was became unlivable. When did Jen stop comforting her when she found her crying on the sofa again? When did they lose the ability to talk about anything other than cycles and hormones and research and pills? Looking for the secrets of supplements, Chinese medicine, or what that woman in Susan's yoga class who had nine rounds of IVF and finally had her baby said worked for her.

'Good for her,' Jen had sneered, pushing her dinner around, 'six more rounds to go and we can be that lucky too.'

Susan called her a bitch, and not in a jokey way. They had never talked to each other like that before. Jen walked out that night and went to her mother's house.

Susan had cried into a plate of organic veggies and free-range chicken. She thought of the books, the blogs, and the YouTuber advice. What was she doing wrong? This wasn't how things were supposed to be.

What no one really tells you, Susan thought, is that what's really best for having a baby when you're in a same-sex relationship is fuck loads of money and plenty of luck. Susan and Jen didn't seem to have any luck and were rapidly running out of money. Having a spare set of ovaries came in handy, but even that wasn't a guarantee of success. Susan wondered how anyone ever got pregnant accidentally. Jen's sister couldn't look at her husband without getting pregnant, and each time, unplanned – a place found at the table for another hungry mouth.

Round three was the one they thought would work; this time, not only would they get embryos (better than round one), but they would be good quality (better than round two) – the desperation of clinging to slow, heartbreaking, body-destroying progress. Round three didn't work. 'Implantation failure', the doctors called it, more negative pregnancy tests (Susan limited herself to five tests this time) and more dashed hopes.

The kind nurses held Susan's hand; she stayed soft with them, a puddle of sorrow like a raw, open wound.

'I'm a bit heartbroken.'

'Oh, pet,' the nurse cooed, 'I'd be surprised if you were only a bit heartbroken.'

Susan had sobbed, full-throated and feral, while Jen held her. Susan never normally showed that kind of despair to Jen. Only the rage seemed to make its way to Jen's door, tightly bound and fists waving, screaming, slamming doors, snapping and snarling at the slightest provocation.

They had stopped talking about names. Or hair colour. Or boy or girl – or how that didn't matter (even though everyone knew Susan wanted a girl). Or what school she might go to. Or if she could sing like Susan, or if she'd look to Jen to learn how to play football or how to string a guitar. It didn't seem to matter anymore. The joy of excitement replaced by the despair and drudgery of injections, scans, blood tests, bank loans and telephone ping-pong with a fertility clinic overwhelmed with desperate, infertile and frantic thirty-somethings just like them.

Susan arrived home one evening, her belly bloated and bruised, her arms laden with bags of supplements from the pharmacy. These would make round four a success. Jen sat at the kitchen table sorting through mounds of invoices, receipts and statements. Her face was pinched and white, and Susan knew she'd been there hours. Her glasses were sliding down to the end of her nose. They stared at each other across the gulf. Jen seemed nervous.

'Susan, if this cycle doesn't work, we can't do another one.'

Susan went to leave the kitchen.

'I'm not having this conversation.'

Jen moved quickly and blocked her exit.

'We have to have this conversation.'

Susan pulled away, but Jen gripped her arm.

'I need you to listen to me, we don't have any money left. We can't spend any more on this for a while.'

Susan began to boil inside and Jen continued in one breath.

'We need to take a break and then try something else in a year or two once we've paid off some of this.'

Susan was full of hormones and pain; she was not about to be talked down.

'I'm nearly forty, Jen! If we stop now, it's over for me. Over. I'm done. We have to keep trying.'

Her voice was shrill, anger and desperation choking out in sobs.

'Maybe this one will work?'

After a while, Jen nodded.

'Yes, maybe this one will work.'

Susan fell into her arms, and they cuddled on the couch, themselves again briefly, united in grief and the barest spark of hope.

Round four was the magic cycle. One healthy embryo, shiny, grade one – that's what you wanted.

'All you need is one!' the fertility instahuns chanted out of Susan's glowing phone.

'All I need is one.' Susan echoed, her mind gripping onto this with every bit of force it had left.

And it did seem like the one. Small and perfect, blobbing around on camera before they transferred him back inside her. The embryologist was soft-spoken, kind and clear. She pointed to the various parts on the camera.

'See this cloudy part? That's what the baby grows out of.'

They oohed and aahed like a pair of loved-up idiots.

'And all the rest, all this shell, etc.? That forms the placenta. It's perfect, girls, it's absolutely perfect. I have a really good feeling about this one.'

Susan was nervous – that dangerous flame of hope warming her. It seemed to make Jen nervous; she gripped her hand as the catheter on the ultrasound injected their future baby inside her.

Jen held her head to Susan's.

'Please work,' she whispered. They were squeezing each other's hands in time. 'Please work, please work, please work.'

Two blue lines. Jen was kicked awake at six a.m. with the good news. Butterfly kisses across her bruised tummy. Love and hope fired. Susan floated through the morning, herself again.

'Fucking hell.' Jen was already jumping into the future, counting up the cost of college funds and school uniforms.

'Bit late to regret it now, babe.'

Susan was enjoying this, watching her wife overthink things. She had already texted close friends with the magic words they'd been waiting so long for.

I'm pregnant.

She pulled Jen close to her.

'I'm pregnant.' The words filled the space between them, closing the gap and electrifying the thread that had always drawn them together.

'I know.' Jen landed a soft kiss on her nose.

'I'm pregnant!' Susan repeated.

'I know!' Jen laughed.

'I'm pregnant, I'm pregnant, I'm pregnant!'

On the couch with Walter, Susan cried herself into a fitful sleep. She dreamed of babies locked in a room far away. Susan and Jen ran towards them from opposite ends of a long corridor, blue and black shadows cast across their faces. The babies screamed, but they ran as though through soup, slow and pointless. Their energy gone, they lay at either end of the hall, staring across the chasm as they panted, spent and lost in their worlds. She awoke with a start and cried hot, useless tears.

She couldn't shove it down anymore. Jen had left, and the cottage pulsated with sorrow. Frank's journals, the photos of dead relatives, the sheets that smelled of her and Jen's last moments together, the towels drying by the fire. Walter yipped at her heels, encouraging her to move, to walk, to do anything rather than soak in her own salty sadness. She patted his head and walked out the front door with him.

Her legs brought her, robotic, to the sandy shore, the dog following close behind. The island was strange now. It flickered in and out like an old TV; the birds' movements were jerky, the sun hazy with static. The weather left the beach empty – even the gulls huddled in their nests from the wind and the spitting rain. She sat on the cold sand staring out to sea. Her denim summer shorts, unsuitable for the day, left her lower legs exposed, the sand scratched her calves and left uneven stamps across her skin.

Then she saw him, her boy with his bucket and spade, and he would glance back at Susan and Jen as they sat reading books on a rainbow-coloured picnic blanket. He would throw his head back and laugh – eyes were brown like hers, his hair that brilliant baby blonde. His body would be small and pudgy in all the right places, skin smooth and smelling like suncream and ice cream and all the things a child in summer should smell like.

He would pick up tiny pebbles and hop towards the waves, holding her hand in his tiny fingers and needing her, loving her. He would look up to her with a smile like hers and a brow like that of some unknown man who made their dreams possible. In her mind's eye, Susan and her little boy, the dream child still hiding in the clouds, looked back at Jen, all tanned and dozing under their raggedy beach umbrella. The warm splash of water on her feet, the joyful scream of her fat, perfect toddler. His small hand slipped from hers, his laughter growing dim as the dream world fell away – all that fuzzy, cosy happiness dissolving – and the cold, wet air of the moment surged up her nose, sharp and real.

Chapter Thirty-one

Jen

Jen stood on Mick's boat, the waves rocking her away from the island. The captain had taken her backpack and offered her a rough hand onto the deck, then left her to her own solitude. There were two other passengers, teenage islanders heading to the mainland for a day out. Their giddy chatter ground through Jen. She stayed as far from them as possible on the small vessel. She gripped the side of the boat as the island and her wife were left behind. Her hands were raw from the salty wind scraping across them. She glanced down, thinking of touching and holding Susan, the now-polluted tenderness they shared. She imagined that other girl touching her, hands raking across Susan's back that weren't hers. She thought of the times Susan had pushed her away, refused her touch, refused to talk, refused to be with her or share with her, or let her into the mess that was her mind. She squeezed her hands on the rail and sobbed out an angry, hurt groan. The other passengers gave her a curious look, but she didn't care.

How could she do this? How could Susan betray everything they had?

She'd been at work when the bleeding started. Susan rang her and Jen flapped around for reassuring words she'd read elsewhere.

'People bleed all the time in early pregnancy, it's probably the blood thinners, it's probably the progesterone irritating your cervix, it's probably nothing.'

The doctors and nurses said the same, at first. 'Your HCG bloods are very reassuring. It's probably nothing. Very common, no need to panic.' Fear distorted the air. Once the clots started, and the cramps, they knew the tiny embryo, their whisper of a baby, was dying. The midwives' faces and words were grim, their tone kind.

'I'm so sorry, but the pregnancy isn't viable.'

No shit, Sherlock – what gave it away? Jen was filled with rage as they sat holding each other's hands. Susan was silent, gaze empty. She's left the room, Jen thought. She seemed to be floating above them, watching this unfold. Jen tried to take control of the situation.

'Is there any hope at all?'

The consultant had joined the meeting and shook her head sadly, still talking to Susan, not realising she wasn't with them anymore.

'I'm so sorry, but no. We can't even really find the embryo in your womb anymore, there's only the sac.'

Pregnancy of Unknown Location. Susan stared at the words written on the blood referral. Her face ashen.

Susan opted for medical management rather than surgery at first. Jen suspected she was hoping for a miracle, the bluntness of a D&C too much to cope with. The medication didn't work the first time. Or the second. The saga dragged on. Bloody pads in the bathroom bin for weeks. Susan on the couch with a hot-water bottle. Multiple appointments, walking past rows of pregnant women holding their content bellies on the way to the early pregnancy unit. At the point where the miscarriage had lasted longer than the pregnancy, Susan's eyes were like round balls of lead.

Jen drove her home from the surgery that finally finished the whole debacle. Susan rested her head against the car window, still dozy.

'I can't do this anymore,' she muttered. Jen glanced over, her hands gripping the steering wheel.

Susan fell silent and seemed to half-doze. They drove past the sounds of children in a local school playground, both of them in their own bubble of sorrow. They stopped at traffic lights. Jen watched a father lift his son, decked out in a giant football jersey, onto his shoulders. She saw her own dreams slipping away in the soup of sadness that flooded the car. She tried to break through Susan's iron curtain.

'Maybe we should check in with Rena again?'

Susan grunted in reply. Jen flailed and said the phrase that always made Susan murderous.

'It'll happen for us someday, love.'

She wasn't sure why she'd said it. She didn't know what else to say. She couldn't breathe, her wife sat drugged and filled with a pain Jen could only imagine. Susan opened her eyes, red and furious despite the glaze still sheening over them. She hissed at Jen.

'You don't know that, Jen. You don't know fucking anything.'

The silence between them deepened further. The next day, Susan had fled.

Jen took a deep breath of sea air; the freshness kicked at the anger and frustration within her. She loved Susan, she really did. She loved how deeply she felt things, her commitment, even her stubbornness with the journey they were on together. And regardless of Susan's barbs and fears, they were in this together. Or had been. Jen wasn't sure what they were now.

What could I have done differently?

It wasn't a fun thought, but a lingering suspicion. A small voice told Jen that perhaps everything that had unfolded on the island, before the island, could have been averted. If she'd been more open, if she'd been more understanding, if she had shared with Susan her sorrow and her hopes. If Susan knew Jen had stopped reading newspapers because of the rage that flooded her whenever she read stories about children being abused, neglected, and mistreated by families that didn't seem to understand the intense privilege of procreation. How Jen cried in the bathroom at work when it became obvious the pregnancy was failing. How Jen confided to her mother her fears that all they were doing was throwing good money after bad in an attempt to outwit genetic reality. But she hadn't told Susan any of that, trying to spare more weight on someone already being crushed by it all. She could never understand the physical torment Susan was going through, the loss of something so deeply connected to her body. But she wasn't sure Susan could understand the misery and helplessness of watching someone you love go through that.

She had the privilege of feeling the loss but being able to forget about it for a brief moment now and then. When it returned, it came with the guilty suspicion that Susan had sensed her moments of lightness. When she lay bare the last few years, she knew she had felt the resentment brewing in her wife. Fair or unfair, it had been there. And now they were here, the boil on their marriage ruptured.

But how could Susan, even with all the pain, all her grief, how could she do this? How could she even kiss someone else, let alone anything else they did?

Jen's brain was stuck in a loop. She glanced back in the direction of the island. It was out of sight, a blanket of fog smothered it, swallowing its cliffs and cottages in a damp embrace.

CHAPTER THIRTY-TWO

—◦◦◇◦◦—

The sand beneath her leeched water up through her shoes and socks; Susan's legs grew wet as she sat, silent and solemn, staring at the sea.

She'd loved being pregnant. In her quiet, darkest moments, she admitted to herself that it had been the only time in her life that she hadn't felt alone in the world. This small dot inside her, barely bigger than a coin, became the cord tying her to this world. She lay in bed and cupped her tummy, talking to the bean, convincing it to stick around just a little bit longer, even as it bled out of her. She hadn't realised how much blood could leave her body without dying – deep red clots and watery gushes. Each time she coughed, or the few times she laughed during those weeks, drove her baby further from her. She understood now, viscerally, how women could bleed to death while giving life. It had been weeks since she had surgical intervention to stop the bleeding, and still she felt that dread of feeling her baby, or the hope of her baby, drain out of her. Of ruining another pair of trousers, another pair of underwear. Having to wash down the car seats after a drive home from a hospital appointment became more than even the maternity pad could handle.

The choices ahead of her lay out like two neat paths through the sand. One path led back to the empty cottage, to the never-ending knowledge of her betrayal and anger, to a life filled with the pain of her stupidity and bad luck. The other lay straight ahead – a cold cleansing immersion and a washing away. The waves roared at her. Her mind roared back. Through the noise, the water called to her, and she saw herself floating, untethered through space and time towards the shore. She stood up. Silky sand gave way to stony shingle, bits of seaweed and foam as the ocean kittened its way onto land. The water gushed into her boots, and her toes contracted as the cold Atlantic water shocked them. She fixed her view on a rock straight ahead, one hundred yards out. It stood solitary, fixed and jagged – hints of morning sun glinted off its shards. Her demin shorts clung, sticky and dark as the sea swallowed her. It pushed against her legs as she waded, her head was clear and calm, feet already heavy. She walked towards her destiny, the lighthouse in the distance calling her home. A sudden high wave washed over her head, clinging her braid to her scalp. She shook it off and kept walking. The water was chest-high, sending the cold down to her bones, the saltiness on her lips, delicious and refreshing. She paused. One more step would put her head under water. She paddled her hands back and forth to keep herself steady, she planted her feet in the sand shifting under her. It seemed the most obvious of solutions – there was a peace that hadn't existed for so long. Jen and Amelia's faces flashed in front of her – a sadness and betrayal in both. She had caused that. She was vaguely aware of Walter barking on the shore. A quick breath and she stepped forward, her feet stumbling into the drop. She sank with the weight of her saturated clothes and boots, allowing herself to fall forward, feeling her lungs emptying and squeezing. It didn't feel like a mistake – even as her body tried to struggle against the darkness. It didn't feel like the pain she had always felt; it was a dull, spreading pain, nothing sharp about it. The world started to muffle and darken, and she gave herself to it willingly.

As she descended, a familiar voice whispered to her, a soft, warm voice full of love and hurt and safety.

'Come home to me.'

The path of cold immersion became clearer as the voice spoke. She was now tumbling through time, searching for the love she had pushed away with her pain.

Jen's face appeared again; Susan's limbs lost their power; her mouth opened and her breath disappeared into the ocean.

CHAPTER THIRTY-THREE

Amelia

Amelia tramped behind the group across the cliffs in the spitting rain, feeling her hair spike up in all the places she didn't want it to. She wiped her hands through it, flattening it against the wind for a moment until it whipped back up again. She pressed on. Her binoculars bashed against her sternum as she marched through the uneven ground. They were heavy around her neck, the weight pressing into her as she squeezed with guilt.

'Trash emotion,' she muttered to herself.

She wished she were alone, with her thoughts keeping her company as she processed the previous few days. Instead, she was babysitting college students who should be old enough to know not to step on certain plants or to avoid squelching their feet in certain parts of the boggy terrain. Fishing nineteen-year-olds out of swamps was starting to get old. These first walks were always the worst of the week – orientation walks, showing them the island, the bogs and nests, the hills and windy spots they would be familiar with by the end of the fortnight. It was like taking a flock of lambs through Mordor.

Susan's face was never far from her mind – the sad mewling of her drunk lover had echoed in her head ever since the night she put her to bed. She didn't indulge in guilt, but still, it irrationally bubbled up at the memory of leaving Susan in her bed to wake up to whatever fear and hangover she might have. That image joined by a new one, Susan's raw terror and Jen's rage as they fled into the night. She had to leave Susan in her own mess. It was too much for her.

'Eh, Miss Dennehy …'

'Amelia.'

'Sorry. Miss Amelia.'

She fixed the spotty blonde with a fluff of goatee with a stare. The students had a year of university under their belts, but still seemed to struggle to shake off the secondary school constructs of their youth.

'I mean, Amelia … are these anything?'

He held up some broken shells, each a vivid blue and smaller than a big man's thumb.

'Robin egg shells. Bit late for them to still be around, but nature is a bit topsy-turvy these days. Nice find, though. Good work, Matt.'

He beamed and returned to his friends. A baby lamb.

There was a deep well of frustration – at herself, at Susan – that threatened to spill forth. Her summer of escape spoiled by being pulled into the gravity of someone fleeing their own situation. In the quiet moments, when she awoke or when the wind stopped whispering, she thought she felt soft lips on her neck.

Luca, another teacher, slid alongside her. His thick Italian hair had grown over his eyebrows.

'Why are you so quiet today?'

Even his voice was charming. They had studied and worked together for two years, growing used to each other's rhythms, their noises and silences. She had learned to understand his thick Neapolitan accent; he had learned to ignore when she did accidental impressions of his Italian. Her mother always said she had a 'musical ear'. It reflected the world around her – useful when imitating bird calls, less useful when engaging in cross-cultural cooperation.

She gasped, ensuring the sheep were out of earshot.

'Oh, Luca, I've been a right dope.'

'This Susan girl, yes? She must be a demon in bed for this type of behaviour.'

Amelia smirked. He wasn't wrong, but that wasn't the point. She raised an eyebrow,, and he laughed.

'You made a mistake, it's not the end of the world.'

'Tell that to her wife.'

They walked on, Luca shouting back to the kids to avoid a marshy piece of the cliff walk – too late for one of the students, slipping into the bog in his white trainers.

'Do you think I should go and talk to her?'

'Is her wife still here?'

Amelia shrugged and shook her head, unsure.

'Then no, *bella*. You stay far, far away.'

'I think I like her, Luca.'

'No, you don't. You just like the drama, and you like that she isn't your stupid cheating girlfriend, and you like to fuck her.'

Luca, like her, was clearly not an old romantic. She couldn't deny it. She thought of the night of the céilí, their walk home under the moonlight. Bodies humming with the need to fuck each other. A shiver floated down her spine. She shook her head and took a deep breath. The present moment rushed back in, the ground beneath her feet, the cries of seabirds on the wind, the smell of salty seaweed rushing up her nose.

She paused, hands on her hips, waiting for the group to catch up with them.

'I just –'

Another sound emerged from between the ragged cries of the seabirds. A sharp noise, staccato, punctuating the legato of the blowing wind. A yap that she recognised.

'Is that a dog?'

Luca asked.

There weren't many dogs on the island. Some of the farmers had big sheepdogs; their deep, cavernous barks didn't match these deranged, terrified rasps.

Amelia hurried towards the sound, which came from the direction of the small beach where they liked to party. The beach where she had wrapped herself around Susan and brought them together in an ecstasy of bad judgement.

'I … I think that's Walter.'

Her feet moved beneath her. She knew without being able to explain why that she had to run faster than she ever had. She reached a ditch and leapt onto the gravel road that led to the beach. Her lungs burned, last night's whiskey slowing her down. Walter's panicking yaps as she turned the corner.

An old jeep sat where the sand met the road, driver's door wide open. Two wet shapes of different sizes moved away from the surf, one half dragging the other. Their clothes hung like sacks on them, shapeless and soaked. Walter danced around their feet, cries still frantic, but tail wagging. Amelia saw the taller figure – grey- haired, saturated – bundled Susan into the car. Walter hopped in, and the passenger door slammed shut. The driver climbed in, oblivious to anyone watching, and Amelia stood at the edge of the beach as the jeep sped over the hill towards the port.

CHAPTER THIRTY-FOUR

Susan sat in her sitting room, salty hair stuck to her face, cold drips snaking down her neck and back. A hot whiskey in her hand, untouched. Walter curled next to her on the couch.

JP and Peggy muttered to each other in the hall. Their whispers carried to Susan's ears. JP's deep rasp.

'Should we call himself over from Skibb?'

Susan's heart sank at the idea of explaining her madness to a doctor. Peggy rescued her.

'Ah, Jesus, no. No need to drag a doctor over here. I'll talk to her.'

'I dunno what she was at. I saw the dog going bananas and went for a look.'

Peggy's voice was softer than she had ever heard it.

'What were you even doing around here? We haven't seen you in an age.'

JP grunted.

'Sure, look. I'll head off there.'

'Go on and get changed before you get a chill.'

Susan saw the reflection of his hulking form in the glass of the sitting-room door. The rippled reflection paused, running its hand over the wallpaper, over the gaps where the photos used to be. Peggy's voice became even more gentle.

'Have you been here since he passed?'

'Not since the wake.'

JP coughed, his footsteps moved away and out the front door. Susan heard it click behind him and knew she was alone with Peggy. An explanation would be required.

She sat staring into the fire as Peggy crept back into the sitting room and peeled off her apron. JP must have called her away from the lunch service. She fumbled with the strings while still watching Susan. She draped the apron over the back of a kitchen chair, pulling it up beside Susan.

'Love, are you all right?'

Peggy's kindness startled Susan. It felt undeserved. She was very aware of her situation and surroundings. She began to cry.

'You don't need to be nice to me … I'm sorry.'

She cast her eyes down. The locked box inside gave a bang.

'You must think I'm a right fucking eejit.'

Peggy sighed.

'You're not the first visitor we've had to fish out of the sea, you know. The scenery goes to people's heads.'

Peggy broke a kind smile. Susan knew she was offering an out, a less traumatic, more reasonable explanation for what had happened. She could nod and smile and agree – it was a whole big misunderstanding, she had walked into the sea to be part of a mystical world of singing crabs and sea witches. One too many tokes of the students' spliffs. A few too many whiskeys first thing in the morning. Susan grunted and gripped the hot glass. Her fingertips burn as she did, and squeezed it harder. The pain focused her mind.

'I didn't mean to … it just kinda happened.'

That was partially true, but she forgave herself the white lie. The tiny smile vanished from Peggy's face. She was in the room with Susan, ready to hear anything. Susan wasn't quite so ready, though. She thought of how she had treated Mick, the chaos she had brought to the pub the last few times she was there.

'I didn't mean for you to get involved in my business.'

That was fully true. Peggy pursed her lips. She reached out her hand and took Susan's, gentle, firm. She ignored Susan's flinch. Peggy's rough hand in hers.

'Oh, *mo stór*, sure you know by now it's my job to know everyone's business.'

Susan laughed. Somehow, that was the oil that loosened the lock. As the giggle died on Susan's lips, her eyes stung – her vision foggy, cheeks hot and burning.

'I wanted everything to stop for a while.'

The clock in the corner ticked as Peggy waited in the space between them.

'I had a miscarriage before I came here.'

The words seemed so small when she said them aloud. A miscarriage. Miss. Carried. Like she dropped a rugby ball. Peggy's face changed, her eyes moistening. Susan inhaled through her sobs.

Peggy squeezed her hand as Susan spluttered out an explanation. A warm wash started to spread over the darkness in Susan.

'I bled for two months after, constantly bleeding and feeling sick, and still testing positive. Eventually, they operated. When I woke up, it was like … it was like I was …'

'Empty?'

They connected, the glow of the stove sitting deep within Peggy's irises. Susan sat in the silence. Peggy bit her lip and continued.

'Before Daniel …'

She paused.

'Daniel's my only one, you probably know that?'

Susan blinked, the sudden change of subject surprising her.

'Um … I hadn't really thought about it.'

'Oh, Susan, you'll have to be a bit nosier than that if you're staying around here. We tried for years to have a baby, myself and Mick. We had some losses, like yourself. We didn't have the fancy doctors or anything, really, then. We didn't have the money for it, even if we had. So we just eh … kept at it.'

A shock of pink across her face gave Susan another surprise. Peggy pulled herself to her feet, then turned towards the Aga.

'Cup of tea?'

She leant against the counter as Susan didn't respond to her, then turned again, her face set. Susan had a sudden fear Peggy was about to give her an 'it'll all work out in the end' speech. Peggy seemed to sense this.

'I know that everyone's situation is different, so I'm not … but what I'm saying is … back then … that pain, that loneliness …'

Peggy's words grew thick, and her eyes stung again. Peggy pulled her chair right up to Susan's legs, sat again, and took her by the hand, enveloping her fingers in her warmth. She looked straight at Susan.

'I don't think you're an eejit at all, my love. You did

what you had to do. And no one else will understand it. But fuck them. If you'll pardon my French.'

Susan was hoarse, croaking out the words that seemed to go around and around her head.

'I've made everything worse.'

Peggy took a deep breath.

'Well, my love, it was fairly bad to begin with, in fairness to you.'

Susan shivered and sniffled her words out.

'But … but … I don't know how to fix things with Jen. Or Mick.'

'He's very fond of you, don't be worrying about Mick, I'll sort him out.'

Peggy stood again, returning to tea-making and pouring two steaming cups, topping them up with milk and a teaspoon of sugar for Susan, who swapped out the hot whiskey, gone tepid, for the hot sweet tea. This felt more manageable; as she sipped, it warmed her, the sugar calming the shivers and helping her brain to mash its pixels back together and form cohesive thoughts. Peggy seemed to consider her next words.

'I know you asked me about Fiona before … I'm assuming you also don't know about your grandmother and her … troubles?'

Peggy paused again and seemed to take Susan's silence as her cue.

'Your grandmother had a loss too. She nearly died. And then Fiona died shortly after, and that finished her off really. My mother, who was an even bigger gossip than me if you believe that, she said she was never the same after that. None of them were.'

The words hung between them, the sadness in the house weaved its way around the room.

'She lost a baby too?'

Susan hated the phrase as soon as she said it. Lost a baby like a bank statement or a pair of earrings. She'd put it in a safe place, where no one knew how to find it. Susan supposed that,, depending on your religious inclination, you might see it that way. The pieces finally falling into place, a small family wedged apart by loss and secrecy.

'My dad always hated it here. He never talked about the island or his mam and dad. Or Frank. It was like they never existed.'

'They definitely existed, my love. And sure, look around you, they're all over the house.'

Susan's hands were tingling, the feeling re-emerging as pins and needles. She shook them, stretching her fingers, feeling the blood flow more freely.

'We always used to slag your dad for being such a snob. But I think …'

Peggy stopped herself. Susan pushed her.

'Go on.'

'… I think that was just his way of coping. If he could blame the island and blame Frank, maybe it was less painful.'

Susan's tears soaked down her face.

'Thank you for being so kind to me.'

'I'm the most underpaid psychologist in the country at this stage.'

They sipped their tea. The ache in Susan had eased to a dull throb. It would return, she knew, when the weight of all that had just been said revealed itself, and she was alone again. She pushed past the last of her pride, not quite done wringing every drop of warmth and guidance out of Peggy.

'What should I do about Jen?'

Peggy smacked her lips together, thinking.

'Is this the worst thing you've ever done to her?'

'It's the worst thing I've ever done in my life.'

There was silence once again, then Susan said quietly, 'and then there's Amelia'.

Peggy's usual sternness returned.

'The first thing you need to do is forget all about her, I'm afraid. She's a big girl, she's probably chasing after someone else already.'

Susan didn't expect that to needle at her. Peggy seemed to notice the flash of hurt crossing her face.

'Just give Jen time, I think. She came all this way to check on you. She's not going to give up on you both any-time soon.'

Susan ran her fingers through her wet hair, the salt starting to collect behind her ears and at the nape of her neck. Peggy pressed a hand against her head, feeling for a fever.

'You've no temperature anyway. You'll need to get showered off, or you'll get a chill.'

Susan said nothing, so Peggy pushed on.

'I'm serious, I know I'm an old fusspot, but you need to mind yourself. When was the last time you had a full night's sleep?'

Susan thought back to her last good sleep, months ago, maybe even years – a deep sleep in bed with Jen, her head in the crook of her wife's arm, her blonde hair strewn across her breasts, their naked bodies pressed against each other.

'If I leave you to it, will you promise to have a hot shower and head into bed? And no more seafaring adventures?!'

Susan realised she was exhausted and that Peggy would be needed in the pub – on a cold,, rainy day, the hungry students would be demanding their hot food and emptying the taps out of boredom.

'I'll be fine. I just need to rest.'

'Sure, you have Walter as well, and you know where I am if you need me.'

Peggy placed a soft, motherly kiss on Susan's head and started to make her way to the sitting room door.

'Peggy?'

'Yes, pet?'

'What happened with Frank and JP?'

Peggy's face darkened.

'Oh, Susan, my love, that's not one for me to answer. And certainly not today. Now, sleep.'

CHAPTER THIRTY-FIVE

—⸰◇◇⸰—

The cold had left her bones by the following morning. She awoke to shafts of sunlight – the summer had returned and was poking its way back into her bedroom, blinding her against the whiteness of its walls. Walter lay at the end of the bed again, his eyes worried and watching her.

'Hey boy, are you ok?'

He crawled up the bed to her, dragging his tummy along the duvet, arriving beside her face and giving her a soft lick on the nose.

'I don't deserve that.'

The cold might have been gone, but the deep sense of disgrace was still lying there like stagnant water.

They got out of bed, and Susan shared her breakfast of eggs and toast with him, made with supplies left on the doorstep by – she assumed – Peggy. The sweet pleasure of morning coffee, its scent bitter and refreshing, lit Susan up. The locked box still creaked within, but its doors were open, and instead of feeling poisoned by its contents spilling about, she felt her breath squeeze through her when she inhaled, like a blockage were dissolving.

She knew what she had to do. She made a list in her head, sipping her coffee and nibbling on the corners of her buttery toast. She felt a slip of worry grow, and grow further as she approached the distillery.

JP was on his knees in a flower bed. He lifted his head

and turned towards her when she opened the gate. They blushed at each other, and JP dipped his head.

'You're still alive anyway.'

She laughed despite herself.

'I am, yeah.'

They stood staring at each other, the island around them singing to welcome back the sunshine.

She sensed the beach and the waves again, washing over her. The hysteria, the release, the soothing darkness descending – and a brief moment of regret. As she started to fade, JP's strong hands had grabbed her underarms, shouting and dragging her as she kicked and wailed back to the shore. He towered over her, his bobbled grey Aran clinging to his large shoulders as he heaved with exertion.

'Jesus wept, Susan, what are you at?'

He had picked his jacket up from the sand where he'd abandoned it and swaddled her like a small child. He kneeled on the beach beside her, his knees sandy, his rough hands around her shoulders holding her up, and she apologising for the snot and tears as he did. He'd whispered to her, rubbing her hair.

'It's ok, you're ok. You're ok now, you're ok.'

Their awkwardness was broken when Walter trotted to JP and placed his two paws on JP's knees. JP stooped to hug the dog and received his kisses. He seemed to remember Susan's presence and looked sheepish. The weight on Susan's shoulders was returning; the tension and worry of the conversation to come were pulling at her again. She went to speak, but JP intercepted.

'So are you all right after yesterday?'

He rubbed the back of his neck.

'I'm ok. I just wanted to say thank you ... for saving my life.'

He coughed and tried to protest. Susan persisted.

'No ... you saved my life, JP.'

He looked her in the eye, his brow still furrowed, his cheeks still flushed.

'How come you were even passing by?'

'Ah sure ... I was eh ... I was dropping stuff down to the pub, you know, some new flavours and that.'

He threw her an awkward look under his brow. Susan let the air thicken between them.

'JP ...'

He looked at her, his face uncertain and full of hesitation. Susan pressed on.

'I'd really love us to have a proper conversation, where we're not angry at each other, and you don't tell me to leave.'

He hung his head. The sadness bubbled up in him – she knew it well.

'I'd like that too.'

A small smile. JP stared ahead, mumbling out his words.

'That's ... that's why I was there. Yesterday. I wanted to say sorry about the other day. The shouting and that.'

'I'm sorry too, about the estate agent ...' She paused, 'and the snooping.'

A hint of a smile played at the edge of his lips.

'I don't blame you.'

'Will you tell me about him?'

JP's face crumpled. He shook his head, and the furrowed brow returned, mask back on. Susan tried to power through.

'JP … I know … I know it's easier for us to just … shut everyone out when we're in pain …'

At this, JP lifted his head, his face inscrutable as he listened.

' … But I think we have to stop doing that. Or we'll both end up in the sea. Again.'

He pulled out a small black hip flask and offered it to her. She shook her head and made a face. He thought for a second, then put it back in his jacket without drinking it.

'Your uncle …' He took a deep breath and swallowed, as though summoning the strength to continue. He closed his eyes and spoke softly, 'your uncle … was the love of my life.'

Susan realised she had known this all along. JP filled with a light she hadn't seen before. Susan puffed out her cheeks.

'Right so.'

They looked at each other, a bridge of love built across their sea of hostility. JP's face cracked first, and then Susan's – laughter rising out of them, raw and unexpected and full of relief.

CHAPTER THIRTY-SIX

---∞∞∞---

Frank

Frank threw his keys on the small hall table in the cottage; they landed with a crash. The tippy-taps of Walter's claws as he ran out to greet him. The dog twirled on his hind legs, thrilled for his owner's return. Frank knew JP would be awaiting him in the sitting-room, tea on the stove, maybe steak and spuds ready to be served if he was lucky. He sensed he had no luck this evening.

He delayed his arrival in the sitting room and tossed his sports bag of clothes into the bedroom. It seemed more bare than when he had left. JP's clothes were missing. His holey socks no longer littered the bedroom floor. Frank had dismissed his growing sense of dread as a hangover after the wedding, but now he accepted it as an omen of what was about to happen. He paused in his bedroom and considered how he could change the course of the river surging towards him. What compromises could he put forward? How much could he offer of himself to try to fix this?

Frank paused at the sitting room and peeked in through the slightly ajar door. JP sat in his chair by the stove, as Frank knew he would be. His hands were steepled together, his fingers butterflying as he seemed to be considering the thoughts that bothered him. Frank pushed the door open fully.

'How's it going?'

JP's eyes were red and angry.

'How was the wedding?'

His tone stayed flat.

'Ah, you know yourself.'

'I don't actually. Never been to a lesbian wedding.'

'Not much different to an ordinary wedding. More vegetarians, though.'

Frank's humour didn't land. He was starting to realise that it might be too late. JP pulled himself out of the chair, lifting the backpack at his feet as he did. He swung it on a shoulder.

'I'm going to stay in the farmhouse for a bit. Handier for work anyway.'

'Ah, JP.'

'No. I've decided.'

Frank's hand reached out; it gripped the beefy forearm of the man he loved.

'Can't we just have a chat?'

JP shook his head.

'No.'

Frank loved JP and his ability to say so few words, the way he could sit in the silence of the dark winter nights with him, Frank telling him stories of the army, or Fiona, or his trip to the mainland. JP listening, sometimes smiling, sometimes nodding, but always listening. Taking him in. Taking in Frank for all he was, not what he wasn't. Now, though, he wished JP would finally open his mouth and say everything he wanted to.

His hand was like a vice on JP's wrist.

'We can sort it out though, yeah? Like you'll be back in a few days.'

JP pushed Frank's hand away.

'In a few days, I'll be even older, and I won't have changed my mind on what I want—'

Frank took a slow, deep breath and looked away. JP held his hand, his fingertips coarse, against his own. The anger was gone, a great shutter of sorrow clamped down.

'– and you'll still be scared.'

Chapter Thirty-seven

Susan was deep in sleep the following morning when three strong taps on the front door disturbed her. The raps revealed Amelia on the doorstep in her boots, her arms folded, her face serious. Despite the return of the sunshine, it was a windy day, her red hair was blowing wildly, giving her the look of a furious siren. Walter strolled out to welcome the visitor, stretching and yawning.

'Amelia ... I'm not sure it's a good idea for you to be here –'

'What the hell, Susan? YOU WALKED INTO THE SEA?'

Susan pulled her in the door quickly before she could shout any more. Amelia stood in the hall, her face still cross.

Her fury stripped Susan bare.

'Amelia, why are you here? Why do you even care?'

'Why wouldn't I care?'

Susan shrugged, Amelia tutted and rolled her eyes.

'You're going to pull a muscle in your eyeballs.'

Amelia's eyebrows were almost at her hairline with frustration.

'For fuck's sake, Susan. OK, get dressed. You'll need your boots. And maybe brush your hair.'

She pushed Susan into her bedroom, keeping her own feet fully planted in the hall.

'Go on, we're going for a walk.'

Susan wondered whether she preferred it when Amelia ignored her.

The sounds of pottering in her kitchen, an occasional clink, and a minor crash that made her cringe while she switched out her pyjamas for leggings and a T-shirt. She dragged the boots over her feet, grabbing her polo-neck, its thick wool hugging down over her neck as she pulled it over her head.

'Now, let's go. Leave Walter at home, he won't be able for it.'

Amelia walked out the front door; Susan and Walter exchanged glances. She pointed towards the sitting room, and he toddled back into the house, leaving Susan to follow Amelia into the wind. They walked together as a duo, Amelia's fury seeming to melt into something else.

'Does everyone know?'

'I don't think so.'

'Everyone probably thinks I'm a lunatic.'

'Are you done making up conspiracy theories about yourself?'

Susan laughed.

'Where are we going?!'

'Just move!'

The pace was stealing Susan's breath; they powered up the hill towards the graveyard, passing bemused tourists as they huffed and puffed. Susan realised how much fitter she had become in the last few weeks;; the knowledge that her body was leaving behind her pregnancy put a sadness on her that tinged the satisfied glow within. The strength in her legs, the muscle returning to her midsection, the slow but steady recovery from blood loss and hormones. It was all great, she supposed, but also sad. The better she felt physically, the further she was from her loss, but also the further she was from the hope that preceded it. She pondered all this in silence, noticing Amelia starting to slow as the hill plateaued alongside the stone wall of the graveyard. They paused by the gate and stood, panting; Amelia offered Susan her flask of water.

'OK … we can slow down now.'

'Why are we power walking up a hill?'

'It's good for our bodies and our minds.'

She recited this like a PSA. It was Susan's turn to raise an eyebrow. Amelia shrugged.

'My mam always took us for walks when we were feeling crap.'

'This explains a lot about you.'

'Fuck you.'

'Fuck you! You just dragged me up a hill.'

'I'm trying to keep you alive!'

Susan rubbed her temples with embarrassment. More tourists strolled past on their way down the hill to the village. Susan gave them an eyebrow salute.

'I'm fine, Amelia.'

'Sure – you threw yourself in the sea fully clothed with rocks in your pocket for thrills?'

'I didn't have rocks in my pockets.'

'That's not what I heard.'

'Now who's making up conspiracy theories?'

They were both silent for a moment. Susan's heart was broken from the last few days.

'I don't know why you're so angry with me. I don't know why you care.'

'I'm angry because you almost died. And what you did, what we did, was terrible, and your wife has every right to hate both of us, and we deserve to feel bad, but you don't deserve to die.'

Amelia stopped, her jaw set and eyes reddening at the corners. She blinked, then continued.

'And I care because I like you, Susan. I enjoyed what we had. I think you're a good person underneath all of … this. And I know it's over and I know we can't be together …'

'I like you too.'

Amelia shook her head and then walked on. Her boots strode into the graveyard, marshy from days of rain. They walked up and over the hill, pausing to survey the land and seascape around them – sunny but with a sniff of wildness still, the wind still strong enough to snatch wisps of sea spray and carry it to them. They threw shy looks at each other, Susan almost whispering.

'Amelia, where are we going?'

'The Wailing Crag.'

The crag was as stunning as it was heartbreaking, the jagged brown rocks keened towards the sea, grasping its stony fingers towards the ocean. A section that could have been a face if the right person looked at it, stared out towards the Atlantic – the arch of its back hunched over, desperate, demented. Susan sat and took it in, perched at a precipice looking down on the unreachable inlet where the Wailing Crag looked upon its pool of loss. The wind squeezed through the sharp rock, the impossible angles and curves releasing a sad whistling into the air.

'Do you think you'll try for a baby again?'

Susan's heart dropped.

'How do you know about that?'

'You're a lesbian in your late thirties, you're obviously struggling with something, when I told you the story of the Wailing Crag you looked like you'd seen a ghost ...'

Amelia took a breath.

'Also, Daniel told me.'

'For fuck sake.'

They sat together, each in the other's presence, listening to their breaths for a moment. Amelia continued.

'When I got here, I was a bit all over the place. Totally out of my body, you know?'

Susan had never considered this concept of not being in your body. She thought about it and so much made sense. Being up in your brain, your thoughts dis-integrating into wisps that spiralled up into the cloud while your body moved without you, careening you into one mess after another. Amelia seemed oblivious to Susan's breakthrough.

'So I came up hcfere to the Wailing Crag, I love it here. She's ... she's so beautiful and so sad, and she isn't ashamed of being sad ...'

Amelia was looking at Susan. Her voice sank through her body, into her heart.

'And then I went to the edge ...'

'Oh Amelia ...'

'Calm down, Virginia Woolf, not like that. I went to the edge, and I screamed my head off.'

'Oh.'

Susan laughed, and and Amelia nudged her in the ribs. 'I want you to do it.'

'What?'

'That's why I brought you here, I want you to try it.'

'Amelia I …'

'Susan, if you keep doing what you always did, you keep getting what you always got. So try something new.'

She thought about it and so much made sense. With no objection, Amelia took her hand and walked her calmly and quietly towards the edge. It jutted out slightly from the wall of the cliff, the water two hundred feet below them in a white frothy mix.

The Wailing Crag stood before them, straight out at sea, leaning away. The wind peaked and dropped through its fingers. Susan heard the whistling, then jumped at Amelia's sudden scream.

'Come on, give a roar!'

A small sound escaped from Susan. Amelia scoffed.

'More!'

Amelia screamed into the wind. Susan pushed a bigger sound from her larynx. Amelia looked triumphant.

'MORE!'

Susan took a deep breath, down through her throat, her lungs, past her diaphragm. The breath swirled around the black pot of ink, collecting in her belly. It mixed with the pain and she drove it all back out. The scream that emerged startled even Amelia. It kept coming, extending, her face wet, her throat burning. The wind wailed up from the crag, joining their voices. Her air ran out, her legs dissolved beneath her, and Amelia's arms came gently around her, guiding her back from the edge.

Chapter Thirty-eight

―❊―

JP

It was six weeks since he had seen Frank. He wasn't sure how long it had been since they'd spoken; their days in the distillery over the last year had been quiet and transactional, only talking to discuss the bare bones of the business. JP had thought about leaving the island more than once, set out on his own on the mainland or somewhere else, but then the azure sky would glance over the waves on a summer morning, or the light would bounce across the heather, and he knew there was nowhere else he could be.

He was lonely and not sure at all if the decisions he'd made were the right ones.

He stood outside the hospital where Frank lay, the elastic of his surgical mask digging into his ears. The masks were always too small for his big ears. He wished Frank were here to take the piss. He knew what a mocking he'd get for being such a softie, turning up outside a hospital that he wasn't allowed to enter, to wait outside a window, for what? A miracle? Or just to be there, to observe the end as best he could.

He spent his time debating what he had been ploughing over for many years. Would he rather be lonely with Frank or lonely without him? Different types of loneliness, he thought, one borne from being an object of shame, the other from his own pride and self-respect.

The question was becoming more moot as the days went by. He booked himself into a B&B near the hospital, the landlady only just reopening after the worst of the pandemic restrictions and thrilled for the business. She spritzed him with hand sanitiser as he walked in and out of the house, and gave him sympathetic sighs as he filled her in on the broad details of his reasons for visiting.

'My great-grandfather was from the islands,' she said, as if it made her like him, 'he moved up to the city in the twenties.'

'More fool him,' he replied, and she tittered.

The coffee shop staff in the shopping centre across the road knew him and started to prepare his cortado when he walked in the door.

'A cortado!' Frank would say, ''tis a long way from cortados you were reared!'

Frank was right, of course. He and Frank had grown up a world away from the one they lived in now. But JP liked it. He embraced it, cortados and kitchen gadgets and all.

He stood outside the hospital, his umbrella in hand, not sure what he was waiting or hoping for. Occasionally, he thought of what might happen if Frank died. Would he be able to keep working in the distillery? Would he be able to keep it going? Would he be able to keep himself going?

Less frequently, as time went by, he pondered what would happen if Frank lived. He closed his eyes and tried to project his thoughts through the concrete of the hospital.

I love you. I miss you. Please get better and come home and we can figure something out.

Could they, though? Could they conquer the fear Frank seemed to sit on?

CHAPTER THIRTY-NINE

Frank

Frank hadn't been able to catch a full breath for weeks. Air clawed its way into his lungs, rasping and scraping along inflamed vessels. The hospital's oxygen mask seemed only to add to the discomfort. In the depths of his fever, he ripped it off his face, flinging it across the room with the only strength he could find that day. Masked nurses tutted and returned it. There was no soft touch on his hair, there were quick, kind words, the door closed, and he was alone again with his raging temperature and the addled visions and memories that plagued him.

The grey wall of the hospital swirled in front of him, explosions of lights and colours as he cooked in his own sweat.

He knew he was dying. He felt life pushing him out of its way. It was trundling on without him. He thought of the island birds, soaring above the Atlantic, the wind filling their wings and their breath mingling with the cool air over the ocean. He thought of the love he once had. He thought of Peggy pulling a pint and patting his hand with a wink.

'That's your last one tonight.'

He thought of Walter and his soft snores, both of

them sandwiched together in front of the stove as the winter rolled in.

Walter had arrived on his birthday. The big 5-0, as JP insisted on calling it. Frank had never seen him so hyper, which made him about as energetic as a normal person on a slow day, but it was unnerving nonetheless. He had awoken Frank with a chocolate muffin crowned with a single candle, murdered a version of 'Happy Birthday' and returned with a tray piled high with a full Irish on the good plates. They sat in bed, tucking in, Frank feeling content despite the unusual start to the day.

'Now there'll be no fuss later, is that right?'

Frank was suspicious of where JP's bursts of energy might lead. For JP's 50th, there had been a strict 'no fuss' rule implemented, but Frank could smell JP's hypocrisy, and he felt a finger of fear running up his spine.

'No fuss,' JP said, unconvincingly, 'just a few pints down in Peggy's.'

'And there'll be no streamers or any of that shite?'

'No streamers.'

'Bunting isn't the same as streamers,' JP tried to persuade Frank that evening. They sat in Peggy's surrounded by red and purple triangles of fabric, and a massive HAPPY 50TH BIRTHDAY FRANK banner. Mick was downing pints beside him. The trad musicians were stacked in the corner and blasting out the tunes.

'No fuss, you said,' Frank muttered at JP.

'Just an oul bit of music. It's your birthday, Frank, you deserve a celebration.'

Mick slapped his back and laughed,

'You're an awful grumpy fucker, Frank Shaw!'

Frank grunted. JP seemed to take no notice, his face in a wide beam. Frank saw him glance towards the bar, the lights went out, the music stopped, and he realised what was happening. A cake with a bonfire's worth of candles emerged from behind the bar, held by Peggy, the young fella Daniel ahead of her, clearing people out of the way. The whole pub sang happy birthday as Frank's face burned. He saw how happy JP was, and his embarrassment and annoyance shifted. The cake landed in front of him, and he did his birthday boy duties and embraced the applause of the pub.

'Speech!!' someone shouted.

'Fuck off!' he roared back, and that was the end of that.

The pub returned to normal. Mick was away getting more pints.

'That's it now, you can relax.'

'There isn't a fecking clown going to pop out from behind the bar?'

'No ...'

'JP?'

'There's one more thing I have to give you, but I'll wait until we're home.'

Frank gave him a wink and JP gave a hoot. Mick returned and Frank sat up straight.

'Now!' Mick said, landing the pints with a splash on the table, 'back to business.'

Frank grabbed the fresh pint, enjoying the foam as it tickled his top lip. He was happy, he was smiling. It struck him out of nowhere, but he looked around, JP sat beside him, Mick and Peggy supplying the pints, music thrumming in his chest, a job he loved finished for the day. It was enough, he realised. He thought about reaching out and grabbing JP's hand, and sharing this feeling with him, but couldn't quite do it. He never had, in public. He guessed that Mick, and definitely Peggy, knew there was more to their friendship. He knew how other islanders gossiped but were always too polite to ask, and he was happy to keep it that way. But JP's hand was so close to his, he could reach out and touch it without even shifting the rest of himself. What would it be like to do that, in the heat of the pub and the glow of his happiness? JP had an odd look on his face, watching him, as though reading his thoughts. Frank wiped his mind of his wild thoughts. He didn't want to give JP false hope. JP, who would tell the whole island if Frank let him. JP, who never seemed to care what anyone thought. JP, who wandered through life to his own rhythm. But it was too late to shove his thoughts back down; he knew JP had read them. When Mick disappeared to change a keg for Peggy, JP held out his hands.

'Will you have an oul dance with me?'

Frank reacted from his instincts.

'Cop on.'

JP drank his pint in silence, and Frank felt the weight of his remorse rising. He pushed it away.

'Thanks for doing all this,' he said, extending a pathetic olive branch. JP was receptive; his unending patience washed over Frank.

'You had a nice birthday?'

'The best.'

Frank shuffled, his mouth dry despite the drink in front

of him. He continued, trying to stop the embarrassment seeping into his words.

'You're the best. And –' he looked around before he even realised he was doing it, 'I love ya'.

JP's beam returned.

They finished their pints and agreed it was time to head home. JP disappeared into the toilet while Peggy refused to take money from Frank.

'Away with you now and get a good night's sleep. And make sure JP gets home ok.'

Peggy gave a wink, Frank ignored it, but had to stop a smirk twitching at the corner of his lips. *Fiona would be only a couple of years older than Peggy. They would have been friends if they'd grown up together. Endless mischief.* Ah, there it was, he thought, his tipsy mind turning maudlin. He wondered what would be the trigger to think of her. He always thought of her on his birthday, even after celebrating thirty-eight of them without her waking him up first thing by jumping on his head and singing out of tune.

JP emerged, not from the toilet but from the door behind the bar, an odd shape protruding under his jacket. Frank was bewildered.

'What in god's name are you doing?'

'C'mon, I'll show you in a bit.'

JP marched past him, holding on tight to the little shape that seemed to throw tiny punches through the fabric. They walked up the hill towards the cottage, JP staying ahead of Frank, only turning his head to laugh as Frank pushed him for answers.

'What's in your coat? What is it?'

'You'll see!'

Frank was getting too old for surprises, but he went along with it nonetheless. Inside the sitting-room, where the stove smouldered and sent an orange glow bouncing off the dresser and their kitchen units, JP opened his coat finally, to reveal a tiny pup nestling within his jumper, its small black eyes shining with fear, its stubby legs quivering with nerves.

'Ah, would you look?'

Frank took the pup in his arms, and the dog whimpered from the separation from the warm body of JP.

'I knew you were missing a dog around the place,' JP said.

Frank's old farm dog, a one-eyed border collie called Jess, had died in his sleep in the very spot they were standing in a few months previous. This dog was certainly not a farm dog. Frank wondered if he'd even manage to walk around the island with legs so tiny. He had the softest ears, little paws that reached out and paddled in the air as he was passed between them.

The dog bed was Jess' old basket, sat amongst the old blankets by the stove. He cried until JP brought him into their bed. Frank laughed and wrapped his arm around the pup between them, stroking his fur until contented puppy snores filled the room. JP rested his elbow on the pillow, head leaning on his hand, his eyes sweeping over Frank and the dog.

'He needs a name,' he said, after a minute of listening to the music of the snoozing pup.

'Jess Two?'

'Oh, Frank, no. He's a gorgeous little fella, isn't he?'

'He's as big a softie as you are.'

'And sure what's wrong with that?'

Frank thought for a moment.

'I'll call him after you.'

'JP Junior?'

'Walter.'

'Walter?'

'Walter, the big old softie.'

Frank coughed in his hospital bed and thought of his soft JP with his sad, hurt face. He thought of their first kiss – it was like touching another world, his fear brushing against hope and excitement.

Another world called him now, too – and he resisted it, rage and grief and the weight of all he'd never allowed himself pressing down on his chest. Out of the corner of his eye, a little girl stood in the corner of his room. He darted a glance in her direction, but she was gone. Shadows climbed the grey walls, seeping, clawing their way into the room until the light collapsed entirely.

His body was iron, immovable. His breath came in shallow rasps, each one a little less. The longing drained quietly out of him, and finally, he let go into the darkness.

Chapter Forty

⸻◦◇◇◦⸻

Susan sat by the shore again at the half-moon cove where her aunt had died. The Wailing Crag jutted from one of the cliffs on the northern arm, as stunning as it was heartbreaking. The jagged brown rocks keened towards the sea, grasping its stony fingers towards the ocean. A section that could have been a face if the right person looked at it stared out towards the Atlantic – the arch of its back hunched over, desperate, demented.

She reached inside her jacket for the most recent journal she had found in the cottage then she solemnly stroked its pages. The business and ledgers had paused – her uncle's concise writing was purely about his life, and what would become his death. She glanced down through the entries:

18 June
Not feeling the best lately. Went across to the mainland to the market and think I might have picked something up.

20 June
Cough is getting bad now. Asked Mick and Peggy to keep an eye on Walter. Maybe I should have asked JP.

29 June
Doctor wants me to go into hospital. He can feck off.

30 June
Going to hospital. Wish JP was here.

Susan turned a page, and Frank's last drawing jumped

out at her, a lovingly detailed sketch of JP and Walter together on the sofa where she sat every evening. They were both cocooned in a delicious afternoon doze. The last entry in the journal stared at her from the page opposite, a single word square in the middle of the paper.

Sorry

The sadness pressed in around her, a shiver down her spine. What was he sorry for? Running from himself? Hurting the person he loved most in the world? Turning away from the things that could have saved him. The echo was uncomfortable and close. There was so much to be sorry for. She closed the journal and patted the cover. Her story wasn't finished yet. Her sorry did not need to come too late.

Susan thought of the cottage, the land, and the poly-tunnels, the cows and the put-putting machinery. She had a growing sense of responsibility to something bigger than herself.

The distillery was resting when she popped by, the package containing the journal and note pressed close to her heart. JP wasn't around, it seemed. She thought about searching for him, but preferred to let her written words be her message:

JP,

The last few weeks have given me so much to think about. I've made some terrible choices but I want to make things right. We both have a chance to continue our lives and learn from all the awful things that have happened or that we have done.

I'm leaving Frank's last journal with you, so you can see how he felt in his last days. He loved you. I don't think he always knew how to show it, but I can tell. His fear and regret over a lifetime of secrecy broke him. I think you were the only thing holding him together for most of his life.

I'm going to ask my solicitor to draw up documents to give you half the business. If either you or Frank had had any sense it would have been yours a long time ago. I'll be in touch with more details when I have them. I think we can make this work.

I'm going to be leaving in the next few days. I need to make things right as best I can.

I can't bring Walter with me, he belongs here on the island. Can you look after him?

Thank you for helping me understand so much about myself and my family.

Talk soon,

Susan

She slipped the parcel in the postbox by the gate. She wandered to the island port, Walter skipping alongside her. Outside Maureen's shop, she paused at the grass-green postbox. She ran a thumb over the letter to Jen, the paper a fragile weight in her hand. She held it to her chest, a final moment of consideration, then gave it a small, decisive kiss and dropped it inside.

CHAPTER FORTY-ONE

———◇◇◇◇◇———

Dear Jen,

I keep thinking about that time we were at the Arcade Fire gig together at Electric Picnic, when I left you by the front of the stage to go for a wee. I waded through the morass of bodies to find you again, pushed my way past drunk girls and drunk guys, teenagers on other teenagers' shoulders, banners and inflatable beach balls, and there you were, pissed and elated, waving your arms. Sometimes, when I'm feeling useless, I think of that look of awe on your face. I think maybe I do belong to someone, to somewhere.

I always found you. I found you that night in the club when we first met. I found you on the day of our wedding when that bloody driver didn't turn up and I had to screech to your mam's house in my wedding dress to pick you up on our way in my car. I liked that we arrived together in the end. It felt more fitting.

Lately I've been so lost. I couldn't even think of how to come back. How to stop this train of sorrow before it went right over the cliff. So I didn't stop it. And now I'm here at the bottom trying to scramble my way back up.

We were happy, weren't we? Until my genetic booby-trap exploded in both our faces. We fell into the darkness and I just kept swimming down. You were always better at seeing the light ahead.

Everything I write here will sound like an excuse. It's not. There is none. I think this letter is what I should have said and written so many months ago. I wouldn't need excuses if I had.

Should I tell you here how sorry I am about what I've done?

I am sorry.

I'd like to not be mad anymore. I'd like our life back. I don't want to push our love away.

When our baby died, and that's what it was to me, no matter how little or how long, it was the baby we loved and longed for and worked for ... when our baby died, I think something broke in me. I was so angry. Why should so many others have that, and not us? There was an animal fire roaring up inside me. After the D&C, it's like the emptiness in me spread out, swirling like ink through my veins. It suffocated all feeling, all reason, all sensation to the world. It made me feel like a stranger in my own body, it made you feel like a stranger to me.

I wanted my own life to pour out along with all the blood.

Even with you lying beside me, your hand on my side, I had never felt so alone.

I remember the day you dragged me out of bed to go to the clinic for a review. I hated you that day. I hated that doctor, and those nurses. I hated myself too. I remember us travelling up the elevator with another couple, and I caught the eye of the woman. We shared a look, like two soldiers in a trench about to go over the top. Her partner looked bored. You were checking your emails on your phone. And me and that woman, we stared at each other, empty. I wonder what terrible things she's done to get away from it all. Or maybe she had the magic cycle the next time. Or maybe I'm projecting.

When the doctor turned around and told me 'at least you know you can get pregnant', I don't know how I didn't kill him. I looked at you, and you were nodding. I don't know if I've ever felt more alone. Another clot fell out of me, pushed out by pure rage.

I shouldn't have kept all of this inside, poisoning me.

I've let it out now, and my heart and mind and body feel like they're working again.

I know I don't deserve your forgiveness, but I don't want to lose you, I don't want you to slip away from me too.

I want to come home. Please let me. I'm sorry.

Love, Susan xxx

CHAPTER FORTY-TWO

—◦◦◦◦◦—

Susan waited, holding her nerve as the days went by, doing silent mathematics at the length of time a letter takes to be posted, to cross the sea, to travel in a big truck, and then a small van, and then finally be walked up the driveway of her beautiful home in the satchel of Tim the postman. How long would it take to be picked up from the hallway by her wife, and then for Jen to read it, to process it, and finally make a decision?

Susan knew fear; she knew anxiety. It burrowed within her spine and her gut, and now it whispered new things – new possibilities. In the silence of the unanswered letter, the reality of a future without Jen unfurled. She held closer to Walter, not ready to send him to JP yet, enjoying the comfort of his soft fur at night, both of them basking in the peace of the last few walks on the island as she waited for the green light to return home.

The reply came in an unexpected way. The cottage, quiet in the daytime, shattered with the ring of a phone. Susan had been ignoring the avalanche of texts, notifications and calendar reminders that crashed into her home screen when she turned it back on, leaving it to one side. Preparing for the real world, she told herself. And it helped – building a slow lifeline back to the mainland, to the life she had run away from. Now that lifeline pulsed with the beep-beep of an incoming call. Susan looked at the name on the screen. Her breath caught. Jen.

'Hello?'

A silence. Susan sat in it. Jen owed her nothing, not even a hello if she didn't feel like it. There was a throat clearing at the end of the line.

'Hey.'

Susan waited another silent moment, then spoke.

'Did you get my letter?'

'Yeah … I'm glad you remembered I exist.'

Jen's voice was cold. Susan let the silence sit again – she could take that hit. Jen cleared her throat again.

'Look. Just come back.'

Susan warmed and allowed herself a hopeful smile..

'OK.'

Silence again. Susan, against her instincts, broke it.

'I love you.'

A sigh on the other end. Jen sounded tired. Susan wondered whether she imagined a slight sniffle in her voice, some tears before she made the call.

'Come back, and we'll talk.'

The call ended. Susan took a deep breath. It was time to go home to her wife, and whatever that meant now.

The island faded out of view as *The Lord and Lady* pulled out of the port. The sea spray kissed her hair, the ocean choppy as the seasons started their transition into autumn. Mick, quiet in the wheelhouse. He stuck his head out of the doorway.

'You'll come back to us, will you?'

Susan was lonesome to leave this wonderful place and this man, and his giant heart.

'I will of course.'

Maybe sooner than you'd think. She turned her eye back to the mainland, knowing that her only option now was to take the next step forward.

Susan's car, covered in bird shit, sat at the pier in Kilbrean when Mick dropped her back to shore. He docked and carried her little suitcase to the Toyota, her own arms full of pots of earth, round pebbles from the beach and some chamomile taken from the distillery, her backpack once again weighing across her shoulders and her neck. He squeezed her close as a goodbye, his big arms pushing the air out of her lungs. His jumper scratched at her face as he held her. He turned, nodded and walked away. She stood there, the temptation to chase him and return to her hiding place threatening to ruin her newfound resolve. She wrapped her fingers around the car keys and wrenched her face towards her unhappy little Toyota, moss and mould gathering at its seams. Rainy mucky days in the little pier's car park had left their evidence across the windscreen and the back windows. The tyres needed pumping, the front lights wiping of the grime and salt build-up from the last few months. The key's battery was dead – a great start – so Susan pulled out the hidden key in the fob and opened the doors manually. The engine ticked and tocked and spluttered. She paused, took a breath, said a prayer to whatever was up there, and turned the key again. It came back to life. She cranked the rickety AC up full, pumping air around and out of the car, the smell of damp turning her stomach.

She gave the car time to come fully alive, and pulled out her phone to explore her notifications. True, there had been a cascade at first – friends enquiring, panicking, worrying. Then it faded in the shadow of her silence. How easily you can fall out of your own life, she thought. That's what she had wanted then, down in the dark pit of her despair. She knew the option of staying away still existed. She considered the road ahead – literal and symbolic – the awkward conversations and the possible outcomes, and knew she could wait in this car park for a few hours and hop on Mick's boat the next time it came by. She opened her messages, found Jen's chat, and wrote a quick text.

'Just leaving now. Be home –'

She paused, then deleted 'home' and returned to her message.

'– back about 4. See you then.'

She agonised over adding an X. She added one, threw her phone into her bag, and then put it on the floor away from her mind and her obsessive, checking brain. She allowed her mind to think for a moment about the worst-case scenarios that might lie ahead, then shook herself back to the present.

She drove. The lanes and small roads of West Cork with its fuchsia pinks, fern greens and montbretia orange flew by her with little notice. Her eyes could only stay on what lay ahead, the phone call, every word Jen had said. They needed to talk, Jen said. The quiet roads and small-town streets soon gave way to the motorway with its monotonous vegetation, the unchanging speed and endless grey asphalt hollowed out a space of boredom where Susan's fears and anxieties could all emerge again and fill her blanks.

She pulled into a petrol station where the end-of-summer chaos was swinging, children and parents grabbing ice creams and burgers and crepes while truckers napped in the car park or sat with a cup of coffee. Susan pumped the tyres and topped up the tank, then joined the truckers sipping lighter-fluid-strength espresso. A family, two women and their small baby, settled for their pitstop at the next table. She sat bolt upright, watching them. They didn't notice her as she swept her eyes over them and their seemingly perfect unit. The love that flowed between the three of them, how enthralled the little girl made both the adults. That sickening feeling in her stomach again, the grief and sadness and the intense, toxic jealousy that made her hate herself and turn all her anger inwards. She chose not to shove it down this time. She let herself feel it. The resentment and the regret flowed through her. She offered it no resistance, just stood and wandered to the bathroom. She stared at herself in the mirror, her eyes were red with hot tears, her hair frizzed from the salt of the last few months. She took in gulps of air and wondered at the future she might have thrown away.

She left the bathroom and smiled at the couple.

'She's a gorgeous baby.'

Some of her sadness broke down in the sunshine of their returned smiles.

Her phone buzzed in her bag as she sat into the car, a text from Jen.

'Ok. Drive safe.'

There was a pause, then the typing bubble appeared and disappeared. It disappeared. No 'x' had been sent, but nothing negative either. Susan allowed a dangerous flame of hope to flicker.

She pulled into the driveway as the evening approached. The garden was neat and recently weeded, still popping with summer colour that had started to give way to autumn golds and browns. The blue borage buzzed with bees stocking up for the long winter. A robin perched on the gate as she pulled her car into the drive, watching her with its head to one side. The heathers still bloomed in the rockery. Susan glanced at the Atlantic flowers sitting in their little tubs on the passenger seat – she hoped they liked it here on the East Coast. She missed Walter already. Perhaps, if they worked past all this, they could get a dog. They needed somewhere to put all the love she knew would still be in their home, if they could get back to where they used to be.

Her neighbour, Rob, strolled past with his white curly dog; it had been a tiny pup when she last saw it. Rob pointed his nose towards the car and gave her a curious nod. She gave him a flat smile. She sat gripping the steering wheel, willing herself to keep moving, keep going. She left her bags in the car, nervous of arriving at the door with too many presumptions, and creaked the doors shut, promising silently to lavish some TLC on the Toyota, once bigger issues were taken care of.

The front door, once blue like a summer sky, was painted midway to the handle in a glossy mint green. Abandoned mid-stroke – no tins of paint in sight. In another life, this well-intended project would have bugged Susan endlessly. But today she smiled. Half-finished or half-beginning, that depends on how you look at things. A light breeze was at her back as she stepped towards the house, her body vibrating with nerves and excitement.

Her legs were jelly, her feet threatened to turn around and run again; fears of rejection, the creeping anxiety that Jen was moving on, building a life without her. Another part of her, deep within, the brave part, the part that drove her all the way back to this, the part that leaned in and kissed Jen in that nightclub, that tried and tried again when all they had got from trying was failure, the part that drove her to stand now, told her to wait, have faith, show your soul to the woman you love, and you can have no regrets if you do.

There are moments in life that exist within the before, the moments before your life changes forever. Susan had experienced enough of them to recognise when she was in one, and knew now to breathe in the last dying breaths of the person she was, before the next moment happened. The moment before she kissed Jen, the moment before she proposed, the moment in Croatia before she decided to answer the fertility clinic's call. The moment before two lines turned blue, and then the one before she sat on a toilet and found blood starting to pour its way out of her. The Susans before those moments no longer existed. Her current self stood in another before now, left on her home's doorstep by the sea, her grief, her recklessness and her island.

She took a deep breath and rang the doorbell.

ACKNOWLEDGMENTS

———∞◇∞———

This novel was both difficult and easy to write at different times in the process, but at all times, I was supported by some of the most wonderful people imaginable.

Thank you to Dee Collins, Carina McNally, and all the team at Mercier Press for giving me the opportunity to get my work into the world and for the support along the way in bringing it to market. Thank you also to Ciarán Gallagher and the RTÉ *Today Show*, both those in front of and behind the camera, for providing the platform to showcase my novel and to yap on national television.

I will always be grateful to the Faber Academy and its scholarship scheme for allowing me to access the Finish Your Draft course and learn so much from my tutor, Dr Natasha Bell. Natasha's teaching on the course, as well as her skilful editing of my second draft,, allowed this novel to jump off the page and helped me find depth when I was nervous to even look for it. Her feedback and insight meant the world to me, and I will be forever grateful.

Dr Kerry Ryan and the Write like A Grrl collective gave me the confidence to call myself a writer a long time before it was justified. Thank you to Dr Hilary Lennon for telling me a long time ago in her creative writing class that she could 'definitely see you writing a novel someday'.

Writing is a solitary pursuit but done best, in my opinion, with others around you to support, guide, and tell you to stop moaning and just get on with it. Thanks to Dialogue and Vibes, and the Magic Writing Hour gangs for the insight and most importantly, the memes. Thanks particularly to Steph Torrance for her endless patience and receptiveness to panicked voice messages.

Thank you to Sophie White – your time, your wisdom, your encouragement, your feedback, and your friendship. I can't wait to sign your copy of my book for a change!

On that note, thank you to all the writers and creatives who have shared wisdom with me throughout this – Anna Carey, Una Mullally, Stefanie Preissner, Louise O'Neill, Maeve Whitehouse-Bolger, to name a few. As a clueless first-time author, it's incredible to have had some of your insights, both big and small, on different aspects of the industry and the process.

Thank you to the first readers of the various drafts along the way, and for your uplifting yet anxiety-provoking texts as you worked your way through it – Maeve Keane, Leanne Harte, Annie Hoey, Hazel Cullen, Etain Kidney and Sinead Kelleher. Legends all. Love to my beloved book clubs, Mnawesome and Buck Club, for the excitement and support. Thank you, Síona and Sarah Elaine, for spending literal hours talking through the plot and helping me see things that weren't obvious. Thank you to Debbie Hickey for the lovely photo session!

I spent a lovely afternoon at the Clonakilty distillery, sipping sloe gin and learning how to make it. Thank you to all the visitor experience team there for answering my many questions.

Sticking with West Cork, thank you to Kathy and Pa for the use of their lovely cottage for the DIY writing retreat that allowed me bring this whole thing together.

I haven't used anyone's story but snippets of my own in this book, but thank you to the many women who have shared their grief and love with me as I've been on the IVF and loss journey. Our stories are worth telling, and it's a privilege to have a space to share a fictionalised version of mine.

To my friends, particularly the Horse Reporters, the Pink Ladies and Sonya Donnelly. I don't think I'd have the courage to write anything if I hadn't known you all. I promise I'll try to make the next book funnier.

Thank you to my in-laws, particularly Joanna, for the endless positivity and healthy piss-taking of the author in the family.

To my own family, especially my mam and dad – thank you for supporting me, whatever I've done, whether it was Buffy fanfic or writing a novel. Please skip over the sex scenes.

My dogs, Minnie and Charlie, were essential to the process. Minnie's name and Charlie's physical characteristics were borrowed for the novel, and all they got was some ham in return.

To Rachel. Thank you for being a rock of support and unwavering belief in my writing journey. I promise I will never run away to an island and have an affair with a young one. Probably.